OUT
OF
NOWHERE

Also by Maria Padian

Brett McCarthy: Work in Progress
Jersey Tomatoes Are the Best

OUT
OF
NOWHERE

MARIA PADIAN

Alfred A. Knopf
New York

Library of Congress Cataloging-in-Publication Data
Padian, Maria
Out of nowhere / by Maria Padian
p. cm.
Summary: Performing community service for pulling a stupid prank against a rival high school, soccer star Tom tutors a Somali refugee with soccer dreams of his own.
ISBN 978-0-375-86580-0 (trade) — ISBN 978-0-375-96580-7 (lib. bdg.) —
ISBN 978-0-375-89610-1 (ebook) — ISBN 978-0-375-86562-6 (pbk.)
[1. Soccer—Fiction. 2. Refugees—Fiction. 3. Somali Americans—Fiction.] I. Title.
PZ7.P1325Ou 2013
[Fic]—dc23
2012005653

Printed in the United States of America

February 2013
10 9 8 7 6 5 4 3 2
First Edition

For my grandparents: Catherine Veronica Flanagan,
Michael Joseph Padian, Margarita Prados Arreche,
and Fernando Claudio Morales, who came with
their hearts and their stories to America

OUT OF NOWHERE

Chapter One

It's like he came out of nowhere.

I was stuck, okay? I'll man up to that. We were playing Maquoit High School. I mean, more than half their guys play four-season private club soccer. Olympic Development Program, that sort of thing. So yeah, I'm in the midfield with the ball and there's no one—repeat, *no one*—open on our team, and Maquoit's big man, the one we call Sasquatch, is bearing down on me. Six foot three, hairy, and he flies over the field. He's about to end my young life unless I dribble forward, right into their two equally behemoth defensive players.

I'm thinking, *Is this what you want, God? Fine. Hurl me headlong into those two Maquoit defenders, who will not only strip the ball from me but lay me out on the green, green grass. Fine. So long, life.*

That's what I was thinking when I heard him.

Not God. I never hear God. I heard *him*. Saeed, the new guy. "Pass *bahk!*"

There was something about his cry, and I don't just mean the accent, that startled me. His voice . . . commanded. So while I

1

didn't see him, I didn't hesitate. I mean, what the hell, there was nobody else open. So I flipped the ball behind me in the direction of that strange voice, then did the unthinkable: I took one step toward Sasquatch and planted my feet. Prepared for the impact.

The sidelines roared, and on my right this blur, this shadow dressed in our team uniform, flashed past me. I watched as he scooped up my pass and moved like blowing smoke, weaving a path toward the goal. The Maquoit defenders couldn't close ranks on him in time. Sasquatch couldn't change direction. I think half our team didn't even realize he had possession, the guy was that quick. So when he lasered the ball into the net, inches from their goalie's hands, and Sasquatch, traveling at forty miles per hour, body-slammed the wind right out of me, I don't think anyone saw the impact. I heard cheering, yelling . . . before I hit the ground.

I don't know how long I lay there, gently pressing each rib and testing for cracks, focusing on the challenge of pulling air into my lungs, before a face loomed over mine, blocking the sun.

"Bouchard? Hey, man, are you dead?"

Alex Rhodes, the Maquoit captain. I hadn't spoken to Alex in a long time. But he has one of those voices you remember. Sense of humor you remember, too. I bent one knee, squinted. A second face appeared next to Alex.

Saeed. He was the first from our team to reach me.

"You okay?" he said.

I nodded automatically, even though I was anything but. I tried to draw another breath and it worked a little better. I had a sense of bodies moving close and a voice telling people to step back. I tried another breath, and it was good, so I nodded again. A hand grasped mine. Pulled me up. And people clapped. Outdoor claps, the sound carried by the wind, like Wiffle balls striking plastic bats. I turned to face him.

He was the kind of skinny you noticed. Like, you could make out the skeleton just beneath the surface. But he was strong. That hand in mine pulled hard, and the muscles of his arms stretched sinewy and tight.

I'd known he'd be strong. I'd sensed it that first day he showed up at school, wearing a Manchester United T-shirt. Everybody in homeroom was asking him, "Dude, where'd you get the shirt?" but he didn't seem to understand the question. Mike Turcotte, who has a knack for communicating in made-up sign language with all the new Somali kids, got Saeed to show him the tag on the shirt's collar. "Damn!" he'd exclaimed. "That's a real Manchester United shirt! Made in England."

While the rest of the guys tried to figure out where in hell a refugee kid with zero money got a shirt like that, I'd pulled up a chair next to Saeed.

"You like soccer?" I'd asked. Pointing to his shirt, I used the English name: "Football?"

Relief flooded his face. He understood.

"Soccer," he repeated, nodding vigorously. He pressed his hand against his chest. "Yes. I play."

As I stood on the field with him, feeling my ribs and wondering if Sasquatch had just handed me a season-ending injury, those words came back to me. It struck me that "I play" was possibly the understatement of the century.

Saeed smiled at me, his lips stretched back against his teeth, bright white in his face. Black, black face. African black, not American black.

"Great pass," he said, lightly punching the side of my shoulder. He pronounced each word hesitantly, as if it were a new food he was tasting for the first time.

"Great goal," I said. Wheezed, actually. It was hard to talk. He turned and sprinted back to his position on the field. The other Somali guys crowded him, laughing and slapping him on the back.

Alex was retreating, too. He winked at me.

"Nice goal, but you're goin' down, Bouchard," he said. Quietly, for my ears only, glancing at the approaching referee: "Even if you do have Osama over there playing for you." He turned and trotted back to center.

Yeah, fuck you, Rhodes, I managed to not say.

The ref spoke to me.

"You need to come out?" he said.

I shook my head. Nothing hurt anymore, and my lungs could fill again. As I walked slowly back to midfield, I scanned the crowd. My mom was in her usual spot, standing in front of the folding camp chair that Dad got her from Marden's. On the other side of the field, Donnie Plourde and the rest of them were taunting a pack of Maquoit fans and acting mad-hammered. He probably was. Maquoit had better score fast and shut him up before a fight broke out.

To the left of Donnie and Co., I saw Cherisse. She had her girlfriends all clustered around her, and she was clutching her hands beneath her chin in this little worried pose. They squealed on cue when I nodded in her direction, and they gave her these little reassuring squeezes when they saw that her boyfriend was still alive. It's something I can never quite get over: the way girls are always hugging each other. Like, even when we change classes, as if years have passed since their last hug and not just the forty-five minutes between math and history.

We didn't win that day—nobody beats Maquoit—but we gave 'em a scare. Saeed scored once more, and I managed a goal. Maybe three seems lame compared to their five, but usually they dominated us. Three to five was a step in the right direction.

After the handshake line and Coach's wrap-up I looked for Saeed. He was at the far end of the bench, slipping a backpack over his shoulders. As I walked toward him, this little kid approached. From the spectators' side of the field he ran straight for Saeed, so fast you thought he was going to topple over. A girl chased him. Well, sort of chased. She wore a long skirt and couldn't move like the kid. She was calling, "Aweys! Aweys, you come back here now!"

The kid closed the distance and jumped on Saeed as I reached them. I recognized him then. One of the little brothers I'd met the day I went to their apartment.

"Hey, man. Well done today," I said. I put my hand out.

Saeed placed the kid on the ground. He shook my hand and smiled.

"Great game," he said carefully.

I laughed. "Actually, we sucked. But we sucked less thanks to you. Where'd you learn to play like that?"

His brow contracted, forming a thin line over his nose. "Great pass," he finally said, nodding at me. Smiling.

"I keep forgetting you don't understand a thing I'm saying, do you?" I replied, grinning back at him. His smile deepened and he looked relieved. Pleased that he was pulling off a conversation.

"You know my brother's English isn't very good," I heard.

It was the girl. The sister, actually. I recognized her, too, although I couldn't remember the name. Sonya . . . Sasha? Anyway, she seemed a little out of breath from chasing the kid. Which probably wasn't easy to do in a skirt. A long, colorful skirt all the way to her sneakers, and a leather bomber jacket on top. She wore big gold earrings that practically hit her shoulders, and unlike most of the Somali girls at our school, who covered up so that the only part of their heads you saw was this small circle of face, she had just a little black scarf tied around her hair.

Unlike her brothers, she wasn't smiling at me.

And unlike her brothers, she spoke great English.

"Yeah, I know," I said easily. "But his soccer kicks ass." Her non-smile deepened to a frown at the word *ass*.

"I asked him where he learned to play," I continued.

She hesitated for a moment, then said something to Saeed in what I assumed was Somali. He looked at me and shrugged.

"I, uh, always play." He shrugged again. As if the outrageous soccer he'd just demonstrated on the field was no big deal.

"Where we come from, boys play soccer all the time," the girl said. "Outside, every day. Saeed also played in the Ramadan leagues."

Ramadan. Now *that* I knew. Only not in relation to sports.

"I thought Ramadan was the month when you don't eat," I said.

One corner of her mouth turned up. She was trying not to laugh at me.

"Ramadan is a holy month in which we fast during the day and eat in the evening," she said. "In Nairobi, coaches form teams during Ramadan, and if you win, you earn money. Or dinner out, at night." She looked steadily into my eyes. "When you're hungry, a meal at a restaurant is a good incentive for scoring."

The way she easily used words like *incentive* made you wonder how she could be related to smiling Saeed.

"Well, thanks for explaining that," I said. "I'm Tom Bouchard, by the way. Tell me your name again?"

She bent to scoop the little guy into her arms. "I know who you are," she said quietly. She glanced quickly at Saeed, then turned on her heel and headed back across the field. Saeed hooked his thumbs in the straps of his pack, nodded once more at me, and followed them.

As I watched them go, I thought, *Wow. That girl does* not *like me.*

It's weird when a total stranger already has her mind made up about you.

Chapter Two

Here's the fact, and I know I'm gonna sound like a jerk, but whatever: girls like me.

Girls like me, and I like girls. A lot.

So the full frontal drop-dead glare and the way-unfriendly attitude I got from Saeed's sister were a first. And undeserved. Not only because I don't usually get that sort of reaction from females, but because I had actually been *nice* to her brother. Unlike probably half the people in our city and most of the kids in school, who would've been thrilled to see them all get back on the buses they'd arrived in.

You gotta wonder who the genius was that came up with the plan to put a bunch of Africans in Maine, the coldest, whitest state in America.

Okay, maybe Alaska is colder. But not whiter. And it's true that the Somalis who began showing up in Enniston by the hundreds started out someplace else. Warm places like Georgia and Southern California. Our town wasn't ever anybody's first bright idea. We'd gotten what's called a "secondary migration" (my aunt

Maddie taught me that term), which is when refugees who have just barely made it out alive from some war zone are dumped in a city where there are plenty of cheap apartments, but as soon as they learn a few words of English, they realize their situation sucks. Like, the guy next door deals drugs and the schools are bad. So they move to a better place. Like Enniston. Which has pretty low crime, okay schools, and loads of cheap, empty apartments.

And empty mills. Big, abandoned textile factories that once hummed and spewed lint and gummed up the river and put a whole army of French-speaking immigrants from Canada, like my great-grandparents, to work. All dilapidated now, except for the ones converted to office space or restaurants serving brick-oven organic free-range something-or-other baked on a crust. I mean, I don't eat that shit, but I have a few friends who landed jobs working in those places, so it's all good.

Anyway, just around the time a bunch of Muslims took out the Twin Towers, a bunch of Somali Muslims started seriously secondary-migrating here. There had been a few of them in town for years, but this was different. Every day in school you saw more of them in the guidance office, these black kids who barely spoke English. They would wander, lost, through the halls, trying to figure out the whole concept of changing classes. The girls would wash their feet in the restroom sinks before lunch, which made them *real* popular with Cherisse's crowd (not). One day I saw this Somali girl on all fours on the staircase landing. Everybody had to step around her, and I heard one guy say, "Dude, what is she doing?"

"Facing Mecca," someone replied.

"Where's Mecca?" somebody else asked.

"It's out by the mall," a third answered, which got a few laughs.

But not everyone was laughing. People were mad. Worried. Especially teachers. Who didn't know what to do with hundreds of kids who just showed up and didn't know English. Hell, a lot of them couldn't even read and write their own language.

My mom and her sister, my aunt Maddie, are very big into the whole immigrant-ancestor thing. They're always going on about our *mémère* Louise and *pépère* Claude, who came here from Quebec to work in the mills. So when the Somali families began showing up in big numbers and people started freaking out, Mom and Aunt Maddie said it was just the "new wave." As in immigrants. Not Blondie, or the B-52s, or that other crap music they listened to when they were in high school.

My uncle Paul, their younger brother, got really pissed off when they said that.

"Our ancestors came here to work. These people came here to collect welfare," he fumed.

Sometimes it's hard for me to imagine how Aunt Maddie and Uncle Paul came from the same family. They're *that* different. He's a total working-class dude, never went to college and proud of it, while she's got a couple of degrees in something and is always going to talks at the local college. Mom says when they were young, Maddie was the most beautiful girl at Chamberlain High School. Voted homecoming queen her senior year . . . then turned it down and boycotted homecoming, calling the whole queen thing sexist and saying that football embodied just about everything that was wrong with America.

My girlfriend, Cherisse, would give up a vital organ or sell her soul to Satan if she thought it'd earn her homecoming queen.

Anyway, I didn't quite get Paul's attitude about the Somalis. Maybe it had something to do with how he works hard and hates freeloaders. He's always coming up with ways for me to earn some cash. Like the day after the soccer game against Maquoit. Paul had a potential two cords of sixteen-inch logs with my name and Donnie's on them. He lives just outside town in this little house he mostly built himself, surrounded by trees, and last winter ice storms took out two big oaks on his property. He'd spent the summer chainsawing them into monster-sized chunks, and he wanted me and Donnie to split and stack them.

When I arrived at ten that morning and walked around to the back of his house, I could hear the mechanical drone and smell the diesel from the splitter he'd rented. He was wearing his red chamois work shirt and had already split a decent-sized pile of green wood into three-sided lengths. Paul is a beast. He'd probably been up for hours, impatient to get started.

"You boys have a late night?" he asked as I approached. Trace of a smile.

"More like an early morning," I replied. He tossed me a pair of work gloves, then turned to the mound of thick logs a few paces away. He wrapped his arms around one of the biggest and heaved it onto the splitter. Then he grasped a lever and pulled. A hydraulic wedge slid smoothly toward the log, nudged up against it, then pressed into and through it. The chunk gave way with a loud crack and two fat halves thudded to the ground. Uncle Paul picked one up, replaced it on the splitter, and aimed the wedge again. This time the oak split into neat, three-sided pieces. He grabbed one in each hand and flung them onto the growing pile.

"Where's Mr. Plourde?" he asked.

"He's coming," I said, trying to sound convinced. I had no idea whether Donnie would make an appearance. In fact, I pretty much doubted it. The last time I'd seen him—nine hours earlier, actually—he hadn't looked like someone who'd be in any shape for manual labor in the morning.

Lila Boutin's big brother had fixed us up with a case of Bud Light, and a bunch of us had headed out to the football field. Some of the girls brought blankets, and we were lying in the middle of the dark field, looking up at the black sky and knocking back a few cold ones. It was one of those September nights—no bugs, not cold yet, with a few random shooting stars that hadn't burned themselves out in August—when you could fool yourself into thinking maybe Maine *isn't* the most dead-end, godforsaken state in the union. That was my mood when Donnie jumped up from his blanket. He shook himself like a horse covered in flies.

"This is so lame!" he exclaimed. "What, are you people just gonna lie here?"

"Sounds good to me," I replied. In the darkness, Cherisse's hands were straying into some fairly interesting places, and I was thinking this was about as far from lame as I could imagine.

"I gotta *do* something," Donnie said, more to himself than to any of us. I could see him move his feet restlessly. See his head tilt back as he finished off his beer.

"Don't step on me, bro," Jake Farwell said, followed by a female squeal and "Ouch!"

"What the hell, Donnie!" I heard Lila exclaim. "You just kicked Devon in the head!"

"Sorry," Donnie mumbled, stepping away from the bodies and

blankets on the ground. "Whaddaya say, Tom-boy?" he added. "Wanna give me a ride?"

"Nope," I managed before Cherisse covered my mouth with hers. Donnie breathed out impatiently.

"Gotta find my man Pepper. Who's coming?" he said. Greg Pepper is this guy who sells weed and lives in probably the sketchiest part of the city. I started to tell Donnie to shut up and sit down and try to find the Big Dipper or Orion's belt overhead, but that's about when Cherisse found my belt, so I wasn't saying a lot to Donnie. George Morin, who's pretty much a stoner and also has a car, got up. "I'm with you, man," he said, and Donnie slapped him five. Then the two of them walked off without another word to the rest of us.

" 'Bout time," I heard Lila mutter. "That guy is so hyper."

"No hating on Plourde," Jake said to her.

"Why the frig not?" Devon snapped, sitting up. She had her hand on her just-kicked head. "The guy's crazy. He's always drunk or stoned, or trying to get drunk or stoned."

"That's funny, coming from someone who's out here drinking beer," Jake replied.

Devon shrugged. "I don't know why you guys defend him," she said. "He's a loser."

There isn't a whole lot that can distract me from the charms of Miss Cherisse Ouellette, but even the wounded Devon wasn't allowed to run Donnie down in my presence. I shifted Cherisse off my chest and raised myself up on one elbow.

"Hey, Devon, can I ask you something? What's your problem with the word 'fuck'? We all know you won't *do* it, but can you not even *say* it?" Burst of laughter, even from the girls.

"Hmm. 'Frig.' Aren't those the first four letters in Devon's other favorite word?" Jake said. I knew where he was going right off, but there was a pause as the rest of them scrolled through their mental spell-checks. Lila got it first.

"Oh my God, that's *so* mean, Jake!" She leaned over to slap Jake but hit Cherisse instead.

"Ouch! Thanks a lot, Lila," Cherisse said, but you could tell she wasn't really hurt. She whispered quietly to me, "What favorite word?"

I pressed my lips against her ear.

"Frigid," I breathed.

She gasped, then tried to stifle her giggles in the front of my shirt.

Meanwhile, Devon got up. She yanked her blanket from the pile and searched for her shoes.

"I have just one thing to say to you people," she said. "Fuck. You."

Jake whooped, then applauded.

"And *you* two," she hissed, turning to me and Cherisse. "Why don't you *fucking* get a room?" She marched off, trailing her blanket.

"Hey. That was *two* things," I called after her. Everyone laughed. Poor Devon.

Not too long after that the beer was gone, Cherisse was making noises about clearing out, and we heard hollering from the parking lot. We didn't know whether it was cops or kids, so we grabbed our stuff and ran behind the bleachers. From there we could see the lot.

It was Donnie. He was standing straight up through Morin's sunroof, whooping like a madman as the car spun donuts. When it turned sharply, Donnie's whole body swung and it looked like he was going to be flung up and onto the pavement. Somehow he held on, and after a victory lap that left the smell of singed rubber, the two of them peeled out and disappeared into the night.

"Guess he found Pepper," Jake said, and we all cracked up.

A few monster chunks into it, Uncle Paul and I had a rhythm. He would heave; I'd manage the wedge; he'd position for the second bite; we'd both toss the splits. Neither of us spoke, which was fine by me. I was enjoying the thought-free zone of splitter hum and repetitive motion. Paul can be good like that. He's happy to work alongside you without pulling conversation out of your head.

Not that morning, however. He'd been at the soccer game.

"I see your coach is starting some of those Somalis," he said. The wedge slid forward. I waited for the crack before speaking.

"Yup," I said. We grabbed the splits. Tossed.

"How's that goin'?" he continued.

"Fine."

Better than fine, I managed to not say, as it probably would have pissed him off. And I sure as hell wasn't going to tell him what my role had been in getting Saeed out on the field.

That day when Saeed wore the Manchester United shirt, I'd told him that if he played soccer, he should come to a meeting with Coach after school. I don't really know how I communicated that to him, because I'm sure as hell no Mike Turcotte when it comes to African charades (that's what we call Turcotte's attempts at talking to these kids), or how he managed to understand, but he showed up. And brought three other Somali guys with him.

After Coach Gerardi gave his talk and dismissed everyone, he signaled me over. Saeed was standing with him, holding a sheaf of papers: permission slips, medical forms. All the things you need to fill out if you want to play sports in high school.

"Tom, this young man says you invited him to the meeting today?"

I nodded. I wondered if I was in trouble. Coach doesn't really talk; he growls.

"Well, he's going to need some help filling out these forms," he said. "Think you can do that?"

I'm captain of the soccer team. Did I really have a choice?

"Uh . . . sure," I told him. "But doesn't guidance have translators who help with that?"

"They're gone for the weekend," Coach said. "He needs these by Monday." He turned on his heel and walked off, leaving me standing there, stupidly, with Saeed.

"Okay, well . . ." I grabbed one of the sheets from Saeed and pointed to a line. "Your mother or father needs to sign here. Their name. That gives you permission to play soccer." I slowed down, pronouncing each word carefully, but he still looked confused.

I tried to imagine how Turcotte would act out "permission slip."

"I got . . . no father," Saeed finally said.

"Mother?" I said.

He nodded. "Yes," he said. "Samira speak English good. So you come. Yes?" He didn't wait for an answer. Just motioned for me to follow him and headed out of the gym.

We walked. Far. And before long I was in a section of downtown Enniston I pretty much never visit. Right near the police

16

station and the skate park and the bread factory, which fills the air with the most amazing smells. The aroma of hot rolls greeted us when we reached his neighborhood, followed us as we trudged up the stairs that snaked along the outside wall of his four-story wooden apartment building.

His door opened onto this little vestibule cluttered with shoes. Saeed kicked his off, adding to the pile. He didn't ask me to do the same, but what the heck—I slipped mine off as well. He shouted into the apartment, announcing his arrival. He motioned for me to wait with the shoes while he walked ahead, then rounded a corner into a room I couldn't see.

A riot of conversation followed, absolutely foreign to me. Somali is a no-holds-barred language. Half the time it sounds like people are fighting with each other, but it's just that they get that animated. The hands go, too, emphasizing each word. I think you'd render a Somali person partially mute if you tied their hands.

Finally Saeed stuck his head around the corner and waved me in.

They were all in the kitchen and looked pretty surprised about me being there. They were in the middle of making dinner. A big pot of something steamed on the stove, and the air in the room felt thick with cumin and curry. There was this old-looking woman who I guessed was his mother, standing near the pot, and a couple of little boys, and a girl about our age. The little guys were dressed like any American kid, in jeans and T-shirts, but the woman and the girl were in long skirts and head coverings. The girl was seated at the kitchen table, reading the papers Coach had given Saeed.

I stood there, awkward as hell, while no one said anything to me. Finally the girl looked up.

"My mother does not know how to write her own name. But I will write for her on these lines, and she will put her mark, and that is good, I think." She stared at me, waiting for my response.

"Sure . . . I mean, yeah. Whatever. It's not like she's signing away his endorsement rights or anything." I laughed at my own joke. The girl didn't smile. Instead, she turned to her mother and began speaking quickly and pointing to the papers. The mother nodded: yes, yes. I shifted from one foot to the other and back again. I didn't understand why I was there. If Saeed's sister could read and all, why had he dragged me home with him?

I watched as the girl carefully wrote her mother's name on the appropriate lines and pointed to where her mother should pen a big X. They did this very carefully, like they were signing a will or something.

After they finished the permission forms, they moved on to the emergency contact card, where you list people to call in case you get hurt and your parents can't be reached. You also have to list your family doctor and dentist, with their phone numbers and emails. Also list your health insurance. If you've got health insurance.

The girl stared hard at this card and frowned. She said something to one of the little brothers, who ran from the room. We heard the door to the apartment open, then slam shut.

"He gets the phone number for the people next door," she explained to me. "But we don't know anyone for the other line. And we don't know any doctor."

There was a plastic clock on the wall just over the stove, and my eyes inadvertently glanced at it. I'd already been there twenty minutes. It takes my parents about five minutes, tops, to complete these papers every year.

"Tell you what," I said. I pulled out the kitchen chair alongside her and sat. I motioned for her to hand me the card and her pen. "I'll put my mother down as Saeed's second emergency contact. And I'll write in my doctor and dentist. When you get your own, you can change it. But for now, this'll work." I pulled the card toward me and plucked the pen from her fingers. She looked startled, but I began filling in blanks.

"That is . . . okay?" she asked hesitantly.

I shrugged.

"Trust me: they don't read these things. They just eyeball 'em to make sure all the lines are filled in." Saeed's mother, watching as I rapidly completed the questions on the card, nodded. She smiled at me. This friendly American, helping her son. The girl's eyes narrowed, but she said nothing.

The last sheet was the medical form. It required a doctor's signature, proving that Saeed had all his immunizations and a recent physical.

Right. These people didn't have a doctor in town. There was no way Saeed was going to find one, schedule an appointment, and pass a physical before the season was half over.

I made a management decision, especially because I was already going to be late for dinner. I scrawled something fairly illegible but slightly resembling my doctor's name on the medical release form.

"Done," I said, slapping the pen down on the Formica tabletop. The girl picked up the paper and scrutinized my handwriting.

"This is . . . not true," she declared, laying the paper down.

"No, it's not," I agreed. "It's a little something we call forgery. And if you want your brother here to go to soccer practice on Monday, you'll let him hand that paper in to the nice lady at the high school athletic office." I stared at the girl. She stared back. Saeed, uneasily watching all this, asked her something in Somali.

Her response was sharp, a rapid-fire staccato of words. I didn't need a translator to tell me what she thought of my helpfulness. Saeed shot back at her, equally fast. Emphatic. The mother looked very concerned.

I stood up. Everyone stopped.

"Let me ask you something," I said to the girl. "Is your brother healthy?"

"Yes, he is fine, but—"

"Then what's the problem? Your mother says he can play, right? You're gonna eventually find a family doctor. And you can go in and change everything on the card after that if you want. But for right now? He's good to go."

She shook her head slowly from side to side, lips pressed tightly together. She wasn't buying this.

I shrugged.

"Whatever. My job here is finished. He needs to hand those papers in on Monday or else he can't play." I turned to Saeed and raised my hand. "Dude," I said. He raised his hand, slapped his palm against mine. "Good luck."

I don't know what happened in that apartment after I left, but since Saeed was out on the field next practice, I guess he won. Come to think of it, so did I. Because he was turning out to be awesome.

Not something I felt like discussing with my uncle.

"I saw your girlfriend at the game," he said. "Danny Ouellette's daughter." He glanced at me as he bent to pick up a split. "What's her name again?"

"Cherisse," I replied, relieved that he was moving away from a possible Somali rant.

He nodded. "That's right. Cherisse. Cute kid," he commented.

I lifted a big log onto the splitter. "Mom's not a fan," I said.

Paul laughed.

"Well, that shouldn't surprise you. You're being careful, Tommy. Right?"

"Yeah, yeah," I said, half muttering. The wedge inched toward the log, but Paul released the lever, halting its progress and cutting the sound.

"I'm serious," he said.

"I know. Don't worry. I'm not stupid, Uncle Paul," I told him.

"I've seen plenty of smart guys get stupid over girls like your Cherisse," he said. "And stupid turns into stuck pretty damn fast, if you know what I mean." He pulled on the lever again and the wedge continued on its path.

I didn't know how we'd gotten into my second-least-favorite topic to discuss with the family: Cherisse. The number one least favorite is college applications and my progress (or lack of progress) toward completing them. This was the first time Paul had started in on me about number two.

Just then Donnie came round the side of the house. He looked like shit. He was wearing the same clothes from nine hours earlier, only more wrinkled. He had his hands jammed in his pockets and this stupid grin on his face. When he got close, you could see his eyes were so bloodshot even the lids were swollen and red. Uncle Paul leaned against the splitter, arms crossed, checking him out.

"Well, good morning, sunshine," he said. Donnie shifted from one foot to the other, then back again. One corner of his mouth turned up as he looked at Paul.

"Sorry I'm late," he said.

"Hell, you're not late. We've got hours of daylight left. You want coffee?" he asked, but it was more like a statement. He pulled off his work gloves and stuffed them into the front of Donnie's shirt before walking toward the house. "Tommy?"

"No, thanks, I'm good," I replied.

As Uncle Paul disappeared into the house, I looked Donnie over. He was pulling on the gloves and whistling quietly to himself as he surveyed the mound of wood.

"So what's the drill here?" he asked easily.

"Are you stoned?" I asked.

"Hell yeah," Donnie said. He broke out one of his big-ass smiles, the type that's been keeping him out of serious trouble for years, because who could ever bust the balls of a guy who can smile like one of God's own angels? Okay, so maybe Sister Marie, our so not-favorite nun from St. Cecilia's Elementary, could. But no one else. I mean it: no one else.

He strode over to the big pieces, bent at the knees, and wrapped his arms around one. He lifted, staggered toward the splitter.

"Dude, you are in no shape to be standing near heavy machinery, let alone working with it."

He half dropped the piece onto the splitter, which shuddered.

"I know, right?" he panted. "Don't worry, Tom-boy. I'm not

so fucked up that I can't carry wood. You handle the heavy machinery."

We worked through a few of the big ones in silence, and when I was confident that Donnie wasn't going to drop a forty-pound log on his foot, I spoke.

"We saw you in the parking lot," I said.

He laughed softly.

"Man, that was a *rush!*" he said. "Morin says he did a donut at fifty!"

"Looked like you were going to fly right through the roof."

"It *felt* like I was gonna fly," he said. "I think I got a little whiplash." He paused, took off one glove, and rubbed the back of his neck. He stood there, inspecting me.

"And what about you and the lovely Miss Ouellette?" he continued. "You manage to get some . . . quality time?"

I grabbed the lever and pulled. The wedge glided.

"Oh yeah." I smiled at him and let his imagination do the rest of the work. Donnie shook his head.

"You are so damn lucky."

"Nothin' lucky about it. I got a way with the ladies. You should try talking to them instead of kicking them. Or taking off to find Pepper. Man, can't you score somewhere else? That guy is not cool."

Donnie shrugged. "He's all right. You're just a little too clean-cut for that side of town. Anyway, Morin had some weed in his glove compartment. We never connected with Pepper."

"So that's what you did all night? Got high and broke the speed limit? Talk about lame. There was Lila Boutin, all lonely on the grass. . . ."

Donnie snorted, signaling what he thought of the lonely Lila.

"Hey, at least I'm not breaking some athletic pledge. Right, Tom-boy?" He didn't bother to hide the edge of annoyance in his voice. Donnie's a habitual screw-up, but he owns it. I think he actually has a little pride of ownership. Not, he enjoys pointing out, like certain jocks who sign athletic pledges but still manage to down their fair share of Bud Light on a Saturday night.

He never comes right out and calls me a hypocrite, but we both know that's what he thinks. Just like I never come right out and call him a stoner.

The screen door squealed open and Uncle Paul stepped out. He carried a mug and a plate piled with donuts. Steam floated from the mug.

"Now *that's* what I'm talkin' about!" Donnie exclaimed. "Breakfast of champions!" He threw his gloves on the ground and walked toward Paul. As he brushed past me, he murmured, "When we're done with this, I want to show you something Morin and I found last night." He walked toward my uncle, enthusing, "You are the *man*, Paul!"

Later that evening, with the wood all split and mostly stacked, I let him show me what he and Morin found. Yeah, I'm that stupid. Or that hopeful. I always hold out hope that when Donnie says, "Dude, check this out!" it's something like a new all-night diner that makes incredible hot wings. Or a great place by the river to hang out on a hot day in July. I want to keep pretending that my best childhood friend, who's always pretty much been a goofball, is still a lovable goofball.

Not some wake-'n'-baker headed for . . . nowhere good.

Chapter Three

Whenever Donnie does something stupid and gets into trouble, my mom says the same thing.

"He's never been as lucky as you, Tommy." She's a schoolteacher in Enniston, so she's seen just about every type of luck, good and bad. Plus she's known Donnie since we were in kindergarten together. Little Catholic boys at St. Cecilia's Elementary. Until sixth grade, when we both switched to public school.

For as long as I can remember, Donnie has come up pretty empty-handed in the luck department. He's been jumping out of his own skin since . . . I don't know . . . the day he was born? He is totally hyperactive, with a processing disability to boot, so school has always been pretty much a disaster for him. He did the whole meds thing, Ritalin and stuff, but whether he took them depended on who had custody that day (his folks split ages ago) and whether anyone was sober enough to remember to pick up his pills at the pharmacy.

Sucks for him. Always has. Not that I'm making excuses for him. Or maybe I am. Isn't luck my excuse? Grades, sports, and girls have always come easy to me because I'm lucky enough to have a good memory, be coordinated, and be halfway decent-looking. Lucky enough to have *my* parents, not Don's. Lucky enough to be born in the good ol' U.S. of A. and not some war zone.

That's one thing you can say about luck: it's not fair.

The sun was setting by the time Uncle Paul released us. Most of the wood was stacked, we had bills in our pockets (he'd paid us ten bucks an hour—sweet), and I told Donnie I'd give him a lift home. As we pulled out of Paul's driveway, I signaled left, toward Donnie's neighborhood, but he reached over the steering wheel and flipped the directional.

"Other way, son," he said. He settled back in the passenger seat with this mysterious smile on his face.

"This had better be good," I said.

"Oh yeah," he said.

"Where am I going?"

"Head out of town. Due east. I'm hungry."

We ended up at McDonald's, and over a Quarter Pounder and shake I got Donnie to tell me what was up.

"So last night? Morin and I drove to Maquoit."

"That's a long way to go to do donuts."

"I know, right. Anyway, near the back parking lot, right next to the refreshment stand—"

"Wait. What parking lot?"

"Dude, the *school* parking lot."

"You went to Maquoit High School? I thought you just went to town."

"That's what I'm telling you. At the *school,* there is this building where they keep all their supplies. I mean, everything from

26

lacrosse goals to rakes. Morin and I were checking it out, and it was unlocked."

I laughed. "Gimme a break, Donnie."

"Seriously, man, there was a latch for a padlock, but the lock was nowhere. I swear." He leaned back, put both hands up, and made his eyes go all round and innocent. I'd seen that look before.

"Fine. The shed was conveniently unlocked. So?"

"We found the paint. And brushes. You know, that they use for their rock and bridge?"

Maquoit High School is not only known in our conference for its over-the-top athletics; it's also known for the rock and bridge. The cement walls that line the old bridge leading into Maquoit, plus this massive rock behind the school, are time-honored spots for painted displays of school spirit. Every time they win something they slap on more black and red. It's so thick, sometimes it peels off in huge, gummy sheets.

"What did you do?" I asked him.

"Nothing. Morin is such a chickenshit. But I know how much *you* love Maquoit, Tom-boy."

He had me there. Years of getting crushed by Maquoit had made me a hater for sure. I could live with the fact that most of their players drilled in a private dome all winter, hired personal trainers, and even traveled to Europe to play. That was just their luck, to be rich and able to afford all those extras. What bugged the crap out of me was that their coach let them run up the score against schools like ours, where none of the guys belong to private club teams. And let them act all chest-bumping proud of kickin' our butts.

"What did you have in mind?" I said.

We waited until it was completely dark before pulling into the school. The parking lot was empty, and I cut my lights as we drove around back. I parked near the rock, and Donnie led me toward a long shadow, which turned out to be a supply shed. One of the doors swung easily open.

"You were telling the truth," I said as we stepped inside.

"I always tell the truth, Tom-boy. It's my downfall," he said. He was stumbling around in the dark. "I'm gonna turn on the light."

An overhead bulb revealed the contents of the shed: nets, goals, balls, grills, tarps . . . gallon buckets of paint. A plastic tub filled with brushes.

"Bingo," Donnie said softly.

It probably took us a full hour to cover the rock in black paint; that mother is huge. We started with brushes, but then Donnie, impatient, just started dumping. Whole gallons. I had to explain to him that if he did that we'd be there all night waiting for it to dry so we could write the words in red.

"See, that's why we're such a good team," he said. "I come up with the ideas, but you know how to execute."

We decided to turn on the headlights of the car just long enough to write *You suck, Maquoit!* There weren't any houses nearby, and we figured we'd do it quick, then peel out. Still, I was starting to get a little nervous; it felt like we'd been there a long time.

"C'mon, let's go," I said when we'd finished the lettering.

"Not until we put all our supplies away," Donnie said. "Cleanup time is the most important time, Tom-boy." He giggled. Like he was high.

"Don, seriously, let's *go*," I said.

"No, really, I want them to find all the buckets and brushes right where they were in the shed." He grabbed a couple of the now-empty paint cans and took off into the shadows. I grabbed the others, plus the brushes, and followed.

Here's the thing about luck: it doesn't have to lock you in. I mean, yeah, it sets you up. Donald Trump's kid is set up for college and yachts, while the kid whose dad got fired from the paper mill is set up for cavities because now they can't afford the dentist.

But you still have choices, no matter how big or small your luck quotient is.

So it was not-great luck that some random cop, on his usual rounds, happened to drive by my dad's car, parked next to the rock, just as Donnie and I were putting the empty paint buckets back in the shed. But it was choice that brought me there to begin with. I could've gone straight home and called Cherisse that night. Taken us both out for a nice dinner and movie with the money I'd earned from Uncle Paul.

Instead, I was in a shed, red paint wet on my hands, a flashlight aimed in my eyes, when a deep voice boomed, "Maquoit police. Put your hands up and step outside."

Chapter Four

Until you've been on the other side of it, you don't know how scary The Law can be. Those guys in the uniforms who visit elementary schools with the cute crime dog . . . what's his name, McNab? McGruff? . . . and pass out goody bags? *Not* your friends. At least, not if they think they caught you doing something. You might have believed once upon a time that their job was to look out for you, but if you cross over? To the bad guys' side? They are out to get you. And all those things you always took for granted, like soccer, your reputation, your future . . . they're suddenly not so sure. It's a whole new world, with a whole new vocabulary.

Like "criminal mischief." That's what Donnie and I did, apparently. They didn't tell us that right away. First, Officer Smiley (not his real name) marched us out of the shed, demanded to know our names and what we were doing, and, when Donnie tried to sweet-talk our way out of it, made us get into his cruiser. I wanted to punch Donnie at that moment. The guy has no sense. I mean, you do not—do *not*—get into long conversations with the police. Simple, short answers to basic questions. Silence, if you're not sure how to answer. Don't lie, but don't offer anything. It's not like I knew this from experience, but when I got my license last year, Uncle Paul took me aside and gave me some pointers based on *his* experience.

I have no idea whether the cop had a weapon drawn. But in the dark, with that tone in his voice, it felt like he did. Next thing I knew, me and Donnie were in separate interrogation rooms at the Maquoit police station, and they were asking me if we'd been drinking, how we'd gotten in, what were we doing there, that sort of thing. Not a warm and fuzzy conversation, despite my best efforts to convince them that, appearances aside, I was an upstanding citizen.

Because the door *was* unlocked (turns out the grounds guy at Maquoit is constantly forgetting to padlock the shed) and we didn't destroy or steal anything, it wasn't breaking and entering. But writing *You suck, Maquoit!* on their rock was considered tampering with someone else's property, and that's criminal mischief. I looked it up online, after the cops finally called my wicked upset parents, who picked us up at the police station. Donnie, too, since no one answered the phone at his house.

That was a fun car ride. First, we had to return to the rock-with-the-still-wet-paint to pick up the car I'd left there. And Don, who just *can't* keep his big mouth shut to save his life, made it even better. We three Bouchards were silent as Dad pulled out of the station parking lot. But not Donnie. He launched right in.

"Mr. and Mrs. Bouchard, you need to know, this was *not* Tom's idea. This was all my fault and I dragged Tom into it because I needed a ride. He actually didn't want to—"

"It doesn't matter whose bright idea this was," Mom interrupted.

"The problem is that neither of you boys realized it was a *bad* idea." She spoke in that way she has when it comes out all quiet but you feel like you're getting screamed at. Actually, you'd prefer getting screamed at. Precise, clipped words, hissed from clenched jaws and razor-sharp. Ouch.

"I'll call John Cantor first thing in the morning," Dad said quietly to Mom.

"Of course!" she said in disgust. "What do you think his retainer will be?"

"Who's John Cantor?" Don murmured to me.

"Lawyer friend of my dad's," I replied under my breath. Even in the dark car, I could see his eyes widen.

"Oh man, you don't think we need lawyers, do you?" he said to my parents. That's when I kicked him. "Ouch! What the heck, Tom?" he exclaimed.

My mother wheeled around in the seat, straining against her seat belt.

"What part of 'this is serious' do you not understand?" she seethed.

When we arrived at the rock, I stayed in the car with Dad. "Sorry, dude," I muttered to Don. You don't want to know the look he gave me, but as he and Mom drove off in the darkness to his house, I figured he deserved it.

Once back chez Bouchard, it took me less than two minutes on Google to find the meaning of *serious:* "A person is guilty of criminal mischief if that person intentionally, knowingly or recklessly: (a) damages or destroys the property of another, or (b) tampers with the property of another, having no reasonable grounds to believe that the person has the right to do so."

Criminal mischief carries up to a year in jail, plus fines. Now *that* sucks. Even if it does earn you epic props at school.

It's not like there was a banner with my name draped over the front doors of Joshua Chamberlain High School on Monday morning, but there might as well have been. I mean, I had spoken to *no one* besides the police, my parents, and John Cantor. Whose fee, if I got charged and he got hired, would be five thousand dollars. That was just to retain him. After that, he'd bill my parents by the hour. So long, college money. What little my parents had saved, anyway.

Oh, and Cherisse. Who called me on my cell late Sunday night. Which, of course, is how word got out. No one can spread a fire faster than Cherisse Ouellette. She programs her phone to simultaneously dial, email, and text everyone she knows the very moment she has a scrap of information worth sharing. And Cherisse knows a lot of people eager to gobble up her scraps.

"That sucks!" she exclaimed when I told her what happened at the rock. Correction: it's what she said after I told her that I was grounded as a result of what happened at the rock. "For how long?"

"Indefinitely," I said. "Hopefully they'll let me out of the house for graduation."

She made a sound bordering on a wail.

"But I can come over, right?" she said. "They'll let you see me?"

I didn't tell Cherisse that she was probably the last person in Enniston my mom would allow over during my groundation.

"I doubt it," I said. "They're pretty mad."

I heard a bona fide wail.

"Look on the bright side," I replied. "As long as I'm under house arrest, I can get my college apps finished. So when they spring me, we'll have more time to hang out."

"I don't want you to go to college," she said in this pouty-little-girl voice. "Promise me you won't go."

"If I don't get the apps done, it's pretty much a promise," I said quietly.

"Yay!" Cherisse said. "But if you have to go, go to U. Maine. So I can visit you. Or maybe I'll go there, too. Wouldn't that be cool? If we went to college together?" I tried to imagine my mother's face if she heard that suggestion.

"Yeah, sure. And who knows? Maybe I'll go for free."

"Free?" Cherisse asked.

"Yeah. All Maine valedictorians can attend the University of Maine for no charge."

"Wait. You're number one in our class?" She sounded skeptical.

"Well . . . no. I'm number three right now. Liz Painchaud is number one. But they'll recalculate in January, so you never know."

"God, that girl is such a dweeb," Cherisse said with a laugh. "Didya see what she was wearing yesterday?"

"Uh . . . didn't notice, actually." There was a pause. I had less than zero interest in talking about Liz Painchaud's fashion mistakes.

"You should totally beat her," Cherisse finally said. "But God, I can't believe I date a geek! Number three!"

"Sorry. Don't tell anyone, okay?"

"But you're such a *hot* geek, Tom Bouchard." Another pause. "Have I told you recently how hot you are?"

"Kind of an oxymoron," I said, laughing.

"What?"

"Hot geek," I repeated. "You know, like jumbo shrimp? It's an oxymoron."

"No, I mean, you're really *smart*, Tommy. Not a moron!" Cherisse persisted.

There was a tap on my bedroom door at that point. Mom, carrying an armload of folded laundry. I signed off with Cherisse (I didn't have the energy to explain that an oxymoron is not a moron), who evidently spent the rest of the night texting most of Joshua Chamberlain High School that Tom Bouchard was a juvenile delinquent.

I would've been good with hot geek.

I hadn't even made it to my first class when it started. Seriously, I walked into the crowded lobby and heard, "Hey, Bouchard! Maquoit sucks!" People laughed. Someone else called out, "Tom, you're the man," and a few others cheered. Of course, the vice principal was hall monitor that morning, and he moved right in. He materialized at my side like he'd been waiting for me.

"That's enough, people," he said loudly. I felt his hand on my elbow. "Tom, you're to head straight to guidance."

Four years at this place and it was the first time the guy had spoken to me. That's because vice principals only deal with troublemakers.

But now I was in that category.

Instead of my guidance counselor's closet-sized office, I was directed to the conference room. This is where they put us when college reps visit and make their pitch to five or six semi-awake students who are less interested in college and more interested in ditching that period's class. Coach Gerardi was there, along with my guidance counselor, Mrs. Swift. And Principal Cockrell. Now, him I'd spoken to before. Usually after soccer games, when he'd shake my hand or slap me on the back.

No backslapping that morning. He was all business.

"Well, Tommy, I have to say I've had better Sunday afternoons," Mr. Cockrell began. "I was on the phone with the principal at Maquoit High School. You don't want to know how long."

"I'm really sorry about that, sir," I managed to say before the expression on his face cut me off. "Furious" pretty much described it. Mr. Cockrell had had to eat major crow on my behalf, and he obviously didn't like Maquoit crow any better than I did.

"Now, when the police released you boys the other night, you understood there might be the possibility of charges, correct?" he continued, keeping his tone level despite the anger I knew simmered beneath the words. I nodded. Inevitability of charges, more like. Officer Smiley made it real clear that no one from Maquoit would cut us slack.

Here it comes, I thought.

"Well, I managed to convince him that since this is the first time you have ever gotten into anything remotely resembling trouble—though I can't say the same for Mr. Plourde—pressing charges would be an overreaction."

A gush of air poured from my lungs. I'd been holding my breath.

"How about 'Thank you, Mr. Cockrell'?" Coach prompted. More growly than usual.

"Thanks!" I said quickly. "So they're going to forget the whole thing?"

Mr. Cockrell held up his hand.

"I didn't say that. I said no charges. That doesn't mean no consequences."

My lungs sucked back in. Shoulders tightened.

"To begin with, we've arranged for you and Donnie to repaint the Maquoit rock. At your own expense. You'll buy the paint and supplies, and paint it after school. And I expect you'll have an audience, if you know what I mean."

Sasquatch. The whole Maquoit forward line. Wearing their Olympic Development Program shirts. Damn. Damn, damn . . .

"You'll also have to do some community service. One hundred hours each. And your graduation in the spring depends on whether you complete those hours."

"A hundred hours!" It burst from my lips.

"You have a problem with that?" Coach Gerardi demanded.

"No," I replied instantly. "But . . . wow. One hundred. I mean, it took me through junior year to finish my thirty." Thirty hours of community service is a requirement at our high school. We each have until the end of senior year to log them all.

"Maybe if you were more involved in the community, a hundred hours wouldn't seem so daunting," Mrs. Swift said quietly.

"Maybe if you were more involved in the community, you might think about how your actions affect the community!" Coach snarled. His face was red. "You are a captain! You represent this school, your team, and this town. I know your buddy Plourde has his head up his ass ninety percent of the time, but I expected better from you! You let us down, Tommy."

Something about the yelling turned my worried-and-humble into pissed-off. I mean, I got the whole role-model thing, and how doing this sort of stuff sets off bad feelings between schools. But it's not like we broke anything or stole anything. No substances were involved. No one was hurt. I mean, c'mon: it was a *joke*.

I looked Coach in the eye.

"I know it was a mistake, sir. It won't happen again."

Coach is no fool. He knew exactly what I *didn't* say.

"I should bench you," he said.

I didn't reply.

"You know why I'm not going to?" he continued.

I paused. It felt like a trick question.

"Because you're . . . fair?" I said finally. I wasn't trying to smart-ass him, but as soon as the words were out, I could see how he might take it that way.

"Because I'm overruled!" he practically shouted. "Our athletic director wants to give you another chance, and I think if you were a less talented player I'd be able to convince him otherwise. But the fact is the team needs you out there, so consider yourself very, very lucky. And make sure your friend Mr. Plourde knows how lucky *he* is. He got off light because he was with you." Coach pushed his chair back and strode from the room. Mrs. Swift and Mr. Cockrell said nothing, eyes focused on the table before them. As if Coach's outburst had been directed at them, too.

The bell signaling first period rang, and I got up. Before I left the conference room, Mrs. Swift handed me a slip of paper. She'd written "K Street Center" and a phone number on it.

"This is an organization, walking distance from school, where you might start to volunteer some hours," she said. "They need tutors for their homework helpers program."

"Thanks," I told her, then folded the paper and shoved it into my pocket. K Street's a long walk from the high school, pretty much in Saeed's neighborhood. But if I had a hundred hours between me and graduation, it was as good as any other place to start.

The halls were empty as I hurried to my first-period class. Then I heard his voice behind me.

"Tom-boy!"

He must have also been at guidance. Separate interrogation rooms again.

"Wait up." Donnie quick-stepped over to me.

"So, didya get the good news?" he said.

"A hundred hours of service plus public humiliation at the rock? What part of 'good' am I missing here?" I said.

"Are you kidding? We are so off the hook! This could've gone down real bad."

"Yeah, that's what they want you to think," I said. "C'mon. We slapped some paint on a rock. Not a federal crime."

Donnie shook his head.

"Not for you, maybe. But they know me, man. And shit adds up. So I was apologizing all over in there."

"And you told me you never lie."

Donnie stopped. Stared at me in the middle of the quiet hall.

"I don't. I *am* sorry. Not for what we did. I mean, Maquoit *does* suck." He laughed a little. Brushed the hair from his eyes. Donnie's hair always seems to need trimming.

"But I'm sorry I dragged you into it. The Maquoit people could have been jerks, you know? Could've wrecked that spotless reputation of yours." He punched me lightly on the arm, then sauntered down the hallway.

I watched him turn a corner at the end of the hall and head in the opposite direction from me.

Chapter Five

Practice that day began with extra laps, which pissed me off.

It was the Somali guys. Again. The same two, Saeed and Ismail, were slow to get laced up, and Coach always penalizes us with a few fast laps around the field if even one person is late. As captain, I try, seriously, to keep an eye out for this sort of thing and keep everybody moving, but sometimes? Motivating the people on this team is like herding cats.

I was matched up with Saeed for quick passes and warm-up drills, which should have put a smile on my grouchy face because the guy is the Tom Brady of passing accuracy. And yeah, I'm mixing my metaphors here, but hey, I like football. It just bugged me that I couldn't say that to the guy. Couldn't even compliment him. First, because there was no way he knew who the New England Patriots were, and second, because his English sucked. I thought he was totally faking it by tossing out a few random words at the right time, like "great pass" and "cool." But most of what everybody said blew right by him.

So late and pissed off were pretty much the themes of the day, and not only because I'd been hauled into guidance first thing and was late for first period. I'd been late to third period 'cause of the lost kid.

He was slumped against the wall in the history wing, this skinny black dude, his head in his hands. He seemed young, maybe a freshman. People were changing classes and walking past him like he wasn't there. Everybody—black, white—just ignored him. I don't think it's because they didn't care. I think we'd just gotten used to the bizarreness of the whole situation. Girls praying on their knees in the stairwells while students stepped around them. Packs, sometimes five a day, of new black faces in the guidance office. They'd wait patiently while Mrs. Swift and Co. buzzed frantically in and out of each other's little cubbies, waving wads of paper and trying to get everyone sorted out. Every single day they had to show new kids how to do totally simple things, like move through the cafeteria line to buy lunch, or open a locker, or change classes when the bell rang. Eventually they'd figure it out. But then more new kids would show up. Every. Single. Day.

Liz Painchaud came up with the bright idea to get all of us in National Honor Society (she's president) to wear these badges in the halls, so that students who needed help could ask us to point them in the right direction. Which turned out to mean *walking* them to class, because they didn't understand what you meant by "Go down these stairs, turn left at the end of the hall, and follow the numbers." Plus you had to put up with the jokers: "Help me, Bouchard! I'm lost! I can't find my way to the bathroom!" Then, after the third teacher gave me crap for showing up late to class, even though I explained I was walking Somali kids to *their* classes, I threw in my badge and told Liz to stuff it. I mean,

I got how hard it was on everyone, and we all needed to pitch in and be patient. But after a while you just wanted a break. You just wanted . . . normal. Even for one day.

Anyway, there he was, a random kid sitting on the floor. People didn't look twice.

I crouched beside him.

"Hey," I said quietly. "You all right?" He lifted his head.

He looked like he'd seen a ghost. I think he trembled. He didn't answer my question; I don't think he could. I didn't know what was wrong with the guy, but it went way beyond not knowing how to get to his next class. He folded his legs up to his chest and rested his forehead on his knees.

I sat with him until the halls cleared out, thinking the whole time that if my third-period teacher tried to give me a tardy slip I was gonna get ugly. As soon as it was quiet, I nudged him.

"Think you can stand up?" I asked. No response. I hooked my hands under his arms and lifted. Surprisingly, he didn't resist. He got to his feet. He let me pick up his backpack. I put my arm across his shoulders.

"We're going to walk to the guidance office now," I told him, speaking slowly, carefully pronouncing each word. No response, but he came with me. He kept his head down and the scared expression switched to just plain blank. Like he had disappeared deep inside himself.

At guidance, I found him a chair and went straight to Ms. Bernier, the woman at the front desk who basically runs the place. I explained the situation, she wrote me a pass for my next period, and as I left I heard her say in a loud, friendly voice to the lost guy, "I'll be right with you, *deah*. Don't worry; we'll get you all fixed up."

Outside the guidance office, I had to take a deep breath and count to ten. I wasn't upset with Ms. Bernier. Hell, I knew her. I was related to her somehow. She and her family are always at the big summer picnic we do at Enniston City Park each year, with all the third and fourth cousins and relatives twice removed, that sort of thing. Berniers and Bouchards and Thibeaults and Pelletiers . . . it's a big party. And she's a nice woman. She's not stupid. And it wasn't her fault that "we'll get you all fixed up" was completely useless to begin to deal with whatever was going on with that kid. But it was the best she could do.

Just like keeping him from getting stepped on was the best I could do. But being totally over our heads like that? Pissed me off.

After drills, Coach set us up for corner kicks. He put our keeper, Pete LeBourdais, in goal, and our best defenders spread out in front of him.

"Okay, I want to run what might be an actual corner kick situation. So in the box right now I want to see Saeed, Ismail, Jake, and Mike. Tommy and the other middies just outside the box. I want you boys to show me how you're gonna get the ball into the goal off the corner kick."

He lined up the rest of the team at the corner, and one by one they sent it sailing to center. Or not. Most of the guys never took the corner kick, so the strikers waiting for the ball were stuck with some pretty lame options for scoring. Which annoyed me. Because I didn't see the point, frankly, of trying to make a play off some weak-ass pass.

Coach Gerardi obviously wasn't seeing it that way. After every kick—which, incidentally, rarely made it near the front of the goal; Pete looked totally bored—Coach was commenting, correcting, suggesting what Saeed/Ismail/Jake/Mike coulda/shoulda/woulda done. Finally he motioned to me.

"Tommy, take the next kick."

I like to stand five steps back for a corner. I raised my hand, signaling that I was ready to go. Then one-two-three-four *pow!* Slightly under and slightly to the side of the ball, with the inside of my foot. It sailed up, not too high, to center. Descended into the scrum of players gathered before the goal. I saw Mike leap into the air to take the header. Ismail jumped, too.

Talk to each other, people! I wanted to scream.

Mike made no contact whatsoever with the ball. Ismail, who clearly had gotten in Mike's way, let it fall. Used his chest, not to deflect it into the goal, but to deaden and drop it. It thudded against him and landed at his feet, and with the top of his foot he sort of caught and kick-flung it forward.

Pete never saw it coming. It was in the net before he could wave at it.

"Whoa-ho!" Coach yelled from the sidelines. "Nice job! *Nice job!*"

He made me do it again (guess he figured it was time to put in someone who could actually kick a corner), and now Saeed got the touch. He didn't head it. But while the ball was still pretty high he used his foot to control it. Touch, settle, two little taps of a dribble forward, then he fired it into the goal. That time, even though Pete was expecting it, it still ended up behind him in the net.

Over and over I set them up from the corner. Sometimes the kick wasn't so accurate, but when I did get it into the box, one of the guys could usually make something happen. It was good, even if some of it was a little unorthodox. Like, Jake and Mike tend to try to take the ball from up high and head it. Saeed and Ismail: no way. Feet, chests, backs, for sure, every which way and some pretty impossible ways, too. But I didn't see that ball touch their heads. Not once. They definitely had some sort of finesse thing going that didn't involve jostling brain cells.

Coach switched us up. He put me in the box and Saeed at corner. The guy stood way back. Like, twice as far as I usually stand. He waited. He took his time. His hand went up and he advanced, deliberately, in what almost looked like slow motion. His foot connected neatly with the ball.

Now, I've never seen angels. When I was a little boy at St. Cecilia's, I used to watch for them. We believed, all of us back then, in angels. In the Tooth Fairy, Santa Claus, leprechauns . . . God, too. We believed and we waited, because that's what kids do. We pretty much would not have been surprised if some big winged dude walked into the classroom one day and began handing out crayons. Or at least flew by the windows outside.

Eventually you figure out Dad's been slipping quarters under your pillow at night and taking your old teeth. Santa Claus brings better toys to the rich kids' houses. God's debatable, and there are no angels.

But when Saeed kicked that ball, I swear: someone guided it. Someone who appreciated the beauty and perfection of a white ball rising from the ground in a rainbow arc. A ball that didn't whiz, didn't soar, didn't zip. It floated. It curved gracefully, the perfect distance away from furiously leaping legs and bobbing heads and waving, scrabbling goalie's hands, until it descended, settling with a soft whoosh, like a waterbird landing on a lake, into a corner of the goal. The net caught it, embraced it.

You couldn't have done it better.

Ismail screamed something I didn't understand and ran toward Saeed. Every guy was on him, the whole team. Mike was losing his mind. Even Pete LeBourdais rushed him. I looked toward Coach, half expecting him to join the swarm, but the guy was motionless. He just stared at the ball entangled in the back corner of the goal.

When our eyes met, there was an expression in his I'd never seen before.

Like he'd just seen an angel.

After practice I got a lift to the K Street Center. You'd have thought they weren't expecting me. I had called, so they knew I was coming, but the crazy-ass chaos that greeted me when I stepped through the doors sure didn't look like homework help.

Sure didn't smell like it, either. More like old sneakers. Unwashed sheets. Unwashed dudes. Seriously, the place was crawling with little kids, but these gray-looking guys in dusty jeans and broken shoes were flopped on some beat-up couch in the middle of the room, staring at the television. Judge Judy, scolding someone. So that was my first mental note about the K Street Center: they don't get cable. Because there isn't a guy on the planet, even if he's an out-of-it guy with broken shoes, who would watch *Judge Judy* if he could flip to ESPN.

It was hard to tell whether the place had been, or still was, part of a church. The front looked like an old church, but everyone entered through the back. There was a grassless yard with a metal gate around it, the ground beaten smooth, like from too many feet, and it swarmed with children. They poured in and out of the building, or wandered down the sidewalk, then disappeared into the maze of four-story wooden apartments that stretched the length of the block. They spilled across the street to play on the swings, the basketball courts, the skate park. In the distance, the spires of the Catholic cathedral towered above every other building.

"Can I help you?" This white girl, who barely reached my shoulder, spoke to me. Her nose was pierced with a round gold stud. Her blond hair was cut close, and a 'random patch on one side was dyed purple.

"Uh, yeah. I'm Tom Bouchard. I'm . . . ah, supposed to be here for homework help?"

Purple-Patch Girl smiled, which made her look older. Older than me, actually.

"Giving or receiving?"

"What?"

"Are you here looking for help, or are you a volunteer?" She waited patiently for my answer.

"Giving. I mean, volunteering. Yeah." I sounded unbelievably stupid. Something about her eyes, really blue, and her question unnerved me. Did I *look* like I needed help? "I called. Talked to somebody named Joe?"

"Cool," she said easily. "Joe is out buying diapers right now, but I can show you where to go." She turned and walked past the TV dudes to the back of the room, where she had to shove a packed rack of clothes out of the way before we could continue down a dim hallway. She wore bell-bottomed jeans that hugged her at the hips and covered her feet, dragging a little on the floor.

"I'm Myla, by the way," she said over her shoulder as we walked.

"Tom," I replied.

"Yeah, you said," she answered. Smiled, but not in a mean way.

"Do you work here?" I asked her.

"Yes. And no. I get paid for eight hours a week as part of my work-study job at Mumford. But I'm here way more than that, so I guess I'm also a volunteer."

"You're a college student?" She didn't fit my idea of a Mumford student: blond girls wearing skinny jeans tucked into Ugg boots, driving shiny SUVs with out-of-state plates and ski racks on top.

We'd reached the end of the hall and a closed door. Hand on the knob, she turned to me.

"You sound surprised," she said.

"No, it's just . . . you're small."

Totally stupid comment. This was off to an epic bad start.

"I know, right? Usually only tall people go to college. But Mumford made an exception in my case." She was still smiling, but now there was a hint of *Hmm, is this guy ridiculous?* in her expression. She pushed the door open to reveal a long room filled with cafeteria tables and metal chairs. Half the seats were taken up by kids, books spread out before them. Some hunched together in small groups; a few stood, leaning over their papers, elbows resting on the tabletops. Others ran around, laughing. Looked like a game of tag was going on. I didn't see any other "helpers."

All the kids were black. Most were girls. I guessed, from the clothes, that they were all Muslim. At least, the girls were. The boys were dressed like any American kid; the girls wore long skirts and their hair was covered.

"Hey! Abdi! What did I tell you?" Myla spoke sharply to a boy who was running. This little guy, who looked like he might be all

49

of eight years old, skidded to a stop. His eyes widened. He tried to look sorry, but those eyes were laughing. I smiled at him.

"This is the quiet and reading room. Play outside, okay?"

Abdi nodded.

"Are you finished with your homework?" Myla continued.

Abdi shook his head.

"Okay, well, Tom here is going to help you get it all done," she said to him. I tried not to look surprised. For some reason I'd been expecting a little more . . . preparation? Some sort of introduction?

And that "all done" part? I had figured on this lasting an hour.

Abdi didn't say anything, but dutifully walked over to a metal chair with a Spider-Man backpack on it and heaved the pack onto the table. He unzipped it and began pulling out crumpled papers.

"Abdi's been having a hard time in third grade," Myla said quietly. "His spoken English is amazing when you consider he's only been in this country for six months. But he barely reads. He's still learning his letters. And you know how third grade is when you stop learning to read and start reading to learn? He is getting *so* left behind."

I nodded, like I got what the hell she was talking about.

"Why don't they just move him into a lower grade?" I said.

She smiled grimly.

"They're placing all these kids based on age, not ability," she said. "If they didn't, half the high school would be in first grade with Abdi. Problem is, there are hardly any ELL teachers in Enniston."

"Sorry . . . ELL?" I asked.

"English Language Learners," she explained. "People trained to teach English as a second language. They've hired a few, but nobody was prepared for how these kids are pouring into the schools right now. Everyone's playing catch-up." She half patted, half pushed me on the back toward Abdi.

"You're good to help out. It's too bad more people in town don't feel like you. Come look for me when you're finished." Myla turned and headed for the door. As she left the room, a little girl jumped from her chair and hurled herself at Myla, wrapping her arms tightly around her waist. The kid was a splash of bright colors and patterns, from her long skirt to her head covering. Myla stopped long enough to return the hug and speak with her.

"Hey. You gonna help me?"

Abdi stared expectantly. His arms were folded across his chest. His legs, which didn't reach the floor, swung impatiently from his perch in the metal chair.

"Sorry. This is my first day," I explained as I pulled up a chair alongside him. I stuck out my hand. "I'm Tom."

He shook my hand.

"I'm Abdi. You a Mumford student?"

"Can't, dude, it's all girls. Besides, I'm in high school. I go to Chamberlain. What about you? College or high school?"

He looked incredulous.

"No way, man! I just a kid! What . . . you crazy or something?"

I shrugged.

"I don't know. You could be, like, a midget genius. What grade are you in?"

"Third grade. I in third grade! Man . . . you crazy!" He laughed. But he'd gotten the joke, and I had his attention. At least for a few minutes. Those feet of his, swinging beneath the table, reminded me of Donnie.

"So what've we got here, Abdi?" I said, lifting one of his papers from the pile. It was almost impossible to read, like it had been smashed into a ball and unfolded again a bunch of times.

"You play sports?" he asked me. He had a thick accent going but spoke in full sentences.

"Do you like sports?" I asked.

He nodded.

"I like soccer. You play soccer?" he asked.

I put the paper down. "You bet I like soccer. I play on my school team."

He jumped off his chair. "Oh man . . . what position?"

"I'm a midfielder. But I can play striker, too."

He was so excited he leaped in the air. "Yes! Me too. That's my position!" I didn't bother to ask him which one. His feet shifted from side to side.

A couple of the girls looked our way. "Shh!" one hissed.

"I think we're disturbing the others," I told him, motioning him back to the chair. "Tell you what: let's take a look at the homework, and when you're finished we can go outside and kick around a little. Do they have a ball here?"

Wrong question. Wrong suggestion. In a flash, Abdi was out of the chair again and making a run for the door. I grabbed him by his T-shirt and reeled him back in.

"Whoa. I think I said homework first, soccer later."

"They do! They have a ball. Myla knows where. C'mon, man, ask her."

It took a few minutes to convince Abdi that I really wouldn't play unless he finished his homework. He looked pretty disgruntled, but I stuck to my guns. There was no way I was gonna face

Myla after only five minutes and admit I was a homework helper failure.

Abdi was working on writing the letters of the alphabet. According to his sheet (which we eventually uncrumpled), this day's letter was R. He was supposed to practice writing an entire page of upper- and lowercase R's, then draw pictures of words that begin with R. I watched as squiggly lines of big and little R's marched across his page. It was messy at first, because he was hurrying to wrap up and go play soccer, but then he actually settled down. He was left-handed, like me.

When he finished with the letters, he pulled out a box of crayons.

"Okay, so: words that begin with R. What can you think of?" I asked him.

He shrugged. He looked down, then away. One foot started swinging.

"What sound does an R make?" I prompted.

Abdi shrugged again. I couldn't tell whether he was just bored and jerking my chain or if he really didn't know.

I floated my tongue in the middle of my mouth and growled at him: "Urrrrr." This cracked him up.

"You *crazy*, man," he laughed. But he did it back: "Urrrrr."

"Awesome, dude! Now let's think up some words. I'll give you a few examples, but you have to come up with some yourself. How about . . . *urrrriver? Urrrroach? Urrrrat?*"

"*Urrrri!*" Abdi shouted.

All the girls' heads shot up. "Shh!" one hissed at him again.

"Uh . . . what?" I said.

"*Ri!*" he repeated. I was stumped.

"You know: *ri*. It like . . ." Abdi scrunched up his face. He was dying to say something but just couldn't spit it out. Suddenly he got on all fours. He started scuttling around the room, going "Naaaa! Naaaa!" loudly. The other kids in the room completely abandoned their homework at that point. Some were yelling at Abdi to be quiet. Others laughed at his antics.

"Is it a sheep?" I guessed. "Baaa? Baaa?"

Abdi stood.

"No, no, not a sheep," he corrected me. "Look." He grabbed a crayon and began drawing. An animal. Four legs. Kind of furry. Sharp hooves. When he added these little horns, I got it.

"A goat?" I said.

He tossed the crayon down. "Yes! Goat. *Ri*."

"Well, why didn't you say so?" I laughed.

He shook his head. "I forget. I get so many words in here. . . ." He struck the heel of his hand on his forehead, a little hard. "Sometimes I forget."

"Yeah, I'll bet," I said. "But are you supposed to come up with *R*-words in English or Somali?" He shrugged. The assignment didn't make it clear. We decided to go with a combo, so in addition to his drawing of a *ri* we added a road and a ring. His pictures were hurried because he wanted to get outside and play . . . and so did I. He stuffed the completed pages back into the Spider-Man pack (I was beginning to understand how they got so crumpled) and ran out ahead of me to find a soccer ball.

Back in the main room an *Oprah* rerun was now on the TV and the gray-looking guys had left. I saw Myla seated in this small, glassed-in cubicle off to the side, behind a desk, talking to someone. I only saw the back of the person, a woman wearing a blue head scarf. I stood in the entrance to the office.

"Hey, I'm gonna go outside and kick the ball around with Abdi for a while, if that's okay," I said.

Her eyes widened. "He's finished? Wow. Good work," she said. Something about her expression made me think finishing homework might be new for Abdi.

"You sound surprised," I said. Second time that comment had passed between us. I felt the corners of my mouth turn up.

"I am." She smiled.

"Did you think I couldn't handle it?" I said. It occurred to me she'd known exactly what she was doing when she set me up with the little man.

Myla shrugged. "Obviously you could." She held my gaze. Blue, blue eyes.

"Bribery works," I continued, not in any big hurry to leave now. "Turns out he's a Chamberlain soccer fan." The woman with her back to me swiveled around. At first I didn't recognize her. Then the expression of dislike on her face reminded me.

"Oh. Hey," I said automatically to Saeed's sister.

Myla raised her eyebrows. "You two know each other?"

"Sort of," I said, at the same moment the girl replied, "He plays with Saeed." Awkward pause. I wondered how much she knew about the Maquoit rock thing.

Probably a lot.

"Remind me of your name . . . ?" I said.

"Samira," she said flatly.

I nodded. "Her brother is an amazing soccer player," I said to Myla.

"So I've heard," she replied. "I need to make it to some of your games this fall. Check out the amazing Saeed. Oh, and you too, of course. Are you any good?" She grinned wickedly. Getting back at me for the "short" comment, no doubt.

"I hold my own," I said easily.

"What are you doing here?"

Samira's question, thrust so abruptly into my pleasant little skirmish with Ms. Mumford Student, startled me. Her voice sounded almost harsh. Accusing.

"Volunteering," I said quickly. "What are *you* doing here?"

Her eyes narrowed and she tilted her head, processing this information.

Myla looked puzzled, at the two of us.

"Samira has been helping out around here with translating," she said. "She's pretty much a lifeline to a lot of new people in this community who don't speak English."

"Oh yeah?" I said. "That's cool. By the way, I see those permission slips worked out. I mean, since Saeed can play and all." *You're welcome,* I managed to not say to her. I mean, what was *up* with this girl?

"It's because you got in trouble," Samira said suddenly. As if some lightbulb had just gone off in her head. She nodded, kind of in an old-ladyish way. "I heard my brother's friends talking about it. You went to that other town and did something and now you have to do service to stay on the team."

I shifted my pack a little higher on my shoulder. I stared steadily back at her.

I was thinking it might be a good time to find out what Abdi was up to.

"Yeah, that's right," I said quietly. No one spoke for a few long seconds.

"So," Myla finally said, "coming here is a punishment?"

"I get to do service *instead* of being punished," I said. "Coming here is my *service*."

Myla glanced at Samira, shrugged, and opened a drawer in the desk. She pulled out a familiar piece of light blue paper. It was the service sheet we need to have filled out if we want our hours officially recorded. She scribbled something on it and pushed it across the desk to me.

"Whatever. I put you down for one hour," she said. "When are you coming back?"

My mind scrolled through my week's schedule. "Tuesday next week?" I asked.

Myla shrugged once more. "We're always here." She returned her gaze to Samira, who had her back to me now. I turned and left. Just walked straight out the door, didn't touch the blue paper, didn't even say thanks or goodbye or anything.

Because now I was super pissed.

Chapter Six

I remember the exact day of the fight because it was really nice outside.

September is pretty much the best month of the year in Maine, which makes the fact that we're stuck in class instead of hanging out at the beach *really* suck, but that particular day? When a couple of the white guys on varsity and two new Somali kids on JV decided to be assholes? Warm, cloud-free, and bright.

We spilled outside after the final bell, and those of us lucky enough to not have to load onto the loser cruiser (aka the school bus) just sort of collapsed on the front lawn. People stretched out, soaking in those vitamin D rays, which, our health teachers had informed us, would pretty much disappear from the Maine skies by November. I had plans to meet Donnie and head over to the hardware store. My team had the late practice, so I figured we could swing by the store beforehand and pick up paint and supplies.

The "untampering" of the Maquoit rock was scheduled for that weekend.

As I waited for Don, this little clutch of Somali girls emerged from the school. Samira was with them; I recognized her right off.

Dress code for these girls seemed to be "draped." Long skirts and a head covering that pretty much looked like another skirt, only you got to have your face sticking out. I had been informed by the ever-informing Liz Painchaud (who was also president of the just-created Civil Rights Club and had been hassling me to join; she'd already snagged Mike Turcotte) that this headwear was called a *hijab*, and that while some Muslims insisted it was spelled out right in the Koran that women had to wear them, other Muslims said it was more of a culture thing and not specifically religious.

Yeah. I got that earful from Liz when she heard me say "head skirts."

Here's what I knew: Saeed's sister was all over the map with it.

Some days she was rockin' the *hijab*; other days the jewelry and a little kerchief. One day it was a sweatshirt and a head scarf; another day that bomber jacket. You never got much skin, and I couldn't say for sure if I'd ever seen her hair, but she sure was stepping out (at least with her clothes) in ways the other Muslim girls hadn't tried. The majority of them dressed more like old-fashioned Catholic nuns, with their wimples and floor-length habits.

The day of the fight was a University of Maine hoodie day for her. I remember first thinking, *Wow, she must be sweating in that thing*, then realizing it was Samira. She and her pack weren't ten feet from me. I automatically raised my hand as they passed.

She saw me. Looked right at me, then through me. Not even a nod.

"Seriously, *what* is your problem?" I think I said it out loud. Must have, because even though she was out of earshot at that point, someone else heard me.

"No problem, bro. It's all good." Donnie's backpack landed beside me with a thud. He flopped on the ground.

"Didn't mean you." I tilted my head toward Samira's retreating back. "I meant her. Saeed's sister."

"Saeed the soccer dude?" Donnie asked. "I didn't know he had a sister."

"Oh yeah," I said. I told him then. About the hostile looks and the stuck-up attitude. As I spoke, this incredulous expression spread across Donnie's face.

"Let me see if I've got this right," he said. "You are dating the hottest female in our high school and you want to know why some girl who goes around dressed in multicolored bedsheets is giving you the evil eye? You care about this why?"

"They don't wear bedsheets. Get with the cultural program, man."

"Whatever," Donnie said. "I don't see why this is getting to you. Who knows what the hell they're thinking behind those burkas? Who cares?"

I stared at him.

"Wow. That sucks. Even for you," I said. Donnie laughed. I shook my head.

"What?" he said.

"That was, like, totally out of line."

His eyes widened.

"Since when did you start getting all politically correct? Please. You know I don't give a damn what color somebody is or what they wear. This is the land of the free and the home of the brave and they can join the club and do fuck-all, as far as I'm concerned. Which still doesn't explain why you're so upset that one girl out of five hundred at Chamberlain High isn't worshipping at your altar."

Ahead of us, the long line of mustard-yellow school buses was preparing to pull out. Drivers had begun flashing their taillights and retracting the little stop signs that stuck out the sides. Only one bus seemed behind the curve; people were still standing on the sidewalk, waiting to climb aboard.

"Besides, when has Tom Bouchard ever given a rat's ass about what some girl *thinks?*" Don continued, grinning at me. He was being a real comedian.

"You know, just because you're a total douchebag about girls doesn't mean I am," I replied.

He burst out laughing.

"What?" I demanded.

"You think dating below your pay grade isn't being a total douche?"

Unbelievable.

"So Cherisse isn't rich enough? Tell me I'm not hearing this."

Donnie shook his head.

"I'm not talking about money. I'm talking about quality. Hey, I mean, I get it! If I were big man on campus with a side of rock star, like you, I'd date the high school hottie, too. But you gotta admit: she's not in your league."

Something was wrong with the bus. Kids on the sidewalk were stepping back to make space for kids who were getting out.

"You sound like my parents," I told him.

He shook his head. "No, your parents want you to date Liz

Painchaud and the rest of the National Hypocrites Society. I just want to see you with someone who doesn't suck."

I tried to imagine what sort of guy would date Liz Painchaud, destroyer of male egos ("You guys are all *idiots*," she likes to say), destroyer of test curves ("Sorry, kids, but Liz got a hundred again"), and destroyer of fun ("Mrs. Wilkins, I know you said we were watching *Gangs of New York* today, but could we review for the history exam instead?"). She is a terrifying person. The type of intellectual snob who will most likely attend the sort of college my guidance counselor keeps pushing at me.

The other bus drivers, oblivious to whatever was going on with the stalled bus, began pulling away from the curb, forming a rumbling elephant line down the long driveway leading away from the school. The other bus was still disgorging students. A few jumped out. Like they were in a hurry.

"How did we even get on this topic?" I asked.

"You were trying to figure out why Saeed's sister hates you."

"Right. You know, you're asking me why I care, and here's the thing: I have to see her. I might have to work with her at that K Street Center. And she's even turning that Myla against me. I mean, I was getting along with her pretty well, then Samira had to make a huge deal about how I was only there because I had gotten in trouble and needed community service."

"I'm sorry. *Who* are we talking about?"

"Myla. She's a volunteer there. She goes to Mumford. She was talking to Samira that first day I went for homework help." I stood up, glanced at my watch. "You ready to hit the hardware store?"

Don looked like he was concentrating on something. "What's she look like? This Myla." I shrugged.

"Kind of a hippie. Pierced nose. Wears clothes the color of dirt. She's really small. I thought at first she was one of the kids at the place."

"Cute?" Donnie pressed.

"Huh?"

He looked impatient. "Is the Mumford student cute? You know, good-looking?" He waited.

"I don't know. I guess."

Donnie made this sound. Like a horse blowing air from its nostrils. "What do you mean, you guess? A guy doesn't guess. Tom Bouchard doesn't guess. You assess. Instantly. Girl in sight: Hot? Not?"

I paused. I thought of something.

"She's got great eyes."

Don laced his fingers behind his head and stretched full out on the grass. Eyes closed, this shit-eatin' grin on his face.

"Mystery solved, dude."

"What mystery?"

"The mystery of why you give a flying whatever about what Samira thinks of you," Donnie said. "You think the older woman with the great eyes has potential, and you don't want her grouchy little Muslim friend saying anything to spoil your chances."

That's when we heard the yelling. The kids on the sidewalk were shouting something. One person was running back toward the school. Then, from the bus door, like they'd been shot from a cannon, four guys popped out. Arms and legs flailing, they were beating the crap out of each other.

Two were white; two were black.

"Whoa," said Donnie, sitting up. "Fight."

The bus driver emerged, and we could see him trying to separate the boys, but he was no match for four furious high schoolers. One of them happened to wheel around, and I recognized him.

Jake Farwell.

"Oh no, those are our guys!" I exclaimed. I sprinted toward the bus. Don followed me.

I took one just above my eye and my nose was bleeding all over the front of my shirt by the time enough of us were able to pull them apart. Donnie had Jake on the ground and was literally sitting on him; the bus driver had one of the black guys in a headlock. I recognized him. A junior varsity soccer player. Somali kid.

As soon as most of the action was over, the school resource officer and Principal Cockrell showed up. We could see them huffing and puffing as they raced across the lawn. The guy I was holding, Roger Pelletier, angrily tried to wrench himself from my grip.

"Cut it out, you stupid fuck!" I yelled at him. My nose wasn't right. It seriously hurt. I was going to be really pissed if one of these jerks had just broken my nose.

"Get your hands *off* me, Bouchard!" he insisted. I pressed my knee into the small of his back instead.

Don and I never made it to the hardware store that afternoon. We got stuck in the principal's office, describing what we had seen, and with the school nurse, who really doesn't do much besides hand out ice packs. Don had this amazing shiner, which started swelling up like a multicolored flower.

"We are so badass," I heard him say at one point, but I was sitting with my head tilted back to slow the bleeding and ice on my nose to prevent swelling, so even though I wanted to laugh, I couldn't. Especially because I was so mad.

Jake was a midfielder. Roger was a striker. Two senior starters on the soccer team, now facing serious suspension time.

And we had a big game on Saturday.

Chapter Seven

Here's the fact: Jake Farwell and Roger Pelletier are assholes.

Yeah, I party with Jake once in a while. I mean, he's my teammate. But he and Roger are well-known jerks. Have been for as long as anyone can remember.

The other two guys? I didn't know them, but word from Ismail was that they were dipshits, too. So what *we* all knew was that the fight on the bus had nothing to do with race or religion. It was just pure asshole-ness.

Of course, "Assholes Fight" is not a newspaper-selling headline in the post-9/11 world. "Ethnic Tensions Flare" sure is. So the night after the fight, a reporter called Coach.

I don't know what Coach said to get the guy to back off, because nothing was ever printed. But the rest of us got an earful at the next practice.

"I know you didn't ask for this," Coach began. "But people are watching us. They're watching to see whether you boys can work together. Play together. Trust and respect each other and become a team. And whether we like it or not, it's a responsibility. And an opportunity."

He said Enniston is a city on a hill, which I guess is right; it seems to get higher in places. But what he meant was that because of our situation, with all the new immigrants coming to Enniston, and most of them Muslim, people were gonna notice what we did. So while four boys fighting in any other city wouldn't be news, in Enniston? When it's white on black? Muslim on Christian? Front page.

The good thing was that we didn't end up in the paper. The even better thing was that as a result of the fight, classes got canceled for an entire day. The not-so-great thing was that instead, we had to do civil rights workshops.

It was kind of stupid, actually, because not only are there hardly any fights at Chamberlain, but the few we *do* have are almost never white versus black. Most are between white guys who start out drinking together on Saturday night, then end up throwing things at each other. Once in a while an American black kid and an immigrant black kid will fight. But a lot of what's going on is actually between the immigrant kids. Old fights they brought with them from Africa. Sudanese kids versus Somalis. Somali Bantus versus ethnic Somalis. I mean, they're all Somali, but some are, like, *Somali* Somali (ethnic) and came to Maine a while ago, while the others, Somali Bantus? These were the dudes showing up more recently. In big numbers.

They didn't hang out together. This was made real clear on workshop day, when Mr. Cockrell and Co. brought in these anti-hate-crime experts (huh?) who started us all off with this big assembly (yawn), then broke us into small discussion groups led by handpicked student leaders (uh-oh). There was no way out of that, me being a sports captain plus a member of the National Hypocrites Society (Donnie's term, not mine). I got to lead a group with

Liz Painchaud—*Gee, thanks, God*—which should have meant I wouldn't have to do much, since she loves to hear herself talk. Saeed was in our group, along with three Somali girls.

"Me and Lila are thinking of skipping this workshop thing," Cherisse had informed me the night before. Not in person. A cell phone conversation from my bedroom, where I was supposedly compiling a list of colleges I planned to apply to. Mom was making the most of my groundation: no Cherisse on the premises, progress made on the apps. "Wanna join us?"

"Where are you going?" I asked.

"Jake's," she said. Giggled. "Like, he's really *hating* suspension. Not. The guy sleeps in, then watches ESPN all day while his parents are at work. Lila told him we're jealous and coming over to par-tay. You in?"

I leaned back into the pillows on my bed, crunching papers that had somehow slipped behind me. I had the Fiske, Barron's, and *U.S. News and World Report* guides to colleges on one side, and a stack of glossy brochures and college viewbooks on the other. I had to admit: all these places looked the same. All the students looked the same, in a carefully arranged, casually diversified way, with just the right number of Asians and brown people sitting next to athletic blondes and frat boys. Everybody smiling and appearing intellectually engaged.

"Love to, but I'm a leader, remember? I even had to miss practice today for my 'training.'"

"Oh, *screw* that, Tommy. What a joke. C'mon." She slipped into her pouty-little-girl voice. "What would you rather do: talk about civil rights with Liz Pain-in-the-ass, or spend time with me in Jake's big, empty house?"

"Yeah, I think you know the answer to that one," I said.

"So . . . ?" she said.

"No can do. I'm already in the penalty box. Skipping school—and you *know* Liz will narc—isn't in the cards for Tom Bouchard right now."

She made this annoyed, feline sound, like someone was squeezing a cat.

"Lame. Lame lame lame," she said. "I've got a *lame* boyfriend."

"I know, right? Where'd you dig up such a loser?" She didn't laugh.

"Uh . . . that was a joke?" I said. Still nothing. The girl was seriously pouting.

"If I were you, I'd come to school tomorrow."

"Right. Give me one good reason," she said grouchily.

"Because from what I hear from Jake, you'll be a third wheel if you and Lila go over to his house. Meaning they'll be in a room and you'll spend the afternoon on his couch watching soaps."

"That's why you have to come with me!" she whined. A real fingernails-on-the-blackboard sound. We ended the call pretty much after that.

Next day, Liz and I were in our assigned classroom, going over the plan for our workshop, when Cherisse sauntered in. There were a dozen students and two leaders in each group, and I'd already seen the list for ours. Cherisse wasn't on it.

"Hey, boyfriend," she said, sliding up against me and hooking a finger into one of the belt loops of my jeans. She stared frankly at Liz. "That is a *great* sweater, Liz. You have to tell me where you got it!"

Liz glanced down at her own chest, as if she were trying

to remember what she'd worn to school that day. It was a tan turtleneck.

"I . . . uh, couldn't tell you, Cherisse. Are you in this group?"

Cherisse rested her head on my shoulder.

"Nooooo . . . I'm next door. But I asked them if I could switch. They said it's up to you guys."

Liz's eyes widened. Other kids were starting to come in. Liz looked at me.

"These groups were carefully put together with gender and racial balance in mind," she said.

"Oh, c'mon, Liz. One more in our group won't matter." I wasn't in the mood to tangle with Cherisse.

Liz shook her head slowly from side to side. I could read her mind. *You are pathetic, Bouchard,* it said.

"Whatever, Tom. Just let me tell them next door that she's in here." She turned on her heel and walked away from us.

"Such a dweeb," Cherisse muttered in my ear. "Remind me why we're heeeeeere?" Semi-agonized tone.

"I thought you were cutting," I said to her.

She sighed. "You were right. About Jake and Lila. She *un*invited me." I laughed.

I glanced around the room. Ellen Fitzgerald from my calc class had just come in. Three Somali girls entered together. A couple of guys I recognized from our JV team. And Saeed. He was the only Somali guy. The only other black guy was some kid named Jimmy who had just moved here from Portland.

We arranged our chairs in a circle and started with introductions. You had to give your name and tell everyone your favorite color, your favorite food, and something you liked to do. This was the rap our trainers had given us the day before. First: intros. Second: talk about ground rules. Third: role-playing game. Fourth: discuss role-playing game.

The idea was that after one day of this, nobody would fight anymore and we'd all get along.

Liz went first. The second she opened her mouth, I was reminded of this woman I once saw on television who did Carnival Cruise commercials. Same sort of high-energy enthusiasm.

"I'm Liz Painchaud, and I love the color yellow! My favorite food is chocolate cake, and believe it or not, I love to cross-stitch!"

"Why wouldn't we believe it?" Jimmy, from Portland. Liz looked a little knocked off track. Probably wasn't expecting questions at that point.

"I don't know. I guess because everybody thinks of me in other ways. Not sitting home doing cross-stitch. I haven't exactly shared that before."

So. Cross-stitch was a big "share" for Liz. Interesting.

"How else do people think of you?" Jimmy asked. Liz flashed me this help-me-out-here look, but I was actually curious to see how she'd answer that one, so I waited.

"Well . . . I don't know," she said, laughing nervously. "But maybe we should keep going. Right around the circle . . ."

Jimmy shrugged. "Okay, Ms. Liz. But I want to get back to you on that." He looked at me. "I think you're next, Leader Man," he said.

"Why do I get the feeling you've done this before?" I said. He smiled.

"Oh yeah. At my old school in Portland? We've got all *kinds* of

71

people." He started counting off with his fingers. "We've got Cambodians. We've got Iranians. We've got Mexicans. We've got—"

"Can we *please* continue around the circle?" Liz insisted. From Cherisse's side I heard a giggle. She'd found a seat next to Devon, and they were doing something on their phones.

"Hey!" Jimmy said sharply. Everyone jumped. He glared at Cherisse and Devon. "Show a little respect. Put those away." People don't usually speak to Cherisse like that.

She and Devon rolled their eyes. One muttered, "What*ever*," but the phones disappeared into their backpacks.

"Next," Jimmy said to me.

"Okay, so I'm Tom Bouchard, and I like a lot of colors, but I guess I mostly like green. My favorite food is steak, and I like to play soccer." I looked to my right.

"I'm Ellen Fitzgerald. Blue. Chocolate chip cookies. Skiing."

"I'm John Gagne. Uh, I'm color-blind, so . . . pass." Everyone laughed. "I like to play pond hockey. And the best food in the entire world, hands down, is *poutine*."

"Say what?" Jimmy.

"*Poutine*," John repeated. "It's French fries, covered in cheese curds, covered in brown gravy. I had it when we went to Quebec this summer, and it is amazing."

"Cheese curds. You mean like cottage cheese?" Ellen.

"No, it's . . . you can't get it here. The closest thing I can think of is those mozzarella sticks you get at the grocery store. But cheese curds are way, way better than that. They sort of squeak in your mouth when you bite them."

"Damn." Jimmy. "You're making me hungry." Everyone laughed again. I saw Liz glance at the clock on the wall.

"Next," I prompted.

"I'm Jimmy Price and I like orange. My favorite food is anything Italian, especially spaghetti. I like to listen to music."

The Somali girls were up next.

"I am Fatuma Hassan." We could barely hear her, she spoke so softly. Everybody sort of leaned forward a little.

"Speak up, girl," Jimmy said. She looked at him. He nodded.

"I like red," she said a little louder. "I like *sambusas*. I like to read."

"Yeah, those are good. I like them, too," Jimmy said.

"*Sam* . . . what?" Ellen asked.

"*Sambusa*," Fatuma repeated. She formed a triangle with her fingers. "Is dough, like this, and you put in spices, and meat. And fry. Is very Somali."

"Goat meat," Jimmy said. "I like 'em with goat meat."

"Yes, that is best, but you can make with other meat, too," Fatuma said. A little louder. She smiled at Jimmy.

"Ewww!" Devon. Or maybe Cherisse. Unclear who said it; they both made these grossed-out faces. "You eat *goat*?"

"Whoa!" Jimmy exclaimed, throwing himself back into his metal chair. He flashed me a what-you-gonna-do-now-man look.

"Okay, that was *totally* inappropriate," Liz sputtered. She'd been holding a clipboard with some papers on her lap, and dropped it. I got out of my seat to pick it up for her. After I handed her the clipboard, I remained standing.

"Maybe we should have gone over the ground rules first," I said calmly. Fake calmly, actually. Fatuma's expression had gone blank, almost as if the comment weren't directed at her. She slouched in her chair, sank a little lower into the loose folds of her clothes.

"And the first rule is *respect*. No matter what anyone says, we all have to listen and respect their contribution to the circle." This was right out of yesterday's leader training.

"So we're not supposed to say what we think?" Devon replied. "She says goat and I'm supposed to say yum? Is that it, Tommy?"

"No, she says goat and you're supposed to listen. Not judge, not mock," I replied. *For once in your life,* I managed to not add.

"Like I said. Don't say what we think," she replied, just under her breath.

"Have you ever eaten goat?" Jimmy challenged.

Devon smirked at him.

"No, and I don't plan to," she said.

"Okay," he said. "Then instead of 'ewww' "—Jimmy raised his voice a few octaves in a dead-on imitation of Devon—"maybe you should say, 'I'm too closed-minded to try new foods, like goat, so I'm going to spend the rest of my life making fun of other people who love this delicious meat.' "

"Okay, *that's* not it, either!" I said. Not fake calmly.

Jimmy put his hands up in surrender.

"You're right, you're right. Sorry." He looked at Devon. "And I apologize to you. That was out of line." He said this politely. A little too politely, but what was I gonna do? Devon stared back at him, silent.

"Maybe you could apologize to Fatuma?" I said to her. She aimed her glare at me and remained silent.

Then: Saeed.

"Tom . . . is okay. Is good question."

Every head swiveled in his direction. Saeed leaned eagerly forward in his chair, looking intently at Cherisse and Devon.

"You don't like goat. Okay! Peoples all different! Maybe if you eat *sambusas* maybe you like goat! I don't know. So now I ask: you eat pig? Somali peoples, we say to that . . . ewww!"

He smiled broadly. No meanness on his face. He was just trying to make a point. *You think we're gross? Hey, that's all right. We think you're gross! It's all good.*

Jimmy burst out laughing. He got out of his chair and leaned toward Saeed.

"Dude," he said, and held his hand up. Saeed slapped his palm. "Couldn't have said it better myself." Jimmy sat.

"Is okay, Tom," Saeed repeated. I glanced at Cherisse, who was staring at me so hard I could feel two holes boring their way through my helpless skull. I sat.

"Okay, who's next?" I said. It was supposed to be the Somali girl next to Fatuma. But then Cherisse stood.

"Hi, everybody. I'm Cherisse Ouellette. I like Chamberlain blue. I *love* bacon." It seemed like she directed the bacon comment to Saeed. "And I'm outta here." With her foot she shoved her chair from the circle. It teetered and almost tipped over backward. She scooped up her backpack and walked quickly out. Devon followed her.

"Good riddance," I heard. But whether that came from Ellen or one of the other girls, I couldn't tell.

"I'm sorry, but are we going to just let them get up and walk out?" Liz, accusingly, to me.

"Pretty much," I told her. "Unless you can figure out a way to get them back in." I was imagining a wrestling, scratching match in the hallway between Liz and Cherisse.

"Next," Liz said instead. Wise girl.

After we limped through the rest of the introductions and finally went over ground rules, we played this Apples and Oranges game. Everybody was an apple, except one person, who was an orange. The orange had to convince the apples to let him join their group, even though he was . . . well, orange.

Liz, still annoyed about the Cherisse and Devon walkout and somehow blaming yours truly, picked me to be the orange.

"I don't know," I said. "I think Jimmy here might have some untapped leadership potential. Plus it's his favorite color."

Jimmy shook his head.

"No, I think you should take a turn at being in the minority. If you know what I mean."

"Okay," I began, less than enthusiastically. "Hi. I'm Tom the Orange."

Half of them went, "Hi, Tom."

"Can I, uh, hang out with you guys?"

"No way!" Liz exclaimed loudly. A bit too enthusiastically.

"Why not?" I replied. "I mean, I'm a fruit. Just like you."

"Yeah, he *is* a fruit," commented one guy. Snickers. Great. I walked right into that one.

"But you're a different color from us!" Liz continued.

"Well, that's because I'm a *citrus* fruit. But hey, I like apples."

"You're not from around here," commented Jimmy. "Where are you from? Portland?"

"No," I said. "I'm from Florida."

"That's too far away. Beat it," said some girl. Friend of Liz's.

"You smell funny," said John.

"You *look* funny," said Ellen.

"You *ooji*," said the Somali girl next to Fatuma. Nasra. Everybody looked at her.

"Huh?" somebody asked.

Nasra seemed very sorry to have spoken. She directed her eyes at the floor and didn't answer.

"Is that, like, a clan?" Liz.

"What's a clan?" John.

"Clan is like . . . family group," the third chimed in. Khadija. "In Somalia, everybody from a clan. You know who you are, who you will marry, where you belong."

"Well, I'm from the Orange Clan," I said, "and I'd like to join your Apple Clan." I flashed Liz what I imagined was a pretty smug look. Thought I was doing a pretty good job "bridging the cultural divide," a term they'd told us in leader training the day before.

"*Ooji* is not clan," said Nasra. "It mean 'hard hair.' It what Somali people from the city calls us. It not nice. Somali people from the city is different from Somali people from the country."

"Bantu, right? Isn't that the word for country people?" Liz. Just dyin' to show off what she'd learned in Civil Rights Club.

Nasra shrugged.

"*Bantu* is white people's word, but okay," she said.

Then Saeed spoke.

"When I come to Chamberlain? On . . . arrive day? Other Somali boy?" He glanced at Fatuma. "Mustafa," he said to her. She nodded knowingly, eyes wide. She was obviously familiar with this Mustafa person. "He go up to me, right here, Tom." Saeed pointed in the direction of the hallway. "He say, '*Jarerah!*'" He sat back in his chair, arms folded across his chest. Like he'd made some big point.

"What the fuck?" I heard the fruit joker whisper. More snickers.

"It also mean 'hard hair,'" Nasra explained. "Like *ooji*. It what Somali people from the city calls us."

"So, like, this Mustafa dude, he doesn't know you, but he takes one look at you and thinks hard hair. Bantu. *Ooji*. Am I right?" Jimmy asked.

Saeed and the three girls nod: yes.

"Damn," Jimmy said.

"Why?" John asked Fatuma.

"They think we are like slaves," Fatuma said. "*Adoon*, they says. Long time ago, Somali people have slaves, from other part of Africa. They say that who we are."

"They don't want us to be same as them," Khadija said. "Even here. They still carry this with them here."

"Not all," Nasra said to her.

"Many," Fatuma replied firmly.

"Can I make a suggestion?" Ellen asked. "Can we ditch the game and just *talk*? I mean, this is actually interesting."

"I don't know—" Liz began.

"Absolutely," I said, cutting her off. "The whole point of the stupid games is getting people to talk. So let's do it."

I'll admit: the workshop got pretty cool after that. It was almost like playing Truth or Dare: you tried to think up things you really wanted to know but had always been afraid to ask. Some of it was stupid, like when John Gagne asked Saeed what he ate for breakfast and he answered "Frosted Flakes," which made everyone laugh. But then they told us they also ate this sweet bread called *anjera*, which was like a thin pancake with sugar. They also drank tea, which they liked super-sweet, almost syrupy. And dates. They ate a lot of dates.

78

Liz got Khadija to talk about why she wore a *hijab*, and Jimmy tried to get Liz to say whether she had a boyfriend or not, but she wouldn't go there. Ellen wanted to know if Muslim kids were allowed to go to prom. I wanted to know what really happened on the bus the other day.

Nasra knew; she'd been on that bus. She said a couple of ethnic Somali guys had been teaching Jake and Roger a few curse words in Somali. They convinced Roger that it'd be really funny to go behind a couple of Bantu Somali kids (or is it *ooji*? I don't know) and say, *"Uf!"* Which Roger, not being the sharpest tool in the shed, went ahead and did, even though it turned out to mean "you smell," but in a super-insulting way. The Bantu Somali kids started swinging, which brought Jake to his feet to help Roger. Meanwhile, the ethnic Somali kids had a good laugh, especially when the Bantu kids got suspended for fighting.

"So they started it, but the other guys got in trouble?" Ellen said when Nasra finished her story. "That's not fair!"

The Somali kids all looked at each other with these surprised, semi-amused expressions. They said nothing; one of them shrugged. *Since when,* their faces seemed to say, *is anything fair?*

The bell rang, and it was time for us to move on to the next planned activity: a "trust walk" set up in the gym. As we moved in a herd along the hall, I could see, through the big plate glass windows, a bunch of the phys ed teachers outside, setting up a ropes course. More games.

"D'you think that was okay?" I heard. Liz, walking alongside me. "That we ditched Apples and Oranges? I mean, I thought the conversation went well, don't you? You don't think the—"

"It was okay, Liz," I told her, smiling. Shiva the Cross-Stitching

Destroyer was wound way too tight, but what the hell. The girl tried. You had to give her credit for trying. "You did good."

"Thanks," she said gratefully, then scurried on ahead of me because she had Trust Walk duties. I was off the hook, at least as far as leadership stuff, for the rest of the day.

Where I was very much still on the hook was in dealing with Ms. I'm-Outta-Here Ouellette. Who, to use Donnie's word, was most definitely in a league of her own.

Chapter Eight

After practice that day we were scheduled for our first team pasta party of the year, at Mike's house. Coach took me aside.

"I'd like you to make sure the new guys feel welcome at the pasta party tonight," he said.

I shrugged.

"I'm not sure they'll come, Coach. They keep pretty much to themselves outside of school."

"They'll come," he said confidently. "I told them you'd drive them."

The Turcottes always host the kickoff pasta feast of the season. Mike's got a totally amazing gaming basement. Xbox and Halo, Ping-Pong, foosball, and a wide-screen TV. Plus his mom always makes the pasta and she's a really good cook. Most of the parents just heat up this thin Hannaford-brand red sauce from a jar, but Mrs. Turcotte cooks real sauce with meat in it for us. She calls it spaghetti Bolognese.

My parents had let me take the Subaru to school, not only so I could finally pick up the "untampering" supplies (the trip Donnie and I had been planning to take to the hardware store having had a bit of a fight delay) but also so I could transport to the party. Grounding didn't extend to team building, service, and other punishment-related activities. When I came out of the locker room, Mike was waiting for me. The four Somalis stood with him.

"Tommy, you got room? These guys need a ride." I nodded, and Ismail, Ibrahim, Saeed, and Double M fell into step with me. Double M was this guy named—seriously—Muhammad Muhammad, but we told him that was way more Prophet than anyone could handle, so Mike came up with Double M. He seemed to like the nickname.

I motioned Saeed to the front seat.

"Saeed gets to ride shotgun for that corner kick the other day," I told them. They looked confused. A little startled.

Right. Note to self: references to guns are not a good idea around people who fled war zones. And are still figuring out English.

As we pulled out of the school parking lot, I took another stab at conversation.

"That corner kick at practice on Tuesday? Amazing." I put my hand out to Saeed, palm up. He grinned, slapped.

"I do better with no shoes," he said.

Okay. So he did understand. Some stuff, at least.

"What, barefoot? You kick better barefoot?" He nodded.

"Yeah, in Kenya? He don't wear shoes," one guy commented from the back. Ismail.

"You mean, like, ever?" I asked.

Ismail laughed.

"No, for soccer."

I tried to get my head around the idea of playing without any protection on my feet.

"Yeah, when I come? To America?" Saeed said. He pronounced it Am-ree-ka. "I want for to play soccer. But I need shoes, you know? And . . ." He paused. Pointed to his leg below the knee.

"Shin guards?" I suggested. He nodded.

"Yes! And guards. And socks. But they are, you know, lot of money?" His voice went up at the end of each sentence. Like he was wondering if he was getting it right.

"So what'd you do?" I asked him.

Ismail answered. "Yeah, so, the guys on JV, we say, 'What size are you? Put your foot out. You look like you got the same foot as Saeed and me.' And, so, they do. So we get the shoes, and when the JV practice is done they give us the shoes. But if varsity practice is first, then we give them the shoes." Saeed nodded. I wasn't sure I got it.

"Saeed and Ismail share cleats with a couple of the JV players," a third guy explained. Ibrahim. This was his second year on the team, and he was rockin' the English in this group.

That explains why they're late.

The thought blossomed in my head. Or maybe not. Maybe the angel that carried the ball into the corner of the goal yesterday just whispered in my ear. *They're late, stupid,* he whispered, *because they can't afford their own stuff, so they share with other players. They pull sweat-soaked socks over damp shin guards, then shove their feet into already hot, wet shoes.* It wasn't the grossest thing I could imagine. Donnie and I once had this contest to think up the grossest thing you'd never want to do but *might* for a million dollars, and we came up with drinking a glass of your own spit. Now, that's gross.

But wearing someone else's wet, smelly gear comes close.

And once you've got the stuff on—hurry, hurry, hurry, you're saying to the guys who are trying to untie, fast—you jog over to the team, where now you're late, and Coach is mad at you and everyone else is mad at you. And the captain of the team is mad at you. Because you made him run laps.

I didn't ask any more questions for the rest of the ride. I just drove us to Mike's house.

Saeed and I sat side by side on the beat-up couch in the basement playroom. It sank low, bringing us to eye level with the Ping-Pong table, where Ibrahim and Ismail smacked the ball at Mike and Evan DeLoach. Ibrahim and Ismail hadn't ever played before, but Mike and Evan pretty much sucked, so it was fair.

We always ended up here after we ate. We'd stuff ourselves, then game. I actually had no interest in playing Ping-Pong. I was waiting for my turn at Halo.

Down there, just playing stuff, felt pretty normal. The Somali guys turned out to be awesome at Xbox, and pretty much no one "plays" foosball—you just spin the handles. But earlier, when we were eating, it got a little awkward.

We were lined up in the kitchen to get food, and I heard them speaking quietly to each other in Somali. They watched the guys ahead of them ladle sauce over heaping plates of pasta, and they seemed really interested in it, but also nervous, which seemed weird. When it was Double M's turn to take some, he just shoveled spaghetti onto his plate and shook a little parm over the top. He was moving right on past the salad when Mrs. Turcotte intercepted him.

"Don't you want some sauce, dear?" she asked. "And salad? I made nice Caesar salad for all you boys." Mrs. Turcotte calls us all *deah*. Like a real old-time *Maine-ah*.

He smiled, shook his head, and kept walking, but Ismail spoke up.

"There is . . . pork?" he asked Mrs. Turcotte, gesturing toward the sauce.

She looked surprised.

"Oh, goodness, no. I use beef. You know, hamburg?"

Ismail nodded and, as he spooned Bolognese over his pasta, called out something to Double M. The guy returned, held out his plate, and let Ismail pour sauce atop the spaghetti.

"They don't eat pork," Mike said quietly behind me. I turned.

"Mom usually mixes some sausage into her sauce, but Coach told her it's against their religion. I mean, it was no big deal for Mom. At least it's not nuts."

"That's true," I agreed, remembering middle school and Nut Kid. He was this guy on our soccer team who had a severe nut allergy. I remember once bumping into him and his dad at the ice cream place in town, where they brought their own scoop so as not to get even the smallest trace of nut oil in the kid's cone. His mom used to show up at practices with Wet Ones and make us wipe our hands as well as all the soccer balls. She even got the coach to make the players from other teams do it before games.

Made you nervous. Like, you were always half expecting the kid to swell up and stop breathing.

"You know those signs we have in the cafeteria?" Mike continued. "Like, the one that says *hilib doofaar*?" I shrugged. I knew the cards he was talking about. Colorful, printed with phonetic

85

spelling that we'd all come to recognize as Somali words, near the hot food on the lunch line. I'd figured it listed the food, sort of the way I taped little pieces of paper with Spanish vocab words around the house. Like *asiento* taped to my dad's favorite chair . . .

"Means 'pig meat,'" Mike said. "Totally *haram*."

"What?" I said.

"Forbidden," he said knowingly, moving ahead for a turn at the sauce. Yeah. Time spent with Somali culture whiz Liz Painchaud at Civil Rights Club meetings was definitely rubbing off on Mike.

As Saeed and I sat together on the low couch, watching the Ping-Pong ball whiz from side to side, we heard something behind us, near the stairs leading into the basement. A scratching noise, followed by shouts. Saeed turned his head, then jumped up.

Mike's golden retriever, Sandy, ran into the room. She was beyond delighted to find so many boys in her house, and that big tail of hers swung madly back and forth. Hair flew off her with every swing. Sandy is a real shedder.

Every Somali guy took cover. They ran—not like they were scared, but more like they were grossed out. As if Sandy were coated in vomit and shit, or had some seriously contagious disease. To make things worse, she thought the guys who were running were trying to play with her, so she followed them. Within seconds, they were dodging and Sandy was chasing. Not good in a crowded space.

"Hey! Who let the dog in here?" I heard Mike yell. "Hold her!" I happened to be nearest, so I grabbed her collar. She had this lolling dog smile on her face, complete with big drippy tongue.

Mike took her from me and pulled-led her from the basement

and up the stairs. Double M, Saeed, Ibrahim, and Ismail stood well away, watching warily as Mike hauled her off.

"Sorry," Mike said as he passed them. "I thought we'd left her in my sister's room. I'll put her outside." Pete LeBourdais and a few of the other guys were giving each other confused looks, but they didn't say anything.

When the dog was gone, I went over to Saeed and Co.

"You guys okay?" I asked.

Ibrahim nodded.

"You know, Sandy's a good dog. She's not vicious or anything."

Double M shook his head in disagreement.

"Dogs *not* good," he told me.

"No," Saeed said in agreement.

"We don't touch dogs," Ismail added.

"You don't touch dogs," I repeated. I wasn't sure I'd heard them right. But they didn't correct me. "Why don't you touch dogs?"

Ibrahim answered.

"You *can* touch a dry dog, but you can never touch a wet dog or let a dog wet you. If you do touch a dog, you have to wash seven times. Or give money to seven orphans. Or feed a poor person seven days. All together, you know? Feed them seven days together."

"Wait. If Sandy over there had come up and licked one of you guys, you'd have had to find an orphan and give him money for seven days?"

"Probably wash seven times would be easier," Ibrahim said.

"Why? What's up with dogs?" I asked him. This was blowing my mind.

Ibrahim shrugged.

"It's in the Koran." He headed back to the Ping-Pong table and retrieved his paddle. Double M followed.

Saeed watched me. Waited. His eyes didn't reveal anything, but they waited for my reaction.

"So, no dogs and no pork," I said.

"No," he repeated. "Is *haram*. You know?" he asked me. That word again, that Mike used.

"Yeah, I'm starting to," I replied. He was still watching me. This was important.

It was also a pretty easy call. I mean, whatev. Locking up the dog and leaving out the pork was way easier than wiping all the balls and scrubbing everyone's hands before every practice and game.

"It's all good, man," I told him. "No worries." I put my hand on his shoulder briefly, then headed to the corner of the room, where it was time for me to kick somebody off Halo.

Chapter Nine

About halfway into our game the next day against Alice Whittier High School, it was pretty clear that life as we knew it, meaning soccer life, had ended.

Here's the fact: we had never, ever, not even when my uncle played for Chamberlain, beat Whittier. They weren't a club soccer powerhouse like Maquoit, but they'd won states a bunch of times, twice in the past decade. They groomed kids early over there, starting with a rec league full of five-year-olds and ending with a varsity team that'd been coached by the same guy for centuries. His players loved him and would burst a lung chasing down balls if he asked them to.

Which explained something. I mean, Coach Gerardi is the man, and he really knows soccer. But our guys slowed down when it hurt. I'll admit it: we had a desire disconnect going that didn't seem to plague teams like Whittier, despite Coach yelling from the sidelines, "How bad do you want it?"

So when the scoreboard read Chamberlain 3, Whittier 2 at halftime? Like I said, something had changed. It *felt* different.

For one thing, Coach had switched the lineup. With Jake and Roger suspended, Saeed and Ibrahim started as center strikers. Mike Turcotte remained at wing, but at midfield, Ismail and Double M flanked me. Coach moved the other two senior middies, Henry Blaisdell and Jonnie Shea, to defense, and the two defensive players they replaced earned front-row bench seats.

Sucked for them.

On the drive to Whittier they were pretty quiet, their faces expressionless, as the bus bounced along the pothole-patched sections of road. They were good players, guys who had worked hard to stay fit, always showed up to practice on time.

But maybe Coach was looking for guys who'd burst a lung. And at halftime, you couldn't argue with the score.

When the horn sounded and we all retreated to the bench, I pulled a fleece blanket from my bag. Whittier's fields are near the coast, and even on warm days inland it gets chilly there. That day was cool for September, and a fog had rolled in. It seeped between the trees, drifted over the soccer pitch like a giant phantom, and wrapped wetly around us. Wet cold is the worst.

Saeed trotted up alongside me. He had scored two of our goals, and I put my hand up to slap his.

His hand was like ice. Even though we'd all been running and sweating, as soon as we stopped that damp cold hit him. You could understand why: the guy didn't have any meat on his bones.

"Dude, you're freezing," I said, as if he didn't know. He nodded, laughing between gritted teeth. I used to do that: tense up against the cold. Then this friend of my grandma's, one from her Franco-lady pack, told me to relax. Told me if I just added a layer or two and didn't exhaust my muscles by trying to fight the cold, I would actually warm up faster. It's counterintuitive, to let your body go limp when confronted with cold.

"*Ça mache!*" she'd said—"that works." In French class, where they teach us Parisian French, not the Canadian French Grandma grew up with, you would say it "*ça marche.*" Almost like two different languages, that's how different the accents are. It was mid-February, the mercury negative something, and I'd driven over to the Tim Horton's where Grandma was meeting her ladies for their Saturday morning coffee. I was helping her take her car to the auto shop, and when I came inside to find them clustered around two tables they'd pushed together, all with their identical beauty shop–teased hairdos, I was shaking with cold. That's when they laughed and told me to relax.

I didn't have the heart to give Saeed the *ça mache* advice just then. Mike had told me all the new kids were having a hard time getting used to the cold. One guy had even tried smearing Vaseline all over his arms and legs to stay warm. I watched as Saeed hopped from foot to foot and pulled a team windbreaker from his pack. They were crappy plastic jackets, more like Ziploc bags. The letters on the back that read CHAMBERLAIN CAVALIERS were peeling off most of them.

Saeed wore his all the time. I'd seen him with it around school. Around town. I wondered if he owned another coat.

"You need to sit in the bus?" I asked him. "They can turn the heat on for you so you don't get all hypothermic." He frowned. *Right. Hypothermic. How about you just say "cold," Tom?*

"Is okay. No bus."

"It's all right to admit it. Maine isn't Africa." He nodded, but stayed put.

"I know! Is so *cold* here!" He shifted his feet from side to side. I got up and slipped the fleece blanket over his shoulders. At first he made like he wouldn't take it, but I stepped away.

"Thank you," he said.

Down the length of the bench the guys were huffing, chugging water. Steam rose off hot backs. Except for two: the bumped defenders. They'd played maybe a couple of minutes, total, and did fine while they were out there. But Coach pulled them as soon as the other guys were rested.

One of them happened to glance up, and our eyes met.

It was like getting hit by Sasquatch all over again, because I was so surprised I forgot to breathe for a second.

He was furious. Which you'd expect, and I didn't blame him. I'd have felt the same way. Except . . . it was like his anger was aimed at *me*. Which was totally unfair, because everyone knows Coach doesn't consult with any of us about his lineups. But there he was, staring at me like he'd deck me if he could. Then Saeed, wrapped in my blanket and still shuffling against the cold, bumped into me, and I got it.

But what was I supposed to do? Sit there and watch the guy freeze to death?

The whistle blew and we headed back out. I felt someone at my elbow: Mike Turcotte. He gestured with his head across the field to a group of guys standing at the corner of the Whittier bleachers. They wore matching black and red.

"That's Alex Rhodes," Mike said. "They got here partway through the first half."

Another sign that things weren't the way they used to be. Maquoit always beat us, and usually beat Whittier, so in the old world

Alex and the Assholes wouldn't have bothered standing around in the cold watching this game. They'd scout somebody like Bangor, a team they usually come up against late in the postseason.

"Let's make it worth their while," I said to Mike. "Keep feeding Saeed and Ibrahim, even if it gets crowded in there. They'll make something happen." Mike nodded, then ran to his position. I looked to see where the ref was, to see if I had time to say something to Saeed.

Not that it would have mattered. First off, the guy didn't need motivation to play any harder. Not hard as in physicality—they don't play that way; it's all finesse—but in terms of effort. He already gave 110 percent. Second, I didn't have enough time and he didn't have enough vocabulary for me to explain who Alex Rhodes was and why Tom Bouchard had so much invested in looking good in front of him.

Hell, I'm not sure *I* even had the vocabulary to explain.

The whistle sounded, and right off you could see that Whittier's coach had made good use of halftime: they gained possession immediately, easily. They took off down the sideline, their man elbowing Double M and knocking him to the ground when he challenged their run.

No call. Nothing, and it clearly deserved a yellow card. I heard shouts from our bench, and in my peripheral vision I saw every Chamberlain player on his feet, shouting. Double M rolled, jumped up, and pursued the Whittier guy, but he was too far ahead to catch. Damn. Less than thirty seconds into it, and they were looking to tie us up.

Henry Blaisdell, in his new and unfamiliar position at defense, challenged. "Back me up, back me up!" he screamed at Jonnie

Shea, because if the Whittier guy maneuvered around him, it would be an open shot to the goal. Jonnie raced behind Henry and put himself in front of the goal. I ran back, tracking the Whittier striker who was trying to get open for the pass.

Then Henry fell. Spectacularly. Stupidly. There was nothing in his way and no one near him, but for some reason his legs went out from under him and he was eating grass. I couldn't see them, but to the left and just behind me I heard the Maquoit guys lose it. Their hilarity was unstoppable. This totally made standing outside in the cold worth it. This would be one to share at the rager later that night: those losers from Chamberlain tripping over their own feet.

I thought, *Is this what you want, God?*

It's bad enough we lose to these douchebags every time—and, yeah, I know douchebag probably isn't a word you often get tossed your way; sorry—but couldn't we for once not look like complete horses' asses in front of them? They get freakin' everything, you know? Couldn't we at least get a little respect? Once?

I hung back; couldn't leave my man unguarded. Jonnie, meanwhile, burned it. He leapt over the still-fallen Henry and hurled himself straight at the advancing Whittier striker. It was a suicide attack, Jonnie insanely deciding to take a yellow—hell, a red card—for the team, and the startled Whittier player let the ball get just a little bit ahead of him.

That's when I heard him. Not God; I never hear him. Saeed. Who could tell, the way a master chess player can read a dozen moves in advance, what Jonnie was going to do and where the ball would go next.

"Tom! I open!"

Jonnie got to the ball and booted it at a sharp angle away from the Whittier player and directly toward me. Two steps and I had it; I settled it, pivoted in the direction of his voice, and saw nothing but green space between me and Saeed. He was waiting for me at the midfield line, and I fired it at him.

I couldn't really tell you what Saeed did next. All I know is he received the pass and then the ball soared. Soared like a kickoff in football, high, arcing overhead. It was a beautiful thing, this trajectory, but then it fell, plummeted, gathered speed as it reached earth. It headed right for the goal. It headed for the top bar . . . no, not quite . . . just under it. Just over the goalie's head. Skirting, by inches, the top bar, until it landed in a tangle of net.

Wow. Thanks.

I sat with him on the ride home. Well, to the extent that I sat with anyone. The guys went crazy, and when the bus driver couldn't get us to settle down he barked at Coach to get it under control or it would be the last time he'd drive the team. Coach whistled (the guy's got a dog-deafening two-finger whistle) and said if we wanted to arrive alive in order to brag about our 5–2 victory over Whittier (more foot stomping and cheers) we needed to sit down and shut up.

It was a little quieter then, and Saeed started rummaging around in his backpack. He pulled out this plastic bag filled with what looked like stiff orange Jell-O. He tore off a chunk, popped it in his mouth, and offered the bag to me.

"Is *xalwo*," he said. "Is really, really good."

I pulled off a piece and gave it a try. Sweet and orange exploded in my mouth.

"It's like seriously intense gummy bears," I said. "*Zal-wo.*"

He nodded, looking out the window.

"I know. Really good," he replied.

I realized I'd stopped trying to figure out what Saeed understood and what he pretended to understand. I just talked to him. Sometimes he surprised me and came up with a string of English that made you think he could speak the language. Other times he faded and I couldn't tell if he was just not getting the words or avoiding a topic.

"So here's a question," I began. "Your sister. Samira. She speaks pretty good English. You . . . not so much." He nodded. Plucked another chunk of *xalwo* from the bag.

"Samira in Amreeka more time than me. I will speak good, too."

"Really. How much more time?"

He thought about this.

"I think . . . one year. She goes with my mother. I goes later."

"Why's that? Why didn't you all come at the same time?"

He sighed. Not like he was going to fade out on me. Like maybe this required more words than he had in his arsenal.

"Okay, my family live in Somalia, right? And in Somalia there is big, big wars and fighting. Like, everyone is gets killed, and the peoples, they just . . . run. You just run, you know?"

No, I didn't say. *I don't know. I have absolutely no idea.*

"There is men. With guns? Who kill peoples outside our house. My uncle? He get killed. My friend? He get killed. I see this. With my eyes." He looked at me. Unblinking. Wide eyes that stared frankly into my own.

"And my mother," he continued, "she just say run! We go . . .

out window. In back of house. And we run! Fast. And all the time we run we hear guns.

"Then we walk, a long time. To . . . Kenya? To this camp. Dadaab. And we stay, with all these peoples, long time. Many years."

"How many years?" I asked.

He shrugged. "I was little boy. Okay. So I got uncle in Nairobi. He say, 'Make Saeed go to Nairobi and live with me and go to school.' And I go. There is school in Dadaab, but it not good, you know? And Nairobi have good school. So I go there. And then UN tell my family, 'You got to leave now.' But I am in Nairobi! But they got to go. So . . . I wait. And in one year I come to Maine."

My head buzzed with questions. If I was getting this right, Saeed was out of town the day his family left for the United States, and it took them a year to reunite with him. That couldn't be right. It was like an African nightmare version of *Home Alone*, with Saeed in the Macauley Culkin role, but instead of fighting off burglars and waiting for his parents to return, he was passing in and out of war zones and trying to cross an ocean.

"Dude. That's unreal," I said.

He held the bag out toward me.

"Is real," he said.

I tore off another piece.

"Samira learn English good in Atlanta," he said. "I don't go there."

"Atlanta, Georgia?" I asked.

"Yeah. That a bad place. My mother don't like it. Samira don't like it. But we got friend. Here. My mother call him, and he say come. Maine is . . . good place. So they come. And then I come." Saeed pressed the seal of his plastic bag closed and returned the candy to his pack. He acted like that pretty much explained it all, but I was even more confused. There were definite gaps in the narrative. Huge gaps. But before I could ask him any more, I heard Mike speaking to me.

"Hey, Bouchard!" he called from a few aisles back. "Did I just hear that tomorrow you and Plourde are painting the Maquoit rock?"

"You heard right," I called back. There were groans the length of the bus.

"Hey, didn't I see some of those guys at the game today?" I heard someone say.

"Yeah, they're next!" another voice replied.

I wished. Wished those words were more than just post-victory attitude. Wished I didn't have to be at Maquoit High School the next morning at 9:00 a.m. I couldn't think of anything in my life that I'd ever looked forward to less. Even having my wisdom teeth pulled last summer trumped it.

"Sucks for you, Tom," Mike said. "Good luck." A few more "good lucks" echoed through the bus.

I noticed Saeed frowning.

"We go, right?" he asked me. I wasn't sure what he meant.

"Go where?" I asked.

"Maquoit," he said.

I shook my head.

"No. Just me. It's not a game. It's payback."

His frown deepened.

"But we the team. We all go." It wasn't a question. It was an assumption.

"No," I sighed. "We the team didn't screw up. Just we the captain. So you're all off the hook for this one."

Saeed pivoted in his seat, got up on his knees, and faced Ibrahim, who sat behind us. They engaged in some rapid-fire Somali, Saeed in earnest. He was speaking emphatically to Ibrahim and nodding at him urgently, but Ibrahim just shook his head and looked pissed. Finally Saeed made a sound in the back of his throat like he was disgusted, too, then put two fingers in his mouth and whistled pretty loud. Coach-like. Everyone stopped talking and looked at him.

"Uh . . . hello," he began.

"Hello," some joker from the back replied. A few titters.

"You know, I am . . . new customer," he continued, "but I think, you know . . . we the team. And all go tomorrow. With Tom. Right?" There was a pause. A surprised pause, actually, because everyone, including me, was thinking, *What the hell?*

"We the team go to Maquoit. Yes?" he said again.

"Did he just say he's a new customer?" I heard someone comment.

"Yes?" Saeed repeated. Loudly that time.

"Damn right!" someone shouted from the back. "We the team!" The bus erupted in laughter, followed by foot stomping and whistles. And before you know it everyone was chanting, "We the team! We the team!"

Saeed slid back into his seat and grinned at me.

"So we all go," he said simply.

He wasn't able to give you a straight story about where he'd come from, but this new customer? He was all right.

Chapter Ten

As it turns out, if "we the team" hadn't shown up, I'd have been out there alone. That's because freakin' Donnie never appeared.

I drove to his house to collect him Saturday morning, but there were no signs of life. His mom's car wasn't in the driveway, and even though I banged on the door and called his cell, there was no answer. I figured maybe he'd gone to the high school, where everyone had planned to meet, but no. Don was either lying in a ditch somewhere or had just blown me off.

All I could think was that it had better be the former, 'cause if he wasn't already dead, I was gonna kill him.

We were five cars in all, and as we pulled into the Maquoit High parking lot we could see a group already gathered at the rock. It wasn't the football-stadium-sized crowd I had feared would show up, but big enough. Pretty much the whole Maquoit varsity soccer team. I recognized Alex Rhodes in the group.

We go back, Alex and I.

Four years ago, the summer between middle and high school, a soccer camp sponsored by Midcoast College. It was just a three-day skills camp coached by players from the men's varsity team. Basically a fund-raiser for them. But for a kid like me? Totally cool to work with college players.

Most of the campers were from away (aka not from Maine) and stayed in the dorms for the three days, but you could save seventy dollars if you didn't sleep over. So every morning my mom drove me the thirty minutes to the college, and every evening she picked me up.

Alex Rhodes lives within spitting distance of the college fields, but he stayed overnight in the dorms, which were reportedly a pizza-candy-and-gaming party until lights-out every night.

He showed up on the first day of camp wearing the T-shirt from his club soccer team, United Maine. He carried a United Maine gym bag. In the mornings, when it was still a little cool, he'd wear a United Maine windbreaker. The camp gave us all free water bottles, but Alex always used the one he'd brought from home: a freakin' United Maine Nalgene.

I didn't know anyone at that camp, but Alex? He knew everybody. He knew guys from Cape Elizabeth and Yarmouth who played on the United Maine team with him. He knew guys from Bangor and Augusta who played on a different club team. He even knew some of the college players. That first day we all walked onto the field? Guys in Midcoast College T-shirts called out to him, slapped him five, and said, "Hey, Alex, great to see you out here!"

We were only fourteen years old, and already it felt like Alex was the most popular kid at a party the rest of us hadn't even been invited to.

As our caravan of cars pulled up close to the rock, Mike Tur-cotte, riding shotgun with me, stated the obvious: "No sign of Plourde."

I had been scanning the group behind Alex, just in case Don-nie had miraculously gotten himself a ride and was waiting for me. No such luck.

"What are you going to do?" Mike asked. I eased the car into a space and turned off the ignition. I looked at him in mock sur-prise.

"What do you mean . . . Donnie?" I said to him. He looked confused for a moment. Then, when he realized what I meant, he shook his head.

"No. Fuckin'. Way." It was the first time I'd ever heard Mike swear.

"Dude, I will owe you *forever*."

"You don't have anything I want, Tom. No way am I taking one for Donnie Plourde."

"Mike, you don't have to say anything. You just have to help me paint. Let them think you're Don."

"I don't even look like him!"

"They don't know what he looks like."

"No, but they know what I look like. I've been playing soccer against these guys since junior high. I'm friends with some of them on Facebook."

"Are you kiddin' me? You friended jackasses from Maquoit?"

"Facebook friends aren't real friends. And I know some of them from Model UN . . ."

Someone rapped on the window. Everyone was waiting for us to get out of the car. Mike stared at the dashboard.

"You're asking me to take one for Donnie Plourde," he repeated. He didn't bother to hide the disgust in his voice. I sighed.

"I'm asking you to take one for the team. Look, all we—"

"The team didn't screw up, Tom. *You* did. Plourde did." He was pissed, but already shrugging off his Chamberlain jacket. If he was gonna pass as Donnie, he needed to lose the varsity gear. He had a black skullcap in his jacket pocket, and he pulled it over his head, down low over his eyes. I checked the overhead compartment where Dad usually stows his sunglasses, and sure enough, they were there. I handed them to Mike.

"I will make this up to you, man."

"Yeah, you will," he said under his breath as he shoved the door open. The rest of the team, all decked out in their team blue, stood outside the car. As Mike and I went round to the trunk to get the paint and brushes, I heard him mutter to the guys, "Act like I'm Plourde." Like a game of telephone, it was whispered through the group.

We all walked to the rock. Someone whistled.

"Good morning, ladies," we heard. Laughter.

Some low-to-the-ground, heavyset guy who was standing with them and looked about my father's age whipped his head around in the direction of the comment.

"We'll have none of that, gentlemen," he said.

Yeah, right.

Alex was standing up front.

At the Midcoast camp, they divided us into little teams and named us after New England schools: Trinity, Williams, Colby, like that. Alex and I both got put on Middlebury.

We beat everyone; Middlebury ruled the camp. Our coach

recognized right off that both Alex and I owned the center striker spots, and if one of us didn't score, the other would. It was sweet, and Alex was . . . amazing. Not only was he just naturally good, but he busted his butt. When we ran laps, he led. When two players chased the ball, he always fought just that little bit harder and won possession every time. He had more desire than I had ever seen in anyone.

And he decided he liked me.

For some reason he chose me as his running buddy for those three days. He'd throw his arm across my shoulders and pull me into his pack for lunch. We'd swim together at pool time. He'd invite me back to his dorm room for the afternoon break, when he'd dig into his duffel for obscene amounts of candy. His door was always open and there was always a steady flow of guys in and out. He was funny and easy to laugh with. He introduced me to everyone, and I imagined I saw a little jealousy in their eyes.

I decided I liked Alex Rhodes.

The low-to-the-ground guy turned out to be their principal. He held a Dunkin' Donuts travel mug. Off to one side there was a small table set up, with a cardboard to-go pot of coffee and a couple big boxes of Munchkins. Maquoit was making a little breakfast party out of this. I glanced sideways at Mike. A bright flush had spread from his neck right up to his cheeks. Mike never gets in trouble. His whole life, and I've known him my whole life, the guy's always walked the straight and narrow.

And that morning he got to be Donnie Plourde.

I walked right up to the principal and stuck out my hand.

"Good morning, sir. I'm Tom Bouchard." He pumped my hand, then turned to Mike. Who smiled, shook, didn't say a word.

Behind the principal and all around the rock, the Maquoit soccer team was a sea of red and black. Like a clone army in their regulation warm-up pants and jackets. Which actually looked warm. Not like our shitty plastic windbreakers with the peeling letters.

I had once asked Coach why we had such crummy crap. I mean, we were all public schools, right?

"They have some pretty active soccer boosters over there," he'd said. "Every year they raise enough money through fund-raisers to outfit the entire varsity team with new warm-ups."

As I watched Mike's face transition from red to maroon, watched our guys shivering in the morning cold while the Maquoit guys popped Munchkins in their mouths, it just hit me how much I couldn't stand those guys. I felt this overwhelming need to get out of there as fast as possible.

"I have a suggestion that could save us all a lot of time and trouble," I said to the principal, who was about to speak. He looked at me a little skeptically but nodded. I cranked open the paint can and gave it a quick stir. Mike handed me a wide brush, and I quickly slapped black over the S and U of *suck*. The rock now read *You ck, Maquoit!*

"How about when that dries in a couple minutes I add an R and an O?" I said to the principal. "Then it'll read *You rock*." He hesitated. Looked a little confused.

"Rock is a verb as well as a noun," I explained. Someone from the Maquoit side laughed.

Alex.

At the end of that three-day camp, when some of the parents came to the final awards ceremony, Alex introduced me to his father. I remember wondering what the guy did for a living, because this was, like, two o'clock on a weekday, and all the guys' fathers I knew were working.

"I've been hearing a lot about you, Tom," Mr. Rhodes said to me. "Why haven't we seen you at any United Maine tryouts?" He was a bigger, wider version of Alex. The same blond hair. Tall and jacked. Wore an adult-sized United Maine windbreaker. I wondered if parents got the gear, too, or if Alex's dad coached.

"Um . . . I don't know," I said honestly. Playing with United Maine was not part of my worldview.

"You could totally make the team," Alex said enthusiastically. "He's way better than Hoover, Dad—"

Mr. Rhodes put up his hand. He gave Alex this reproving look.

"We don't run down our teammates, son," he said.

Alex stared at his father. His face had gone blank. Like he hadn't heard the correction. Smooth, no emotion, except for his eyes. They started blinking, fast. As if Alex had something in his eye he was trying desperately to blink away.

"We haven't posted the dates yet, but tryouts for the fall season are always in August," Mr. Rhodes said to me. "Just go to the United Maine website. I hope we'll see you out there." He and Alex turned to go, but not before Alex threw an arm across my shoulders.

"It's gonna be you and me on that front line!" No trace of the blink as he spoke then. Just the confident grin I had gotten so used to that week. As if there were no question about my trying out, making the team, and spending the next four years collecting trophies with him and his friends from Cape Elizabeth and Falmouth and as far away as Bridgton and Kittery.

As he stepped forward from the rock and spoke to the princi-pal, Alex Rhodes resembled a bigger, wider version of the eighth grader I had met at soccer camp years ago. He had turned into a slightly blonder, not-yet-balding clone of his father.

"I think that'd work," he said. "Especially if their team chants it while the paint dries."

"We didn't come here to sing, Rhodes," I said immediately. He smirked, shrugged. I knew for damn sure he didn't care what we did. He was just playing with us.

"I believe we can dispense with the chanting," the principal said. "But if you're fine with this suggestion, Alex, then we can go ahead with it."

"Whatever," he said.

As we waited for the black paint to dry, the principal filled the air with blather. No one was listening. Mike had his head ducked, half facing away from the Maquoit players, who, if they recognized him, didn't say anything. Meanwhile, our guys were shifting their feet, silent. No one offered us donuts or coffee. I *so* wanted out of there.

Alex stepped in close to me.

"Why do I get the feeling none of this was your idea, Bouchard?" he said quietly.

The expression on his face and the tone of his voice were al-most . . . friendly. From one captain to another. Old camp buddies, right?

The night after that camp ended, I'd pored over the United Maine website with my parents. I remember their gasps when they clicked on the fees button. My parents are both schoolteachers, so while we're not rich, we're not poor, either. Still, the cost of playing for that team was a showstopper. End of conversation. *Sorry, son, but we're not that family.*

Long after they'd gone to bed that night I continued scrolling through the photos on the website. I found pictures of Alex and his teammates playing in Virginia that spring. They'd won the eastern under-15s and were posed in front of the goal, their noses sunburned, hair plastered with dried sweat, and this big honkin' trophy in front. I found John Hoover in the picture, the striker who Alex said wasn't nearly as good as me.

I'd stayed up pretty late going over those pictures. When I shut the computer off, I'd promised myself to never visit the United Maine website again. And I never did.

Standing with him beside the rock that morning, paint slowly drying, I wondered if we would have ended up right where we were at that moment if we'd been United Maine teammates. Would I have messed with their stupid rock if we were practicing in the dome together the next day?

He looked at me curiously when I didn't answer him.

"I don't get you, Bouchard," he continued. "You're not an asshole. And this was a completely asshole thing to do."

"Maybe you don't know me as well as you think, Alex," I said pleasantly. I went over to the paint and laid one finger gently on top. Came away black. I suppressed the urge to blow on the rock. "Mind if I have a donut?" I walked over to the Munchkins box and surveyed the flavors. Picked out a chocolate glazed and popped it in my mouth.

"Thanks," I told him.

He shook his head in wonder.

"You just gotta hope this doesn't screw you out of a tip for college," he said. "I heard your coach was pretty mad." I shrugged. I would have loved to know where Alex got his insider information about how mad Coach Gerardi might or might not have been.

I would have loved to know whether some college was recruiting *him*.

Of course, he volunteered the information.

"It's lookin' like Amherst for me," he said softly. So his teammates couldn't hear. "My dad spoke to the coach yesterday. Said I'm on his list." I nodded.

It figured. Alex Rhodes would be the sort of guy who'd have an admissions deal with a college before the rest of the world had even sent in their applications.

"Congratulations," I told him. "I can see you in purple. Remind me . . . what's their mascot? The Little Lord Fauntleroys?" Alex colored. The Amherst College mascot is Lord Jeff, named after the college's founder, Lord Jeffrey Amherst. Who had made a name for himself handing out smallpox-infected blankets to the Indians back in colonial days.

Damn. I had definitely been spending too much time reading college guidebooks. But still: the Jeffs? We both knew it was freakin' ridiculous.

And way more than I had up my sleeve in the college department.

"I think this paint is dry." Mike Turcotte. Who was even more eager than I was to get the hell out of there.

"Go for it, man," I told him, and Mike pried the lid off the red.

The two teams were strangely silent as Mike painted the letters *R* and *O* in front of the *CK*. The black was still a little gummy, but the red didn't run.

Principal What's-His-Name was making final blathering sounds, and we were pressing the lids back on the paint cans when Alex delivered his parting comments. He stepped in close and spoke quietly, for my ears only.

"I feel sorry for you, Bouchard. You could've been good, but instead you're stuck in a crap program. Playin' with Osama over there." My glance automatically shifted to where Saeed stood, a little off to the side of our group. I didn't think he'd heard Alex.

My anger was quick, deep, and familiar.

"You know what, Rhodes?" I said, loud enough so that a few of the guys standing right near us could hear. "Eat shit."

A satisfied grin spread across Alex's face.

"What was that, Tommy?" he said. "What did you just say?"

"I said, how about a little friendly *bet?*"

This I said clearly as I looked at the principal.

"How about," I continued, "if we beat you guys next time around, you all have to paint your own rock. I'm thinkin' . . . instead of 'Maquoit' you paint in 'Chamberlain.' So it'll read *You rock, Chamberlain!*" The suggestion drew some energetic clapping from my guys.

"Yeah, but what do we get out of it when we win?" Alex declared above the clapping. Big cheers from Maquoit. This was feeling more and more like a dueling pep rally. The principal looked uncomfortable.

When the noise died down, I spoke.

"If we lose, which we won't, by the way, I'll come back. Alone. And I'll paint whatever the hell you want on your rock."

Even the guys on my side liked that one, especially because

they sure didn't want to come back. If Maquoit beat us, I was gonna be on my own.

Everyone started to leave. I gave the principal the unused brushes and what was left of the paint. The Maquoit guys knocked off the last of the Munchkins; Alex and I made a point of shaking hands over this latest deal. Mike was already in the car.

As we pulled out, he looked at me skeptically.

"I feel sorry for you, Tom," he said. Which was strange, that he would repeat what Alex had just said. What was it about me that generated all the pity?

"Why?" I asked.

"Because our next game against Maquoit is scheduled for the second week of October. Right smack in the middle of Ramadan."

This sick, cold feeling settled in my stomach. Trust Mike to know that. Trust me to . . . not. To not know that precisely when we had to take on our biggest, toughest opponent in the conference, our best strikers would be running . . . no, staggering . . . up and down the length of a soccer field after fasting all day.

At that moment I felt sorry for me, too.

Chapter Eleven

When I was little, I went through a stage when I pestered my folks for a sibling.

We knew a lot of big families. Kids-spilling-out-of-the-house families where there always seemed to be a new baby and there were a lot of toys. The televisions were always on in the houses of big families, tuned to Nickelodeon and Disney and, if there were older kids, MTV: all stations my vigilant parents refused to purchase on their cable contract. There was always a pan of something freshly baked and just lying out for the taking in big families, and lots of. sugary drinks in the fridge. In the backyard, older brothers were always organizing the games, or spying on the girls, or building something with a rusty whatever-they-found-in-the-garage, which often resulted in a bloody gash, a trip to the emergency room for stitches, and a tetanus shot, which, if you weren't on the receiving end of all that treatment, was pretty exciting.

Our home, by comparison, was dull. Healthy snacks stocked in the cupboard, sweets served only after dinner for dessert, books outnumbering toys, and PBS the channel of choice. It never occurred to me that these were conscious child-rearing decisions my parents made: I figured we just didn't have enough kids, and as a result, the "fun factor" was way too low in our house.

"It doesn't work that way," Mom said when I told her I wanted an older brother. "You can only get younger brothers at this point."

"Okay," I said. "I'd like . . . two."

"And of course," she continued, "you might wind up with sisters. Little sisters."

That option had never occurred to me. I'd seen plenty of little sisters in the homes of the big families, and as far as I was concerned, they were a complete drag. True, a few could swing a bat and sink a basket as good as anyone, but for the most part little sisters were whiny tattlers, convinced the boys were forever up to no good.

When I didn't respond, Mom played her trump card.

"And you know, Tommy, you really almost already have a brother."

"Who?" I asked her, bewildered.

"Donnie," she said. "He's your best buddy, and an only child, too. You're more like brothers than friends."

And that's how it rolled. I think my parents would have been happy with more kids, but that's not how things worked out for them. Meanwhile, I stopped bugging them and focused instead on the brother I did have.

At first he looked out for me. That's because he was bigger for a long time, one of those early growers who shoots up fast, then stops, and ends up short or only average height. But back when we were five, he was bigger and bolder, egging me on to take my training wheels off, or climb the tree, or swim in the deep end.

I was actually sort of shy, a little timid, and Don, with his pre-school swagger, would pull me along. No one dared mess with me, because otherwise Donnie Plourde, the biggest kid on the playground, would mess with them.

Things started to change in third grade because that's when school changed. You were expected to know how to read. Fill out worksheets quietly. The kids who couldn't sit still weren't so cute and "kinetic" anymore. They were disruptive. Undisciplined. Dumb. All of a sudden, Timid Tommy was in the driver's seat, while Donnie was sitting in the corner, the nuns' favorite place to put him. I would finish my work fast, then volunteer to help him with his. In the cafeteria, I was our table's monitor and always overlooked Donnie's "violations," like getting up and walking around, or leaving trash behind. I would pick up his trash. Wipe up his spilled milk.

Maybe that didn't really help him in the long run. Especially because by senior year in high school, most of us were pretty tired of wiping up his spilled milk. Even me, and I knew him better than anyone. Sometimes it felt like the things that happened to him happened to me. I'd wince when he scraped a knee, cry when he got cut from teams, feel the same rage when his deadbeat dad, who was supposed to show up with Red Sox tickets for his birthday, failed to show at all. On the rare occasions when Don's dad did show, he was usually drunk. Or with a new girlfriend.

Still, there was a limit. And Donnie leaving me to face Alex and Co. by myself at the rock was *so* not cool.

After we finished up at Maquoit, I gave Saeed and Ismail rides home. I was headed to the K Street Center and they both lived nearby. I doubted there would be much homework help needed on a sunny Saturday afternoon, but with ninety-nine hours of service ahead of me, I figured I could find something to do there. Maybe Myla would let me count hours spent playing soccer with Abdi as service. . . .

That section of town used to be one of those old Franco neighborhoods. Walking distance from the river and the old mills. As we drove down Saeed's street, I saw all these French names on the little convenience stores and businesses tucked between the apartment buildings: Thibeault's Market, Morin's Grocery, Coulombe's Auto Repair. Now they faced Somali grocery stores advertising specials on goat meat and international phone cards.

One word caught my attention.

"What's *halal?*" I asked Saeed, pointing to one storefront. The word was scrawled in black marker on a piece of paper taped to the window.

"Is good," he replied. "Is . . . okay. For the Muslim peoples."

"Is in Koran," Ismail added. "What is *halal*. What is *haram*."

That word again.

"Like, dogs are *haram*," I said.

"Dogs is not clean," Saeed corrected. "Pig meat is *haram*." I sighed.

"Okay, so what's *halal?*" I asked them.

"Goat," they replied at once.

"If is made *halal*," Ismail added.

"Wait. So goat is not automatically *halal?* You gotta do something to it?" He nodded encouragingly. Like the stupid Amreekan was finally getting it.

"Yes, is *way* you kill it make it *halal*."

"But pork always *haram*," Saeed added.

"Sounds kosher," I said, grinning. They looked at me blankly. "Never mind," I said. So much for humor.

When I pulled up to the curb in front of his building and started to get out, Saeed looked surprise.

"I'm going to the K Street Center," I explained. He said something in Somali to Ismail, they clasped hands for a moment, then Ismail disappeared up one of the dim staircases that ascended like a maze between the apartment buildings. Saeed fell into step with me.

"Why you go to Center?" he asked.

"I have to help out. Volunteer. Because of what I did at the rock," I told him. He laughed.

"That is good. Lot of peoples need help there. Samira work there. You know?"

"Yeah, actually, I did know that." It occurred to me that this was as good a time as any to ask him about his sister.

"You know, Saeed, I get the impression she doesn't much like me. Samira." He frowned.

"Samira like all peoples," he said.

"Not me," I said. "I think she's still annoyed about the permission slip thing. Do you remember?" Saeed stopped walking. He looked thoughtful.

"You not know Somali girls," he finally said. "Somali girls is . . . different from Amreekan girls."

"I understand, but some things? Especially in the girl department? Some things are the same." I laughed, a little. Saeed did not laugh with me.

"Somali girls different."

Something about his expression wiped the smile right off my

116

face. He didn't have the English to bridge the gap between our respective understandings of girls any more than he had the English to explain how one slaughtered a goat according to the Koran. But he did have enough body language to make one thing very clear: the gap between us was deep. Like, Grand Canyon deep.

I changed the subject. We talked soccer for the rest of our walk.

The Center was alive with kids when we arrived, and I was beginning to suspect the place was never quiet. They raced in and out, spilling onto the sidewalks and running across the street to the big municipal park where there were benches, swings, and a basketball court. Somali women sat on the benches, a few holding babies. I felt like they'd been sitting there since my last visit.

When we walked into The Center, we practically crashed into my little pal, Abdi. "Dude!" I said to him. He skidded to a stop. He was about to reply, but then he saw who I was with. His expression took on something like awe. He said something to Saeed in Somali that made Saeed laugh. They went on, back and forth for a few sentences, leaving me completely in the dark, until Abdi turned to me.

"Tom, man, how you know Saeed?"

"We play soccer. How do you know him?" Abdi looked amazed. "Man, *everyone* know Saeed!" He ran outside, zipped across the street without looking, and disappeared into the sea of children milling around the park.

Saeed meanwhile had walked ahead of me. The room was full of kids trying to blow up these cheap balloons that simply wouldn't blow up, and in the thick of it I saw Myla's blond cropped head. She caught sight of me.

"Tom Bouchard!" she exclaimed. "Look, guys, just what we need! A pair of strong lungs." She wove through the kids toward me, holding out a limp blue balloon.

It was stupid, but Donnie's comments about my supposed thing for Myla popped into my head at that moment. Hot? Not?

Here's what was really weird: neither. She was just herself. This little person wearing flip-flops and khaki pants that ended halfway down her calves. Her toenails were painted bright red.

I took the balloon. It was a little damp at the opening.

"Hmm. How many kids just put their mouths on this?" I asked her. She flashed one of those oh-give-me-a-break looks and rummaged in the package for a fresh balloon.

"Just me, Mr. Germs," she said, holding one out. I backed up and raised the first balloon to my lips.

"Oh, *your* germs are good with me," I replied. She colored, which, I admit, was my intention. *Yes, Ms. Mumford Student, this is how we roll.*

I blew. For a moment the balloon resisted, and I realized I was going to wind up looking like a complete idiot with my cheeks puffed like some chipmunk with his pouches full of nuts, but then it yielded into this long, narrow tube. A few of the kids shrieked, and then they started jumping up and down and holding their balloons toward me.

Myla turned out to be an energetic balloon animal maker, so after I inflated and tied off each one I passed it to her and she transformed it into a mouse . . . a fish . . . an alligator. Her creatures didn't actually look like any of these animals, but the kids didn't care.

"So I guess I don't have to tell you that no one around here is doing any homework," she said at one point.

"Yeah, I figured as much," I said with a shrug. "But you'll put me down for a few hours of heavy labor with balloons, right?"

"Dream on, Captain Bouchard," she said dryly.

"Now, *that's* what I'm talkin' about," I said. "Captain. I've been waiting to get a little respect around here."

She laughed.

"Don't kid yourself. You're just my assistant balloon boy. Hey, everyone!" she shouted. "This is the last, and I want you to guess what animal it is!" The kids shouted the names of animals that didn't look anything like the balloon knot Myla had created, which reminded me of a slug with warts, but she handed it to a girl who called out "cat," so what did I know? Anyway, once the balloons were gone the kids drifted outside, and it got quiet.

"Wanna help me sort cans?" Myla said, heading for the kitchen without waiting for my answer. I followed her.

The industrial-style kitchen in the back of The Center had big ovens and long metal counters. You could cook enough food in there to feed an army, but it looked like they were only using it for storage. Namely, dozens of cardboard boxes and paper grocery bags stuffed with canned and packaged goods.

"A local high school did a Stuff the Bus project and gave us some of the food they collected," Myla explained. "I'm sorting through it, pitching the crap, and trying to put together boxes we can give out to new refugee families. You know, staples to get them started?" Myla peered into a box, rummaged, and pulled out a can of peas and a crushed bag of something labeled Splenda.

"For example, *this* is crap," she said, holding up the Splenda and unceremoniously dumping it in the metal trash can next to the counter. She held up the peas. "*This* is food you can use." She shook her head in disgust.

"Some people think cleaning out their cabinets once a year and donating their garbage counts as charity," she said. She shoved a box toward me and I began emptying the contents onto the counter.

"Once," she continued, "we got a load of donated used toys. Books. Some plastic stuff which was still okay once you gave it a good scrub in the tub. But there was this doll? One of those super-expensive American Girl dolls? With a busted face. It looked like someone had taken an ice pick to her eye. I couldn't believe somebody thought that sad, scary doll would be a decent toy for a child. But I guess some people think if you're poor, you'll be happy with anything. That you *should* be happy with just anything." Myla pulled cans from a paper bag on the floor. She was fast, and sorted as she went, into corn, beans, tomatoes . . .

"Dolls creep me out," I commented. "I don't get why girls play with them."

"I know, right?" she laughed. "And a broken doll? Totally creepy." She shuddered. We sorted in silence for a few minutes: boxes of mac and cheese, instant cake mix, SpaghettiOs . . .

"So how'd you find out I'm a captain?" I couldn't resist asking her. She shrugged, not looking at me.

"Samira. We had a conversation about you after you left the other day."

I put down the cans I was holding and forced a smile.

"Hmm. Why do I get the feeling that didn't go so well for me?" She laughed.

"Yeah. Samira's definitely not your biggest fan."

I felt my smile fade.

"Okay. Enlighten me. *What* did I ever do to piss her off?"

Myla stopped sorting as well.

"Let's just say she doesn't think much of your taste in women."

Wow. Completely unexpected response.

"Huh?"

"She knows your girlfriend," Myla explained. "So I guess it's a case of guilt by association."

"What did Cherisse do to her?" I asked. Then I was instantly sorry. I hadn't planned on telling Myla that I had a girlfriend. Saying her name confirmed it.

"Nothing directly. I don't think she even knows Samira. But apparently your girlfriend is part of a group of white girls who told a teacher that Somali girls were gossiping about them and mocking them to their faces in the classroom, in Somali. They made a real stink about it, so now your school has an English-only policy in the classroom. If immigrant kids so much as say 'Can I borrow your calculator?' in their own language, they get detention."

This was news to me. I didn't have any Somali kids in my classes. But Cherisse, who was about as far from the honors track as you could get, had a bunch of kids in her classes who had just moved up from the annex. That was the basement floor, where they put everyone who couldn't speak or write English. The day care was down there, too, for girls at our school who had had babies but still wanted to earn their diplomas. They'd drop their kids off in the morning, then head upstairs to homeroom.

"I never heard anything about this," I said.

"Welcome to Girl World," she said, and laughed. "It's right next door to hell."

"Yeah. Sucks for you, I guess," I said.

She slammed the can she was holding down hard on the metal counter. Put her hand on one hip, and cocked her head. I couldn't really tell if she was insulted or pretending to be insulted.

"Excuse me: I'm no girl. I'm a college *woman*."

Okay. Pretending. Phew.

"Oh. Oh, pardon me. *Ms.* Myla."

"Much better, *Captain* Bouchard. I see you're getting the hang of things around here."

We sorted in silence for a few minutes after that. But something was bothering me.

"Can I ask you something? What's wrong with making the classroom an English-only zone?"

She put her can down again. Now she looked serious.

"Do you not get how this shuts them down? Especially when they barely speak our language? For them, not knowing English is like being gagged and blindfolded at the same time."

"That's why they need to learn it. Hey, my grandparents spoke French. It was their first language, and they didn't get detention for speaking it in school. They got whacked with a ruler!"

"Wow. That's enlightened. They should try that at Chamberlain," Myla remarked.

I breathed out impatiently.

"I'm not saying it's good. I'm saying it's reality. You gotta speak English if you want to get ahead in this country. And you know, things are way easier for the African kids than they were for my grandparents. At least Saeed and those guys can speak whatever they want in the hallways and the cafeteria."

Myla didn't answer me. We both returned to stacking cans in silence until she finally spoke again.

"I think, Tom, Samira assumes that if you date someone, you must be like them and share their views. And she doesn't think much of your Cherisse."

I couldn't argue with her there. I also wasn't about to explain my interest in Cherisse Ouellette, which had little to do with her views or opinions about anything.

"You know," I replied, "enough about me. Where are you from?"

She looked surprised. "Minnesota."

"Wow. Why?"

She paused for a moment.

"Huh?"

"Why did you come to Enniston, Maine, of all places, for college? Why didn't you go to, like, Carleton or Macalester or Hamline or something?"

Myla burst out laughing.

"Ooh, somebody's been reading *Fiske's Guide to Colleges*! Tell you what, I'll say the state and you name every college in it."

"Sounds like fun, but I'd have to kill you if you did that," I said shortly. Myla looked at me curiously.

"My parents teach at Carleton," she finally answered. "So it would've practically been incest to go there. Besides, I needed to get away. And Mumford is awesome."

"Yeah, but Enniston?" She grinned.

"What's wrong, townie? You don't love your city?" I shook my head.

"Not a relevant question. It's like asking, 'Do you love having skin?' I mean, I guess. But sometimes I want to crawl right out of it. And I can't imagine somebody else wanting to crawl in." All of a sudden this conversation felt serious.

But Myla could hang with it.

"Sure," she replied slowly. "Enniston is like a part of you. But you're ready to move on. And it seems weird that this place you need to dust is someone else's moving on."

I was so surprised that she got me before I completely got myself that I didn't even know what to say. So I just nodded, like a complete idiot, and unpacked more canned corn.

"So where do you want to go?" she continued.

I shrugged.

"Seriously," she said.

"I don't know," I answered.

She gave me a look.

"It's late September of your senior year and you don't have a game plan for after you graduate?"

Ms. Myla didn't realize she'd wandered into a minefield. Talking about the future was not my favorite topic.

"Who says I need a game plan?" I asked. Her eyes narrowed.

"What the hell is a game plan, anyway?" I continued. "What's wrong with just finishing this year, graduating, then looking around to see what I want to do next? Maybe I'll get a job, work with my uncle." I reached the bottom of my paper bag and pulled out one last jar. Hot Chipotle Chili Cocoa Mix. It was in this artsy shape, and made in Santa Fe. I searched for an expiration date: three years old.

"Crap, right?" I said, holding it up for Myla to see. Before she could reply I hook-shot it into the trash can. The glass shattered loudly against the aluminum. We both flinched at the sound.

"A job is a plan," Myla said quietly. "What does your uncle do?"

"Fuck-all," I said with a short laugh. "He has a big-ass plow on his pickup, so he clears driveways in the winter. He can build pretty much anything. Refinish wood floors. Install windows. Doesn't make much money, but at the end of the day he's actually accomplished something. His favorite thing to do, however, is fight with his sister—my aunt."

"What's she like?" Myla asked. With her foot she slid a packed cardboard box along the floor so that it rested between us. We unloaded the contents.

"Like you. Smart. Went to college. Into helping people. You might even know her. Maddie Thibeault?" Myla shook her head.

"And which one of them are you like? Your uncle?"

Even a blockhead like me could pick up on the irritation in her voice. I took a deep breath.

"I don't know who I'm like. Nobody. All of them. Stuffed into the same body."

"Like a big sausage casing," Myla commented into the box.

"Listen," I said. "All this college talk drives me nuts. *Way* too many people have an opinion about my future, and if I have to hear one more word about SATs and sports tips and applications, I'm gonna spontaneously combust."

Myla didn't answer, but instead methodically placed food on the smooth metal counter. When the carton was empty, she pressed one foot against it and shoved it, hard, across the floor, so it skittered into a corner of the kitchen with other empty containers. She aimed those enormous blue eyes in my direction.

"Think of going to college as a privilege instead of a punishment that adults are inflicting on you and I'll bet filling out applications won't seem so bad," she said evenly. I felt my face color.

"You know, Captain, outside of your family I doubt anyone much cares where or whether you go to college," Myla continued. "But as a healthy, smart white male growing up in one of the safest, most prosperous countries in the world, you know what? You have a moral obligation to do something worthwhile with your life and *not* be an asshole. Just sayin'."

Chapter Twelve

Later that afternoon Donnie texted me. While I was driving home from K Street, and yeah, I know I shouldn't drive and text at the same time but I only typed when I stopped at a light.

Got messed up last night. Woke @ noon. What happened @ the rock?

I texted back: *F U.*

I realized this was pretty cold. He could've been lying in a ditch for all anyone knew, and I didn't even ask if he was all right. But it only takes five characters to text "sorry" and I thought I deserved that much.

My phone vibrated again.

Let me make it up to u.

I replied at the next light: *In enough trouble already. Go f yourself.*

Next it rang. I considered turning it off. But I didn't. Story of my life with Donnie . . .

"Dude," I heard him say. "I propose G-rated, highly legal fun. It's all my brain cells could handle at this point, anyway."

"Why would I want to spend any time with you?" I asked.

I heard his short laugh.

"Because you love me. And because for once in your life I'm paying."

"No way. What, you rob a bank?"

"Somethin' like."

"Seriously, Don."

"Seriously, Tom-boy, you have five seconds to lighten up and let me take you out or I'm calling George and he gets to eat dinner with me at Michelangelo's tonight."

I paused. Donnie never has money. This couldn't be good. But I really liked the barbecue chicken pizza at Michelangelo's.

"Don't ask, don't tell, huh?" I said to him.

"You got that right. Pick me up at six."

"Don . . . no. I'm grounded, remember? Unlike you, who continue to go out and get ruined. And have yet to do a single hour of community service."

"Exactly. You're suffering, man. And it's my job to ease that suffering. *That's* my service. My guidance counselor is going to give me hours for it." He was trying not to laugh.

"I'm hangin' up now, Plourde."

Five minutes later I was a few blocks from home when my cell went off again. Mom.

"Hey, honey, where are you?"

"Pleasant Street. I'm really close."

"Donnie just called here. He sounded like he could use a little family time. I told him we'd relax your grounding conditions so that he could join us for dinner."

The guy is *epic*. He knew my mom had a soft spot where he was concerned.

128

"Let me guess: I should go pick him up."

"And stop at Michelangelo's on your way home. He wants to get you a pizza."

Donnie lost his license within six months of getting his license. His first two tickets were for speeding in a school zone. The third, license-losing infraction was an OUI. The good news was that everyone in Enniston could breathe easier now that there was one less Plourde on the road (his father and uncle were both "experienced" drunk drivers). The bad news was that Donnie always needed a lift and could never manage to hold down any sort of job because he didn't have reliable transportation.

Jake and I tried to help him out as much as we could, but during soccer season Donnie leaned on guys like George Morin. Greg Pepper, if he was really stuck. But even Donnie used Pepper, who was a couple years older than us, as a last resort. "Man, if we get pulled for a bad taillight or something, I don't know *what* the cops would find in Pepper's trunk!" he once commented to me.

You couldn't talk sense into him. He knew he was screwing up. Felt bad about it, too. But Donnie Plourde was a walking Greek tragedy. Heading down some dark path the Fates had determined for him, and he was hell-bent to see it through to the fiery finish.

I said that to him once, and he laughed.

"See, that's what I love about you, Tom. Everybody else falls asleep in school, but you put the classics in context. And make me out to be a Greek hero."

"A tragic hero, dumbass," I replied, which only made him laugh harder.

We didn't get to Michelangelo's until five-thirty, and on a Saturday evening people were already standing in line. We'd called ahead for the pizza, but they were backed up, so Donnie and I had to hang out for a while. As we waited, my phone vibrated in my seat pocket. I pulled it out and read the incoming number on the screen: Cherisse.

"Hey," I said when I flipped it open.

"What's up, boyfriend?" I heard.

This greeting was a huge improvement over the previous forty-eight hours. Following workshop day she'd hung up on me five . . . no, six times. When she finally did take my call, she yelled at me for embarrassing her by asking Devon to apologize to Fatuma. From there, she'd moved on to weepy and accused me of secretly having a "thing" for Liz Painchaud. Unbelievable.

A little part of me was actually grateful to be grounded and forbidden to see her, but I'd be damned if I'd actually admit that to my mom.

"Not much," I replied.

"Where are you?" she said.

"Michelangelo's. Gonna pick up some pizza for dinner. Donnie's with me." I heard this whiny sound. Petulant. Displeased.

"Gee, thanks for inviting me!"

"I can't invite you. I'm grounded."

"Michelangelo's with Donnie doesn't sound very grounded." I looked at Don.

"Help me out here," I said to him. "Tell Cherisse my mother ordered me to pick you up and get pizzas."

He took my phone.

"Don't believe a word he says, Cherisse," Donnie said. "We're here with two other girls and his mother has no idea where he is."

I grabbed the phone back.

"Cherisse?" I said.

"I hate that guy," she said. "Tell him I hate him."

"Hey, did you hear we beat Whittier yesterday?" I said instead.

"Whoop-dee-doo," she replied.

"Hey, it's a huge upset. The guys were losing it on the bus."

"That's great, Tom. I'm so happy for you. I'm gonna go wash my hair now. Because it's not like I have anything else to do on a Saturday night, with my boyfriend supposedly grounded but still managing to eat out with his friends." She signed off without even saying goodbye.

"She hates you," I told Donnie as I snapped my phone shut.

"She'll get over it," he said contentedly.

Michelangelo's is cool. It's in one of the old mills downtown and it's got these high ceilings and brick walls everywhere and the food is awesome. I like looking around and trying to imagine the place when it was a working mill. Imagine the din of giant looms and oily machines. Lint floating like snowflakes.

Mom tells me when it first opened, she wanted to take her grandmother, Mémère Louise, there for lunch, but the old lady refused. She'd already gone to a mill restaurant in Brunswick with a friend, and it upset her. Apparently when they renovated the place they kept the original floors. Sanded them down and waxed them to a high polish; everyone said they were beautiful. But Mémère knew those floors. Recognized the shape of the windows. The columns supporting cavernous ceilings and dredging up memories which no amount of framed local art or bistro-style furniture could hide. She couldn't eat; they had to leave.

I have no problem eating in a former mill. To me, it's like eating in a museum. Where someone has just baked an oven's worth of garlic bread.

After a while we stood near the hostess station, in view of the dining room. It was packed; lots of families with their little kids coming to get an early dinner. I felt someone tug on my sleeve.

Myla. I didn't recognize her at first. She wore eye makeup and these big hoop earrings. Instead of her usual handwoven, practically edible clothing, she was rockin' the dressed-up-for-a-Mumford-student look: black tights and a long sweater. Boots, with spiky heels, that made her seem taller.

"Hey," she said, a little hesitantly. "Thought I recognized you."

We hadn't parted well. After she'd made the asshole comment earlier that day, I'd stormed out. Think I kicked a box of groceries on my way. Heard something crack.

"Hey," I said back. "Are you waiting for a table?"

She pointed into the dining room.

"I'm over there, with some friends. We're taking my roommate out for her birthday."

I glanced in the direction she pointed, to a long table packed with college girls. A few of them looked our way, and when they saw me staring they giggled and nudged each other. Myla frowned. Shook her head at them almost imperceptibly.

"We're just getting takeout," I said, turning away from the girls. "This is my friend Donnie."

Mr. Plourde had snapped to attention. He knew exactly who this was.

"Hi, I'm Myla," she said, extending her hand.

He didn't miss a beat; he took it.

"Myla from the K Street Center?" he said politely. "I've heard a lot about you."

Myla looked genuinely surprised. She blushed. I'd never seen her off balance until that moment.

"Oh. Well. Hope it's not *all* bad," she said, laughing nervously.

"Not at *all*," he said pointedly, and smiled his most charming Donnie Plourde smile, which, like I've said, worked on virtually everyone except for Sister Marie. And Cherisse. Devon. Come to think of it, it didn't work on any girls at Chamberlain.

Myla teetered on her heels. She turned to me.

"I was actually gonna call you. I was totally out of line this afternoon, and I want to apologize."

It was my turn to be surprised. I'd been thinking I needed to call her and apologize for being a jerk.

"Yeah. Me too. I was gonna call *you*. Even though I don't have your number." We both laughed. "I guess I don't take criticism very well."

She shook her head.

"I was out of line," she said. "Two years ago I was in exactly your position and I was freaked out. Totally stressed. So it's pretty unfair of me to judge how you're handling things."

Two years. So she's a sophomore.

"I also think . . . you know, I work with so many kids who would give anything to be in your shoes and go to college that I start to get judgmental. I shouldn't do that."

"Really, Myla, it's okay. I could probably use a little judging every once in a while. Hope I didn't break anything when I walked out." She grinned.

"Another jar of that chili cocoa," she said.

"Oh. Good," I said.

Myla laughed. She began backing up, returning to her friends.

"Anyway, I'll see you later, Cap. Enjoy your dinner," she said. "Nice meeting you, Donnie." She ducked her head, then sort of quick-step-skipped across the crowded dining room. We watched her go, and once she was seated, Donnie sighed. He put a hand on my shoulder.

"Son," he said, "you have a problem."

Chapter Thirteen

Donnie didn't just stay for dinner. He spent the night. Joined us for mass the next morning, and went with us to breakfast at Grandma's house afterward.

I wonder now, if we'd known what that brunch was going to be like, we might have both taken a miss. That's because it was the first Sunday after The Letter. First time my aunt Maddie and uncle Paul were in the same room since The Letter appeared in the Enniston paper.

Don knows about my aunt and uncle: their fights are epic. Their name-calling is epic. Like, Paul calls Maddie a pseudo-intellectual bleeding-heart liberal. My mom says that's his way of saying she went to college and votes for Democrats. Maddie calls Paul a right-wing Neanderthal, which Mom says is her way of saying he votes Republican and hates taxes.

Dad just says they're both incredibly rude and pigheaded and he's glad he married the only member of the family, besides Grandma, who is reasonable.

Anyway, it could have been a Sunday just like any other

Sunday, except that in the Friday paper the mayor of Enniston had published a letter, addressed to the entire Somali community, asking them to please tell their friends and relatives who might be thinking of moving here to . . . not. She said Enniston was maxed out and needed a break from all the new immigrants. She asked them to exercise some discipline.

To be honest, that edition of the paper arrived and made its way into the recycling without my notice. Guess I was too busy kicking Whittier's ass with the help of my Somali teammates to read the news about how maxed out we all were. Too busy painting the rock, making balloon animals, and sorting cans. I mean, was this really news? Hello, people. Stop by Chamberlain High School on any given day and watch new kids who barely speak English get handed schedules they can't read.

Did the mayor think she was telling us something we didn't know? Did she think this was going to help?

Maybe instead of writing letters she could have come up with something actually useful. Like hiring someone to direct traffic in the hallways at our school and steer all the wandering kids to their classrooms.

Instead, we got a Molotov cocktail tossed into a crowded room. A match struck in a gunpowder factory. A Peterbilt kissing a Mack truck on the interstate.

That was The Letter. And that was brunch.

Mom, Dad, and I always go to the eleven o'clock mass. That's the one with the Praise Band. The good music, as Dad puts it. As opposed to the tuneless choir at the eight o'clock that adds ten minutes to the service with all the extra warbling. The Praise Band's songs are lively and we're usually out of there in exactly one hour, which is good. Timing is important to Catholics. I once met a guy who always found the shortest mass possible. He ended up going every Sunday to the Catholic service at the local hospital chapel. Twenty minutes, start to finish.

My grandmother goes to the French mass at the cathedral on Saturdays at four o' clock. This way she can make brunch for everyone on Sunday morning as she listens to her favorite radio show: *La Revue Française,* two hours of Franco programming, mostly music. She says it helps her hang on to her French.

Grandma spoke only French for the first five years of her life, which is hard to imagine because she speaks perfect English now, without a trace of a French accent. But when she does speak French, she could pass for a real *Québécoise.*

She says up until the day her mother, *Mémère* Louise, passed, she dreamed in French. But the night after they buried her, after *Mémère's* funeral mass, the dreams switched to English. That very night. Grandma always tells that story dry-eyed, no drama. She's that kind of no-nonsense lady who brings in her own wood and doesn't think twice about driving during an ice storm. Mom gets all teary when she tells it. She's pretty emotional about the whole Franco heritage thing. Grandma, on the other hand, actually *lived* it.

Anyway, take-out pizza and a night on the pull-out couch, followed by church and family brunch, isn't a big draw for most guys I know, but Donnie seemed almost hungry to tag along. It had been ages since he'd slept over; I couldn't remember the last time. When we were little, I think he slept over most weekends.

He was lucky I didn't kick him out of the car pre-pizza, because as we drove from Michelangelo's with the hot pies to my house, he started annoying me about Myla.

"She likes you," he said. In that singsongy voice I hate.

"You saw her for thirty seconds. You can't tell what she thinks."

"Uh, you can totally tell if a girl likes you in thirty seconds," he said. "She was doing that squirrelly thing."

I almost drove off the road.

"Squirrelly thing? What are you talking about?"

"You know. When they're near a guy they like, girls move differently. They sort of . . . you know." Donnie started doing these contortions, twisting his face into this strange half smile, wiggling his shoulders. I burst out laughing.

"They have spasms? Maybe that's what girls do around *you*, but I'm unfamiliar with the squirrelly thing."

"Trust me. I have special perceiving powers. Like, the way I can always tell when somebody's gay? Even if he hasn't come out yet, I know it before he knows it? It's my gaydar. Well, I've got girldar, too. And that Myla likes you."

"Don, you don't have radar, gaydar, or girldar. You just have dar. Which is first cousin to duh."

"Okay, so I'm not going to punch you for that while you're driving. The fact remains: you have a problem. It begins with the letter C. And I don't have to tell you about all the sorts of dar she's got."

"Seriously," I said.

"And it's gonna start going off like a freakin' car alarm, buddy."

"Uh, why's that?"

"Because not only does this Myla like you. You like *her*."

He knocked it off by the time we got to my house. For the rest of the night he was actually decent company, probably because he hadn't had anything to drink for the previous ten hours. We stayed up late watching the Red Sox smoke the Yankees in extra innings, and because I didn't feel like driving him home he just crashed on the couch.

The next day, the smell of baked meat and strong coffee greeted us when we arrived at Grandma's. Donnie had borrowed a clean shirt from me and tucked it neatly into his jeans. His hair was combed back and still damp from the shower. A big smile broke over Grandma's face when she saw him. She was sitting in her little living room with the starched lace curtains in the windows. There isn't a pin out of place in my grandmother's house; even her garage is cleaner than most people's kitchens. Every fall that garage is draped with long braids of fresh garlic and onions she pulls from her garden and hangs to dry.

"Quelle surprise!" she said, holding one hand out toward Donnie. He grinned as he bent toward her and kissed her lightly on one cheek.

"Hey, Mrs. Thibeault," he said. "It's really good to see you." He settled into the armchair alongside hers like there was nowhere else he'd rather be. Mom and Dad each gave her a breezy kiss before heading straight into the kitchen, where they knew a large pot of coffee awaited them. As I leaned over to kiss Grandma, we heard my mother exclaim.

"Wow! *Tourtière!* What's the occasion, Mom?"

Grandma smiled. Her *tourtière*, an amazing combination of meat, potatoes, and vegetables surrounded by crust and baked in the oven, wasn't usual Sunday brunch food.

"No occasion. Except it's my grandson's favorite and I was in the mood. Or maybe I just had a feeling we'd have special company today." She reached over and squeezed Donnie's knee. I seated myself on the couch. "And guess what I made for dessert?"

"No clue," I replied.

"Maple sugar tart," she said.

"Oh wow," Donnie said. He sighed contentedly. Grandma's maple sugar tart—this mixture of *real* maple syrup and cream, thickened, then cooled in a pie crust—is the best thing ever. She said when she was growing up her mother couldn't afford maple syrup, so she'd make it with brown sugar, but the authentic *Québécois* recipe calls for the real thing.

"How was your show this morning?" I asked her.

"It's always wonderful, but I'll confess I only half listened to it. I switched to the talk radio channel. Everyone was calling in about the mayor's letter." I glanced over at Don, but he shrugged.

"What letter?" I asked, just as the swinging door between the kitchen and living room yawned open and Uncle Paul, mug in hand, entered.

"The long-overdue letter," he said. A bit loudly. He settled on the couch alongside me. His glance fell on Donnie.

"Mr. Plourde," he said. "Looking wide awake and neatly dressed. Welcome."

If you knew Paul, you'd have recognized the tone. A certain politeness with edge. Like someone who was either spoiling for a fight or had just had one.

Grandma pursed her lips. She didn't look at Paul.

"In Friday's paper there was a letter from the mayor asking the Somali people to please not encourage any more immigrants to move to Enniston," she said. As she spoke, Mom and Dad joined us. "She said the city was overwhelmed and really couldn't afford any more new families."

"Amen," Paul said, raising his coffee mug in a mock toast. Grandma frowned.

"Actually, I don't recall the word *please* anywhere in her letter," my mother said primly.

"As if *that* would make a difference," Paul said.

"Have you boys not heard about this?" my father asked, surprised. "Weren't we just talking about it last night?"

"They ate dinner in the den, watching the game," my mother reminded him.

He sighed.

"Gotta read more than just the sports section, guys," he said.

"Wait," Donnie said. "The mayor says we've got too many Somalis and they should leave?"

"No, she's saying we can barely afford the ones we've got and we can't afford any more," Mom explained. "She's asking them to . . . well, what exactly *is* she asking?"

Grandma got up from her chair.

"I've got the article in the kitchen," she said. "And I also think our *tourtière* is ready. Why don't you all go sit down?" Mom followed her; the rest of us moved into the dining room. Paul carried the Sunday paper to the table, as always. No one ever objects to this. I once commented that if he could read at brunch, why couldn't I text? To which Aunt Maddie replied, "Because we *want* to hear what you have to say, hon."

I pointed Don toward my usual spot, next to Grandma. Dad was already rummaging through her sideboard drawers for more silverware and another place mat. I pulled a chair up for myself.

"All I can say is it's about time somebody spoke up for this city," Uncle Paul said as he eased into his seat.

"How is picking a fight with the Somalis good for this city?"

Dad asked. "Things are tense enough as it is. C'mon, Paul. Use your head."

"The mayor just put into words what everybody's thinking," Paul replied. "Enough is enough."

"I still don't get what she wants them to do," Don said. "Move?"

Paul grinned.

"That would be a start," he said.

Shut up, I wanted to say. *For once in your life say something useful instead of picking a fight.*

"Uh . . . can we wait until after the soccer season is over?" I joked instead. Taking on my uncle wasn't part of my skill set.

"Yeah," Don agreed. "The Somali guys on the team pretty much rock. Don't want to lose them."

Mom, Grandma, and now Aunt Maddie entered, carrying dishes. I hadn't realized Maddie was in the kitchen.

It explained Paul's mood.

The hot *tourtière* was placed on a trivet next to Grandma's place. Salad and bread appeared; there was a big pitcher of icy water and another of orange juice. A thermal carafe filled with hot coffee was positioned on the sideboard. Everyone sat, crossed themselves, bowed heads for grace.

Bless us, O Lord, for these thy gifts which we are about to receive from thy bounty through Christ, our Lord. Amen.

We always do the grace in English, but sometimes Aunt Maddie and Mom ask Grandma to do it in French. I don't know why, maybe for my benefit? *Bénis-nous, ô Seigneur . . .* At any rate, whether we pray in English or in French, Grandma always follows the amen with *Bon appétit!* I know it means "good appetite," but in my head I always think: *Dig in!*

As we passed salad and bread and Grandma served up big portions of the pie, Maddie spoke.

"Sorry if I'm a little out of it," she said breathlessly. She sounded as if she had just been running. It's what she does when she's either super-stressed or overly excited. Or both. A lot of times she's both. "I was out till all hours last night, then on the phone with Yousef most of the morning." Yousef is one of her coworkers at Catholic Charities. He's from Africa, but he's not Somali. He's actually been in this country for a while.

"And what were you and Yousef cooking up this morning?" Paul asked amiably.

Here it comes, I thought.

"We're trying to organize a group to draft a response to the mayor," she said. "Actually . . ." She reached into her pocket, pulling out her cell phone and glancing at it briefly. A real no-no at Grandma's table. "Mom, I may get a call and have to leave. We're preparing something for the paper tomorrow."

"That shouldn't be hard," Paul said. "How about 'Dear Mayor Smith: You are the *woman*! Enclosed please find a campaign contribution'?"

I saw Aunt Maddie's glance move quickly in my mother's direction, then away. Two rosy patches appeared on her cheeks. No one spoke.

"I mean, I'm just a taxpayer who works for a living, so what do I know?" he continued. "But it seems to me that the mayor is on to something. Like, why are we giving handouts to illegal aliens who would have been better off staying put in their own country and getting jobs?"

"It's kind of hard to apply for a job when a member of a rival clan just cut off both your arms with a machete," Aunt Maddie replied evenly. "Which is why they're refugees, not illegals."

Uncle Paul didn't miss a beat.

"You know, Maddie, as awful as that is, it's not our problem. We've got our own problems, and we don't ask other countries to solve them for us."

"These people have fled war zones, Paul. Where is your compassion?"

"People who were born and raised in this town are on waiting lists for housing, while these folks show up by the busloads and are handed a clean, free apartment and a check from the government every month while they sit home, have children they can't afford, and pray to Allah . . . what? Six times a day?"

"Five," my mother corrected, smiling brightly. She took a big bite of *tourtière*. "Delicious, Mom," she said.

"Thank you, dear," Grandma said.

"Yeah, Mrs. Thibeault, this is amazing," Donnie added.

Paul slammed his hand down so hard on the table our plates jumped.

"Am I the only person in this family who doesn't have his head up his ass?" he demanded. "Did you not watch, along with the rest of the world, when those towers went down? Who do you think these people *are*?"

"Paul, stop it, please," Grandma quavered. Mom put her hand over Grandma's.

"They are our neighbors," Dad shot back. "They are Donnie and Tommy's classmates. Teammates. They are women and children—"

"Take a stroll down Main Street some Friday afternoon, Bob,"

144

Uncle Paul interrupted. "It looks like freakin' Little Mogadishu. It is packed with unemployed, Muslim *men*—all lookin' pretty able-bodied to me, by the way, Maddie—filing into this unmarked storefront. A few doors down from the senator's office. I mean, it's unbelievable! We've got jihadists meeting next door to a U.S. government office and nobody seems to give a damn!"

"That's their mosque, you idiot!" Maddie practically yelled. "They keep it unmarked so as not to attract attention from morons like you!"

"A hundred guys all walking in the same direction on Main Street isn't my idea of a low profile, Maddie."

"They go there to pray on Fridays. How is that any different from the crowds outside the cathedral this morning?" she fired back.

"How do you know they aren't in there making explosive devices that they'll strap on their backs next time they go to the mall?" Paul shouted.

"Stop. Please," we all heard. Grandma. Everyone turned to her. Her eyes brimmed.

Here's what you never want to do: make Grandma cry. You feel like absolute shit. Because she is probably the nicest person in the world, and if you've made her sad, you must suck. Big time.

"Enough! Both of you!" my mother said loudly. "Donnie, I apologize for our family's bad behavior. This is no way to act in front of guests." She said that last part with emphasis. As if she could shame my aunt and uncle into speaking respectfully to each other.

"Oh, don't mind me," Don replied cheerfully. "This is nothing compared to when my parents fight. And the food is *way* better." He smiled at Grandma.

That's the thing about Don. He's either a complete idiot or really smart about emotions. Because that made Grandma laugh.

"Sweetheart, you are welcome in my house *anytime*," she said to him. Then she looked at Paul and Maddie. "You two . . . I'm not sure."

They shut up after that. Maddie ate fast, then left in a hurry; we could hear her phone, set on vibrate, buzzing every few minutes as another text came in, but she didn't look at it. Paul left soon after her. Neither stayed for dessert, which suited me and Don just fine. We ate obscene portions of the tart, and Grandma gave him a big slice to go. Nobody said another word about the letter, the mayor, or the Somalis.

Except Don, as I drove him home.

"So, you think Saeed is a terrorist?" he asked.

I laughed.

"Yeah, right. A real card-carrying member of Al Qaeda."

Which sounded pretty funny when you said it out loud.

Of course, how the hell did we know what terrorists looked like? Acted like? And whether or not they played soccer?

Chapter Fourteen

Abdi was upset.

At first I thought it was because I was late. Practice went way over, and by the time I got to The Center, most of the kids doing homework had finished up and were already in the park across the street. But Abdi, who usually led the pack outdoors, sat inside with Myla at one of the long tables. Both wore very serious expressions. He was swinging that foot, and occasionally kicked the leg of the table. Hard.

I hadn't seen Myla for three days. Since the night at Michelangelo's. For some reason my homework help hadn't overlapped with her schedule, which was funny because the kids gave me the impression that Myla practically lived at The Center. They would see her or talk to her or text her every day; she was that big a part of their lives. Mr. Bouchard, however, hadn't caught a glimpse of Ms. College Student. Which made me wonder if she was avoiding me.

Which made me wonder why I was wondering.

I didn't want them to, but Donnie's comments sounded in

my brain as I approached Myla and Abdi. She looked up and a pleased, relieved smile broke over her face.

Blue, blue eyes. Yeah.

"Hey, guys," I said casually, dropping my pack on the floor alongside Abdi. "Sorry I'm late. Coach kept us for sprints."

"Hello," Abdi muttered. He didn't look up. He stared sullenly at the table. This was very un-Abdi-like behavior.

I crouched down to his level.

"What up?"

He pushed a crumpled piece of paper toward me.

"Man, that homework you did with me? It all wrong!"

I smoothed the paper flat and examined it. There weren't any comments. Just big red X's wherever Abdi had come up with a Somali word that began with *R*.

"Well, it's not *all* wrong," I said. "See, you got *river* right. I guess this answers our question, huh? They wanted just English words."

Abdi shrugged. The expression on his face bothered me. It wasn't just mad.

He seemed discouraged.

"Abdi, look at me," Myla said gently. He wouldn't. She glanced at me, and I could tell this was bothering her, too.

"Your work is not bad. Your work is good. It's okay to get some red X's. That's how you learn. See, next time you'll get the answer right." Abdi's head shot up, startling both me and Myla.

"What wrong with Somali word?" he demanded. "They want word with *R*, and *ri* got an *R*. That teacher, she makes no sense. She dumbass!"

I choked back a laugh. In his limited lexicon of English, you had to wonder where he'd heard this.

Myla looked severe.

"We talked about this," she said evenly. "No disrespecting teachers. Now, I'd like you to take your paper and go over there." She pointed to a table at the end of the room. "You spend some time fixing your homework on your own, then come back here to Tom and me and we'll go over it." Abdi grabbed the paper and slouched off to the other end of the room.

"I wasn't sure whether to scold him or correct his grammar," I said, sliding into Abdi's vacant seat. "'She *is* a dumbass.' Not 'She dumbass.'"

Myla pretended to punch me on the shoulder. Her fist lingered. Pressed into me a little longer than it had to. At least, that's what I imagined.

"That's not helpful, Cap," she said. Her breath smelled like peppermint Altoids. She'd pulled her hair over one ear with a green plastic barrette shaped like a frog.

"You know I'm kidding, College," I said quietly. She looked at me, surprised. It was the first time I'd used the nickname for her that'd been bouncing around my head. "What's going on with him?"

Myla sighed, glanced over her shoulder once to make sure Abdi wasn't listening, then leaned in closer.

"Probably more than I know," she said. "To a certain extent I think he's just frustrated. Really frustrated. I wonder sometimes if he might have a learning disability, because he's pretty verbal but is having a hard time learning to read. But how do you diagnose a learning disability in someone who doesn't have the basic language skills you're testing? I mean, the schools don't even have the staff to teach all the kids who need ELL, never mind learning-disabled kids who need ELL!"

"Especially 'cause we're so maxed out. Right?" I said.

Her face clouded over.

"*Don't* get me started on that," she said.

"Agreed. Let's stick to Abdi."

"Who may be dealing with a little PTSD on top of everything else," she said. "I've been wondering about that."

"PTSD?"

"Post-traumatic stress disorder. It's like what soldiers returning from combat have. People who have experienced some deep, usually violent trauma. You wouldn't believe what some of these kids have been through."

Across the room, Abdi had his back to us and was hunched over his paper. That foot was swinging in a wide, sweeping pendulum beneath the table. He knew we were talking about him.

I didn't know a thing about PTSD. But I did know what happened to sad little boys.

"You know my friend you met the other night? Donnie?" I said to her.

She nodded.

"Charmer," she commented.

"Yeah, you're probably the only female in a thirty-mile radius who would say that. But anyway . . . he's had it tough. Parents are screwups, and he's always had trouble with school. But the worst thing is at some point he started to believe he was stupid and just decided to party on, you know?

"Anyway, Abdi sort of reminds me of him. I don't know what he's been through, but the thing that's gonna hurt him the most is if he doesn't think it's worth trying anymore. Can't let little dudes give up, you know?"

Myla stared at me from across the table. Like she saw me for the first time. "You actually give a damn, don't you?" she said.

I shrugged.

"Nah. I'm just here to log service hours. And argue with you. By the way, are you dating anyone?"

The words were out of my mouth before they fully registered in my brain.

This is it, God. The perfect time for the apocalypse. End the world, now. Or how about just a big, gaping hole that opens up and swallows me?

As usual, God didn't answer.

Instead, two bright red patches appeared on Myla's cheeks. Her mouth twisted into this awkward grin.

"Are you asking me out?" she said.

"No. Absolutely not. I'm just curious."

"Because I hear you already have a girlfriend," she said.

"That would be true," I said.

"And you're a high school boy. I'm a college *woman*."

With a plastic frog barrette in your hair, I managed to not say.

"Yeah, but you could be into the whole cougar thing, you know? Mature woman, young guy? We could pull it off. Especially because I'm taller than you."

"Everyone's taller than me."

"Also true. You're avoiding my question."

Myla looked down, picked at her fingernails. Short nails painted navy blue. A little smile played out around her lips. A thought occurred to me. A pretty wild thought, but . . .

"Wow. You *are* seeing someone."

She still didn't answer.

"Is it . . . another woman?"

Her head snapped up.

"Oh. My. God. Are you for *real?*" I couldn't tell if she was laughing because she thought this was funny or totally offensive. "Do you think the only reason I might reject you is because I'm a *lesbian?* 'Ooh, watch out for that Tom Bouchard, ladies! Only a *lesbian* could resist him!'"

"No! Of course not. I'm sure you have plenty of reasons to reject me." Pause. "But if you were, that's cool. A lesbian, I mean. Not rejecting me. That wouldn't be so cool."

"But of course, you weren't asking," she said sarcastically.

"No. Not a chance. You scare me. I'm going to go sit in the corner with Abdi now and practice writing words that begin with R."

"Like *ridiculous*," she suggested. *"Rude."*

"Retreat," I added. I picked up my backpack and headed toward Abdi.

She tossed out one parting comment: "I'm not, by the way." Then she got up and went into the little glassed-in cubicle, shutting the door.

So . . . not seeing anyone, not lesbian, or not rejecting me?

She called that night. She launched right in, didn't even say hi. Like nothing had happened between us a few hours earlier.

"I have a brilliant idea, Cap."

"I'm sure you do."

"A project. A self-esteem-building, totally cool project for Abdi. And you are going to help him."

I was lying on my bed surrounded by paper. I had an essay due the next day on *The Scarlet Letter,* and I'd been spending the last hour going round and round in my head with Hester, Chilling-worth, and Dimmesdale. *Okay, brain, reorient, because it's time to do a few more rounds with Myla. . . .*

"Lay it on me."

"A dictionary. A Somali-English dictionary, every letter from A to Z, with pictures he's drawn, plus words in both Somali and English."

"Wow. Our little guy is having trouble with the letter R and you want him to write an entire dictionary. I love that idea. Really."

I heard her sigh impatiently.

"Don't be obtuse. I'm thinking picture book. Two words per page, twenty-six pages."

Were there twenty-six letters in the alphabet? I started count-ing on my fingers: A, B, C, D . . .

"Tom, are you listening?"

"Yeah, yeah . . . sorry. I'm . . . Hester Prynne. Do you know her?"

Long pause from Myla.

"Name's familiar. Didn't she date some guy named Dimmes-dale? Seriously, Tom, what do you think?"

"I think everything you say is brilliant and I'll do anything you want. I'm your community service slave. But right now, I'm thinking about this essay that's due tomorrow on *The Scarlet Let-ter,* and—"

"I know a guy who will take the finished pages and laminate them and bind them. It'll look like a pretty real book by the time he's all done, and then Abdi can give it to his teacher. For the class, you know? It'll be like this thing that celebrates *both* lan-guages, and shows that he knows *both.*"

I thought about that for a minute. It was a cool idea. Something Abdi could definitely do and be proud of. He was a good little artist. His pictures would look neat, all bound up in a picture book.

"I think it's great, Myla. I think you've come up with a really, really good idea."

"Thanks," she said. "So you'll help him?"

"Absitively posilutely, College."

"There's just one hitch."

"Uh-oh."

"I want Samira to work with you guys."

I couldn't help it. I laughed.

"Yeah, right, she's gonna do that. Not. Have you forgotten she's not my biggest fan?"

"She's already on board."

I didn't expect that. And I'll admit, it was not a welcome surprise. I had less than zero interest in spending time with Samira the Fun Suck.

"I can handle Abdi alone," I said.

"It's not about handling him. It's about doing the Somali part of the book. You wouldn't have a clue, Cap, and Samira would have a good feel for the right words to choose. Plus she'd get the spelling right. Plus I'd like Abdi to have a positive experience being directed by an older girl. And watching how you respect and work well with a girl. You'd be a good role model for him."

Something about this felt like a setup.

"Let me guess: you're getting extra-credit points in your I'm-gonna-make-the-world-a-better-place class if you get me and Samira to work together. Am I right?"

"What if I agree to go out to dinner with you? Will you do it then?"

That came out of left field. This woman was full of surprises.

"Seriously?" It was the first word out of my mouth.

She laughed. Giggled, actually. At me. She couldn't have been laughing *with* me, after such a stupid-ass response.

"I want to try that new Somali place on Market Street. You can take me there."

"Oh, can I? Will I pay?"

"Of course. But I hear it's not too expensive, so you're good."

"And when are we doing this?"

"We can talk about it tomorrow. You are coming tomorrow, right?"

"How 'bout Friday? I've got late practice and . . . another commitment tomorrow."

"Great. Friday it is. Thanks, Cap." She hung up before I could say another word.

And there I was, with a date that was actually a bribe. With a girl who was not my girlfriend and was possibly a lesbian. At a restaurant I'd never heard of, for an undisclosed amount of money, time and day unknown. I'd have to keep it a secret from Cherisse (who would freak if she found out), bypass my parents (because I was still grounded), and deal with a sullen Somali girl (who hated me).

So why did it feel like Christmas in October?

Chapter Fifteen

The other commitment I'd mentioned to Myla was *Survivor* with Cherisse. Eight o'clock on Wednesday nights. She never misses an episode and informed me that after blowing her off for pizza the other night I could make her happy by watching it with her.

Life is easier when you're on the right side of Cherisse. So even though I had a big physics test the next day, I agreed.

I told Mom that she was coming over to study with me.

Mom was *so* not fooled. Cherisse didn't take physics, and even though I'm pretty sure my parents didn't have a printout of the girl's schedule, they knew Cherisse Ouellette wasn't the physics type. We carried our books into the den off the dining room and closed the French doors, which have these very nice privacy curtains, but Mom kept popping in: first with lemonade, then with a basket of corn chips.

"Ooh, thanks, Mrs. B.!" Cherisse said when the chips made an appearance. She's the only person in the universe who calls my mother "Mrs. B." Mom smiles with her mouth closed, sort of this straight line running from ear to ear, whenever she hears "Mrs. B."

"You're very welcome, Cherisse," she said. "You kids have everything you need?"

"D'you guys have salsa?" Cherisse asked. "I love salsa with chips."

Mom raised one eyebrow in this high arc. Along with the straight-line smile, it was a pretty intimidating look. Dad calls it the Scary Franco Momma look. It's the look *her* grandmother used to control eight screaming children. Genetically coded right there on my mother's face. I recognized it from old photographs of *Mémère* Louise.

"There's a jar in the fridge, dear. Go help yourself," Mom said. Cherisse bounded from the den. Mom folded her arms across her chest.

"Seriously, Tom?" she said.

"What?" I replied. "She likes salsa."

The other eyebrow shot up. That was the "I'm Not Stupid, Son" Scary Franco Momma expression.

After Cherisse turned up as my junior prom date last spring and we started going out (Facebook official), Dad took me aside for a "talk." Actually, it was more of a non-talk. He didn't demand to know if we were sexually active, but . . . practically. Instead, he spoke in code, dancing around the questions you couldn't help but ask yourself when you met Cherisse.

"How did you two meet?" he asked, aka *She sure as hell isn't in any honors classes with you, is she?* "I don't think we know her parents," he said, aka *They don't live on our side of town and aren't among the 25 percent of Enniston residents who graduated from college.* "I hope you're being responsible, Tommy," he said, aka *I sure hope you're abstinent, but if you're not, I hope you're using protection, even though I'd be the last Catholic in Maine to suggest it.*

I didn't hold it against my parents for getting squeamish about the S-E-X question; most parents don't handle it well. But I did hold it against them for being intellectual snobs. A girl like Cherisse Ouellette wasn't part of the master plan they'd mapped for their college-bound son, and from the second she walked in the door Mom was tight-lipped and unfriendly.

"I'd like the doors left open a crack," Mom said. "And it's a school night, so company has to leave by nine." She made this pronouncement just as Cherisse returned holding the Newman's Own mango salsa.

"This was all I could find. We usually get Pace," she said, plopping alongside me on the couch. She hadn't brought a bowl, so she unscrewed the lid and dumped some salsa over the chips in the basket. I made a point of not looking at my mother's expression over that move. Mom walked out, leaving the doors about three inches ajar.

"She seems uptight. Everything okay?" Cherisse asked between chips.

"Yeah, it's all good. She just knows I've got a test tomorrow." I pulled the heavy physics textbook across the coffee table toward me. I glanced at the clock. I had forty-five minutes to review an entire chapter before *Survivor* started.

"They still mad about the rock?" she asked.

"I think the question is 'Will they ever *stop* being mad about the rock?'" I replied. "Rock madness is now part of the daily drill. I think she just wants to make sure we're actually studying."

Cherisse squinched a little closer to me on the couch. She whispered in my ear, "I don't think she likes your girlfriend." She gently took my earlobe between her teeth. Her lips were cold. Like the mango salsa that just came out of the fridge. I turned to kiss her, and her mouth was half open. She tasted like chips.

"She likes my girlfriend just fine," I said, but instead of kissing her again I turned back to the book. I needed to at least *look* at the stuff, if not learn it.

Cherisse made this pouty face and threw herself back into the cushions.

"I don't think *you* like your girlfriend," she said.

I smiled but kept my eyes on the open pages.

"I like my girlfriend just fine," I told her. "What I don't like is failing physics."

She bounced back up. The lips were near my ear again.

"I'm a bad influence," she said quietly.

"Yup," I agreed.

She kissed me behind the ear. Planted a trail of kisses down my neck.

"I'm a distraction," she continued. She placed one hand on my knee and slowly began sliding it up my thigh.

"Definitely," I said.

The French doors swung open. Cherisse's hand shot to her side.

"Almost forgot napkins." Mom in the entry, holding a thick white wad. Her eyes flickered briefly over the scene. Cherisse had gone rigid. Mom dropped the napkins on top of my physics book and as she exited spread the doors open wide.

"Whatever," Cherisse grumbled, pulling a notebook from her backpack.

A few minutes before eight Cherisse was searching through the couch cushions for the remote and I'd only made it through one of the sections we were getting tested on the next day. It was clearly gonna be another sleepless night for Tommy: I'd stayed up way past midnight the night before finishing my *Scarlet Letter* essay. Plus I kept having all these weird dreams. About a certain Mumford student. I'd dreamt she came to The Center on Friday wearing a *hijab* and a long skirt, and it was embroidered all over with ornate letter *L*'s.

"I'm going to wear this to the Somali restaurant tonight," Myla said in the dream, "so they'll know I'm a lesbian."

Clearly, my brain was on overload, trying to process all the junk going on in my life. Not the least of which was my overwhelming sense of Catholic guilt that I needed to come clean with Cherisse and tell her about Myla. Although I wasn't sure what I'd tell. Was I "seeing" her? No. Were we friends? Hardly. Did I even find her attractive? Well, yes. She was adorable. Different. Surprising. In a good way.

Yeah. I would have to say something. I just didn't know what. Or when.

As I marked my place in the textbook and began clearing papers off the coffee table, I heard the kitchen door open and shut, followed by slightly raised voices.

"I'm sorry, Maddie, but the kids are working in there right now," Mom said.

"Oh, pish! They can take it up to Tommy's bedroom," I heard Aunt Maddie say.

"Uh, *no*." That from Mom. Then footsteps headed toward the den, and the sisters appeared.

"Busted!" Maddie crowed when she saw the television on.

"Your mother thought physics homework was going on in here." She flashed Mom this smug smile, then settled herself beside Cherisse on the couch. "My TV's broken," she explained. "And you know I can't miss *Survivor*."

It's hard for me to get my head around how someone like Maddie, with such high-minded ideals about practically everything, can be such a reality-TV junkie. But she's obsessed with *Survivor*—a little trait, my dad likes to point out, that makes her human. "Otherwise," he says, "she'd be insufferable."

As Maddie snuggled in, Cherisse unearthed the remote, and the part where they show what happened on the last episode started rolling. Mom had the pissed-off-and-defeated expression going. She always hates the way Maddie barges in unannounced. Bosses her around, like they're still kids.

"I am *so* glad they voted off Bobby T. last week," Maddie said to Cherisse.

"Totally," my girl murmured in agreement.

Mom turned on her heel and walked out.

"Now she's mad at me," Maddie commented without removing her eyes from the screen.

"Yeah, welcome to the club," I sighed.

She didn't reply until the commercial break.

"So, how's it going?" she said when the Geico gecko appeared. There was that certain something in her tone. *Open up to me, Tommy*, it said.

"Fine," I auto-replied.

"Honestly," she said. I shrugged.

"It could suck more, I suppose. At least, that's what everyone keeps reminding me."

"Can you believe he has to do a hundred hours of community

service?" Cherisse said. "For, like, a joke? Just pouring some paint on a stupid rock?"

Maddie frowned.

"Sweetheart, am I really hearing this? Do you not get what Tommy and the amazing Donnie Plourde did?"

Cherisse rolled her eyes. She reached for another handful of chips.

"Okay, I'm not going to waste my breath," Maddie said impatiently. She turned to me. "Your mom tells me you're volunteering at K Street?" I nodded.

"Have you met the guy who runs it, Joe Faulkner?"

"No, I've mostly been working with a student volunteer there. Everybody talks about Joe, but whenever I'm there, he's out."

"I know him—he's awesome. When you do meet him, make sure you tell him you're my nephew," she said.

I nodded. Maddie knew every do-gooder in Enniston.

"I'm helping kids do homework there."

Maddie smiled.

"You'll be great at that," she said. She reached for some chips. The smile vanished.

"Eww! Who spilled salsa in the basket? It's leaked all over the coffee table." She grabbed a few napkins from the wad and started mopping salsa.

"So here's a question," I said as she mopped. "What do you know about Somalis and dogs?"

Maddie scrunched the wet napkins into a tight ball.

"They don't touch dogs," she said simply.

I slapped my knee.

"Now *how* did you know that?" I demanded.

She shrugged.

"I know Somalis. I've been to their homes; they've been to mine. And when they come to my house I have to lock Ginger in the bedroom." Ginger is her golden Lab.

"Why do you lock Ginger up?" Cherisse asked.

"They consider dogs to be unclean animals. If they touch a dog, they have to wash seven times, or—"

"Give money to seven orphans, or feed a poor man seven days," I filled in for her.

Maddie grinned.

"See? You've learned something," she said.

Cherisse burst out laughing.

"Oh my God! That is seriously the stupidest thing I've ever heard!"

Wow. If I could have magically made a giant hole appear that would have swallowed Cherisse right then and there and saved her from the storm she'd just unleashed, I . . . might have. One part of me was sort of curious to see what my politically correct aunt would say. But another part of me felt that no one, not even I-say-things-that-make-me-sound-dumber-than-a-bag-of-sticks Cherisse, deserved to be in the crosshairs of Maddie on a shooting spree.

My aunt attacked.

"Stupider than immaculate conception? Stupider than transubstantiation? Papal infallibility? How about the ascension of Mary? Now there's one of my favorites. You know, when the mother of Jesus doesn't just die and rot like the rest of us, but the skies open up and she floats to heaven?"

Cherisse stared at her, dumbfounded. Probably wondering what the hell Maddie was talking about. I was pretty amazed that they'd gone from Bobby T. to the foundational beliefs of Catholicism in under five minutes. But a Maddie rant can happen that fast.

"Let me ask you something, dear. What do you think you're doing every Sunday at mass when you take communion? Oh, never mind, I'll tell you. You are eating flesh and drinking blood. Not a symbol. The. Real. Thing. *That's* what Catholics believe. The priest gets up there on the altar and does his host thing, and poof! Flesh. Blood. And not just anybody's. It's Jesus. That belief is what separates us Catholics from the rest of the Christian crew. Now, if you went up to one of those Somali kids at your high school and told them the basic tenet of your faith was something they could most closely equate with cannibalism, what do you think *they'd* say?"

Cherisse looked like she might cry.

"Gross?" I suggested. But nobody laughed.

"That's the stupidest thing I've ever heard," Aunt Maddie said evenly. She settled back into the cushions. On the television, Jeff Probst explained what the contestants had to do in order to win immunity. I was guessing Cherisse would've considered walking over hot coals to earn immunity from my aunt right then. I considered saying something. Something comforting to poor Cherisse. Something to Aunt Maddie, letting her know how annoyed I was at her not only for butting into our evening together but also for practically gutting my girlfriend.

For some reason I didn't. Then Aunt Maddie abruptly got up and left the den. She closed the French doors behind her on the way out.

"You didn't tell me your aunt was a bitch," Cherisse said nastily.

There are moments in life when the fog suddenly lifts. Aha moments. Lights-on moments. They don't happen often, and in my case, not nearly as often as they should. But Cherisse's comment sparked one of those moments.

And I realized it was time to vote her off the island.

Chapter Sixteen

At practice the next day, I told Saeed about Project Abdi. He hadn't heard of it.

"Samira didn't tell you we're going to be working together?" I said. We were warming up with passes: sharp, accurate kicks, beginning at ten feet apart, then slowly stepping back and increasing the distance.

"No," he said, shrugging.

"It's not like it's a huge deal or anything. But I figured, since she knows you and I are friends, she might have said something."

"No," he repeated. Fired a pass at me. I took a few steps back.

He had something else on his mind. Right before practice started, Coach called all the Somali guys over. Nothing bad. He wasn't angry or anything. But he seemed to be explaining something to them, and they were all nodding. Then practice started as usual, but Saeed seemed to have a cloud hanging over him.

"What birthday you got, Tom?" A strange question, coming out of nowhere.

"November fourth. Pretty soon, actually. Why? When's your

birthday?" Bam! I lasered one back. Saeed stopped it, settled it. Looked at me.

"Don't got one."

I smiled at him.

"Of course you do. You're here, right? Alive, on this planet?" I signaled with both hands: *C'mon, pass back.*

He kicked. He shook his head.

"No," he said.

"No, you're not alive?"

"No, I . . . don't know. Don't *know* it. It in rain season, my mother say. But I don't know when that in Amreeka." He stepped back. I passed to him.

"What does it say on your birth certificate?" I asked.

He frowned. Shook his head, uncomprehending.

"Papers, from when you were born?" I tried. Saeed looked at me like he couldn't really believe what I'd just asked him.

"Tom, we got no papers."

"Dude, you must have something. I mean, what do you use for identification?" He didn't answer. "ID. Like, your Chamberlain card?"

"Yeah, ID," he said, nodding. "I got green card. That it." Stepped back. Kicked to me.

"So isn't your birthday on your green card?" I asked.

"It say January one," Saeed replied.

"Seriously? You're a New Year's baby? That's cool. Around here, if you're born on January first, you might get your picture in the paper. See, you have a birthday. We'll have to throw you an epic party this New Year's Eve!"

Saeed didn't seem impressed by my proposal.

"We all January one," he said. "All Somali peoples."

"Yeah, right." I grinned at him. I fired the ball.

Saeed picked it up. He walked toward me. No one seemed to notice that we'd stopped drilling.

"In camp, at Dadaab? When you gets to leave, you answer a lot of questions. But some things, you don't know. And some things we got no paper. So for everyone, for birthday? They January one."

"Saeed, that's ridiculous. Even if you don't have birth certificates and papers, why didn't you just *tell* them your birthday?"

"I don't know, Tom! No one know!" He sounded like he couldn't believe how stupid I was being.

I mean, I got that in a refugee camp you didn't have nice file cabinets with your paperwork all neatly put away. And all the things we do with our babies over here? Wrapping tiny plastic hospital bracelets around their wrists, or putting their pictures in the newspaper if they manage to be the first one born in the new year? Not a lot of that happening in refugee camps. I'd seen the photos of how Saeed and families like his had lived in the camps . . . in these little houses they made from branches and sticks. Carrying water in plastic jugs. A lot of them had run for their lives with nothing but the clothes they were wearing. So yeah: no birth certificates.

But I didn't understand why he didn't just *know* the date.

Then something occurred to me.

"Saeed," I said. "What was Coach talking to you guys about?"

"They asking how old we are. Monday we bring green cards to a meeting at school. But I do that, you know? When I come, first time? So . . . I don't know."

"Who, Saeed? Who is asking how old you are?" He shrugged.

"I don't know. Some peoples."

"Mr. Bouchard! Mr. Bashir! I don't recall excusing you from drills!" Coach's voice boomed at us.

Saeed turned to run back, but before he could slip away I grabbed his arm.

"Saeed. Do *you* know how old you are?"

He hesitated.

My heart sank.

"Eighteen," he said, then trotted back to position. I watched his retreating back. The guy was so damn thin. You could see every sinew in his legs, his bony knees. He didn't grow up like we did, with slabs of bloody steaks on the grill and endless amounts of butter and milk. He ran like a gazelle, but he was slight. He could've passed for sixteen.

Or an undernourished twenty.

You can't play high school sports if you're twenty. Hell, you can't stay in high school. It's called aging out, and you either have to go to continuing ed or get your GED if you want to graduate.

You sure as hell can't show up out of nowhere and start beating all the white guys whose parents have been dragging them to soccer fields and watching their games and paying their club team fees since they were five and scarcely knew how to kick a ball in the right direction.

At least, not without answering some tough questions.

For some reason I was actually on time for homework help that afternoon. Or maybe it wasn't such a mystery. Maybe I had some incentive to get my butt right over to the K Street Center. I must have been moving fast, because I managed to shower at school, change into a clean shirt and jeans, and still arrive before Myla and Abdi.

Samira was already there.

It wasn't one of her *hijab* days. Instead, she'd tied her hair in this Chamberlain blue bandana. She wore a long-sleeved Chamberlain T-shirt that said VARSITY GIRLS SOCCER, plus big gold earrings. Peeking out from under her long skirt I saw sneakers and the cuffs of a pair of warm-up pants.

She sat at one of the long tables and had set out a stack of blank white paper, an old soup can filled with colored pencils and markers, and a box of crayons. Good thing one of us came prepared.

"Hey," I said, pulling up a chair across from her. She didn't glare, which I took as a step in the right direction.

"Hello," she replied. She leaned to one side, rummaging through the backpack she'd placed on the floor. She pulled out a slim paperback with a bright orange cover and placed it on the table between us.

"Just get off practice?" I said, gesturing to her shirt. Joking. I knew Samira didn't play sports.

But then she smiled. A real smile.

"I am manager of the girls' soccer team now," she said.

"Seriously?" I said. I tried to imagine Samira hanging with the jockettes on our very blond and fairly aggressive girls' soccer team. The rumor was that they could beat us boys, but we never agreed to play them. "When did that happen?"

"Yesterday," she said. "My cousin, Fatima? She plays on the JV team, and sometimes I go watch her. When I was at her game yesterday, the varsity coach saw me. And she knows I am Saeed's

170

sister. So she asks me if I know the rules, and I say, 'Sure, I know the rules! I watch my brother all the time.' So she asks me if I can help with the book. You know the book?"

"Sure," I told her, my surprise growing. The book was where you kept track of the team stats throughout the game. You had to know the players and the game really well in order to accurately record all the assists, goals, penalties, whatever, for the book.

"So I help her that one time, and then she asks if I would like to do it all the time. And be manager. So I said okay."

"Cool," I told her. "So now you'll go to all their games. Away games, too?"

"Yes, but you will have games at the same time, so we can still work with Abdi together," she said. It took me a second to catch up with her. She'd moved from soccer to scheduling to Project Abdi in a single bound. She'd also switched from smiling to businesslike in a nanosecond. She picked up the paperback she had placed on the table.

"Do you know this book?" she asked, handing it to me.

"A *Somali Alphabet*," I read aloud. "*Alfabeetadda Soomaaliyeed*."

A sound emerged from Samira. I looked up to see her hand over her mouth. She was struggling not to laugh.

"*AL-fah-BAY-tah-dah SO-mah-lee-ED*," she said carefully, lowering her hand.

"Right. Like you said." I grinned at her. I flipped through the pages. It was a kid's book, almost looked like a coloring book because all the illustrations were black-and-white pencil drawings. On each page was a letter and a Somali word starting with that letter. Each word had its own picture, and a definition in both

English and Somali. "Looks like Abdi's project has already been done."

"No. But this is a good model for him, and is probably good for you, too," she said. "See, this book teaches people Somali words, but is also good for Somali children who learn to read." She reached across the table and turned the book over in my hands. On the back cover was a photograph of a Somali woman reading it to a child.

"With Abdi, we make a book with the English alphabet, but instead of one picture and one word for each letter, he will do *two*. One English, one Somali."

"You've already got this all figured out, don't you?" I said to her. I opened the book again. Coincidentally, to *R*.

"*Ri!*" I exclaimed. "My old friend the goat."

Samira looked at me like I had two heads.

"Long story," I muttered. "But listen, Samira, that sounds great. Seriously."

She shrugged.

We sat silently as I slowly turned pages. I glanced at the clock. Myla and Abdi were late. Samira looked perfectly comfortable just sitting there, saying nothing.

"Samira, when's your birthday?"

She startled, as if I'd woken her from a deep daydream.

"Birthday?" she asked.

"Yeah. The day you were born."

"June twenty-first," she said without hesitation.

I closed the book.

"Okay. That's messed up."

Her brow wrinkled.

"I don't understand."

"Saeed just told me that all Somali people have the same birthday. January first. So how come *you* were born in June?" Her forehead smoothed.

"Oh. Yes. January first. That's the birthday on my green card, so it's the *official* day. But my mother says I was born in a rainy season, so I think maybe June."

I shook my head, mystified.

"And the twenty-first?"

She smiled shyly.

"It's the same birthday as Prince William. So . . . I choose it."

I stared at her.

"Prince William?"

"He is very rich. And handsome," she said. Like that made everything clear.

"Samira, I just don't get why you people don't know your birthdays."

She sighed, completely exasperated with me.

"Tom. My mother does not read. My father did not read. When I was born? In our house, in our farm? No one writes down the day. No one *knows* the day. And then you get to the camp and even if you do know, you have no paper to prove it! So when the UN people fill out the forms? And ask us questions? They guess the year for how old you are, and put January first for everyone."

"So every refugee kid in our school has a January first birthday?" I asked her.

"If they come from the camps, yes," she said.

Wow. Who knew?

"Why you asking me this?" Sometimes she drops a word.

"Just something Saeed was saying. I get confused with him, you know?"

She nodded.

"English is hard for him," she said.

"But not for you," I pointed out.

"I am good at school," she said. "And I go to school. At Dadaab. Saeed, he just played around all day. All he liked was soccer and being with the boys. So my mother sent him to Nairobi, to be with our uncle and go to school. But he still didn't like it!"

"He said he was in Nairobi when you all got the word that you could leave the camp," I said. She nodded. "Why weren't you all there?"

"Sometimes . . . we were. Sometimes we went to my uncle. Because the camps are very, very dangerous. At night, you just stay inside because sometimes these people? Who are not Somali? They come into the camps and they steal and they fight. Even just to get water during the day is very, very dangerous."

"So why didn't you just stay in Nairobi?" I asked.

She sort of smiled.

"Because in the camps, there is hope."

"Hope? Sounds like death."

"In the camps you might get called. By the UN. And you get a green card and leave. You don't know when and you don't know where. We thought maybe Australia, but then they send us to Atlanta, Georgia. I never heard of Atlanta, Georgia! But it's America, so . . . great. But Saeed? He was with my uncle. And when we got called, we had to leave. He was in Nairobi. But we had to go."

Yeah. *Home Alone: African Nightmare Version*. Well, not quite alone; he was with his uncle. But the rest of the family? Gone.

With an ocean between him and them. I didn't have a chance to ask her how they'd made it from Atlanta to here, or how Saeed finally made it to the United States, because Myla and Abdi finally arrived and were heading toward us.

The little dude had a big happy smile on his face and shouted "Tom!" when he saw me from across the room. Myla wore these long, loopy earrings that hit her shoulders, and the same little sharp-heeled boots I'd seen her in at Michelangelo's. Clearly, she was in going-out-tonight mode, and it was all I could do to not just get up and hug her hello. Instead, I pulled my thoughts from imagining all the shit Samira and Saeed had lived through, and shifted to the work at hand: crayons and homework and third grade in America. College girls . . . no, *women* . . . who kept you guessing.

Still, you had to wonder if a four-story walk-up in Enniston, Maine, was really the hope Samira and Saeed and the rest of their family had been holding out for.

Chapter Seventeen

My expectations for the evening with Myla started out very high. But I had good reason to be hopeful: lip gloss.

In addition to the earrings and the boots, which could have been part of any night-out-with-the-girls outfit, she was wearing lip gloss. A dead giveaway.

See, girls think they look good with lip gloss, and if a girl is trying to look good right before going out with you, well . . . that's good. Even though in fact lip-glossed lips taste fake and plasticky when you kiss them. And gloss feels gross and sticky on your face. I mean, for a decent kiss I'm willing to put up with a lot, but if anyone ever asked "Gloss or no gloss?" I'd vote for none every time.

Cherisse was a big glosser, something we used to fight about. She had this one brand that reminded me of strawberry Vaseline, and once, after a particularly long kiss, I gagged. She got all insulted, even after I apologized and explained it wasn't her, it was the gloss. Didn't matter; she marched off in a huff.

Here's the thing about Cherisse Ouellette: don't make her mad. Let me tell you, Shakespeare was channeling this girl when he wrote, "Hell hath no fury like a woman scorned." After I voted her off the island the other night (*not* a pretty scene), she kept sending me these random, rude texts, like "You're an asshole," or "Hate u!" I didn't respond. Didn't even read them after a while, but she couldn't help herself, so they kept coming.

Anyway, despite my antipathy for gloss, I'll admit: when Myla walked in with the stuff on her lips and the cute I'm-going-out-tonight clothes, I moved, imaginatively, to the post-dinner possibilities. Tom Bouchard was feeling very optimistic about life.

Then it all crashed and burned.

There we were, cleaning up after a pretty good session with Abdi. Our guy had his Spider-Man backpack on, Samira and I had wiped the table and put away the art supplies, and Myla was shutting off lights when the roller coaster, which had been doing a nice, steady climb, took a downward plunge. I heard Myla say: "Hey, Samira. Tommy and I are going to grab something to eat. Want to come with?"

Played. Completely, totally played. I couldn't believe my ears. I thought, *Bouchard, you're an idiot. She wanted you to work on this project and lured you in, making you think there was more to it.*

Seriously, College Girl? Is this how we roll?

Frankly, I thought I deserved better. We'd made it through the letter C, which was no small feat. A had been fine: *apple* and *aqal* ("house" in Somali). B was *boy* and *babaay*, "papaya." But C was a challenge. I'd suggested *cat*, which turned out to be the pet of choice among dog-avoiding Somalis, but to go with *cat* Samira wanted to do *cilaan*, which is henna, that stuff women use to paint their hands. Abdi was up for drawing a hand covered in tattoo-like designs, but then I stepped in.

"Problem, guys. That word doesn't make a C sound. You just pronounced it 'EH-lan.' Sort of like the girl in my calculus class, Ellen Fitzgerald."

"Yes, but it begins with C," Samira said.

"But it sounds like 'eh,'" I said. "I think we need words that make the same sound."

Both of them stared stubbornly at me.

"Tom, *cilaan* is good," said Abdi. "I make a really cool picture."

"*Cilaan* is a good word for people to know," Samira said. "We use it at weddings and special days. We use it to dye hair. Sometimes men use it to dye mustaches and beards."

Abdi nodded and began drawing.

"Whoa, whoa," I said. "I get all that, but isn't the point here to teach the sounds the letters make, and show their similarities in each language?"

Abdi kept on drawing.

"Well, no," Samira said. "The point is to show differences, too. It's important to show differences. We are not all the same, and the letters don't always make the same sounds."

Huffy. That's how my grandmother would have described Samira's tone with me just then. "Now, don't get huffy, dear," she says when an argument begins to brew, or she picks up strains of annoyance. That's how Samira was acting. Pissed, with a side order of stubborn and a sprinkling of self-righteous.

And this was only C.

"Problem, guys?" Myla was sitting at the next table, doing spelling homework with a group of little girls. And eavesdropping on us.

"No," I said, just as Samira said, "Yes." Abdi, still drawing, grinned.

"I think," I said carefully, "we are having some creative dis-agreements over the purpose of the assignment."

Samira shook her head vigorously.

"There is no disagreement! You are wrong," she said firmly.

Myla looked highly amused.

"Wow," I said. "Works and plays well with others . . . not."

"*Cilaan* begins with C and *cat* begins with C," Samira replied. "Abdi draws the pictures. What is the problem?"

"The problem is, who is this thing for?" I answered. "I think it's pretty clear it's for the kids in ELL, who, like Abdi, are learn-ing *English* words and letter sounds. Let's not confuse them with Somali pronunciations, okay?"

"And I say it is for kids in ELL *and* for white kids who don't know Somali words. Both can learn from this! When you were Abdi's age, did you know about *cilaan,* or henna, like you call it?"

"When I was Abdi's age, none of you people lived here and I had no clue what henna was, to answer your question. I'm still not sure what it is. Looks like you girls are drawing on yourselves with Magic Marker."

Samira leaned back in her chair. She looked helplessly at Myla.

"Who is *right?*" Samira demanded.

"You both are," Myla said pleasantly. Her eyes shifted to the clock on the wall. "And I'm hungry. Are you guys almost done?"

I caved on *cilaan* right then and there, figuring the "date" was about to begin. Then, as we cleaned up, Lip Gloss Girl invited Fun Suck Girl to come with. Unbelievable.

Granted: Samira and I were getting along better, if this ses-sion was any indication. Getting along well, actually. But it wasn't

179

easy. For starters, you never knew what you'd get with her. Like, with the clothes? One day she might be rockin' the *hijab;* another day it was a long-sleeved Celtics sweatshirt. But her outfits were nothing compared to her opinions. As she started to relax around me, she started throwing out opinions. And she had a lot of them. Especially about guys.

"Boys are too lazy," she commented.

Abdi was drawing an apple.

"Huh," he said, not bothering to look up. "I being lazy now? No."

"You only do this work because Myla makes you. And we help you. But, Abdi, you must learn to do your work on your own. By yourself."

He shrugged. It gave me the feeling he'd heard this riff from her before.

She kept going as he colored.

"My brothers? When they get home from school, what do they do? If the weather is good, they go outside and play soccer in the park. If the weather is bad, they are inside playing games on Xbox. When I come home, what do I do? I help clean. I fold clothes. I do homework. Do they do homework? No. My mother has to yell at them to make them not be lazy about homework."

Abdi's head snapped up.

"Your brothers got Xbox? Lucky!"

I burst out laughing.

Samira looked severe.

"Will they be lucky when they don't finish school? When they don't get jobs and no one wants to marry them? No."

Wow. Seriously opinionated. I couldn't resist prodding her.

"Hey, Samira. I play soccer after school. I game. And I'm third in my class. So what the heck?"

She frowned at me. Narrowed her eyes at Abdi.

"Maybe some American boys are not so bad. But Somali boys? Lazy."

"Huh," Abdi and I said at the same time. He glanced sideways at me. I kicked him under the table.

After Abdi left, the three of us walked to the restaurant, which turned out to be this no-bigger-than-someone's-kitchen place on Market Street. Actually, the girls walked together, side by side, chatting away, while the Guy with the Wallet, aka *me*, followed. To say I was doing a slow burn would be putting it mildly.

We could smell the restaurant before we saw it, and when we arrived we peered inside through the front glass window. There were bright lights and Formica tables, a scuffed linoleum floor, and all sorts of weird stuff hanging on the walls, like framed Somali money, photos of monkeys and giraffes, and inspirational sayings painted on pieces of wood. Pictures of the various menu items were taped to the wall, along with the prices. I counted three tables, total, and two of them were filled with groups of Somali men.

Samira balked. Her feet could have been cemented to the sidewalk outside.

"I think I won't go in," she said. "You two go."

"Okay, see you later," I said at the same time Myla exclaimed, "Oh, c'mon, you need to help us order!"

Samira shook her head. She stared through the plate glass window into the front of the restaurant.

"No, thank you, I think I'll go home." She turned to leave, but Myla grabbed her arm.

"Samira! Seriously, we want you to join us."

Speak for yourself, College, I managed to not say.

Samira's eyes returned to the front window and I followed her gaze. I could only see men. Several looked through the window back at us.

"Are you not allowed to eat here?" I asked her.

She frowned and shook her head.

"I'm allowed. I'm just . . . shy."

Shy my ass, I thought, recalling the battle over *cilaan.* But here's the thing: outside the restaurant she was a different girl from the one who'd been handing down judgments about lazy boys and going head to head with me over the alphabet book. I wouldn't have called it shy. I'd have called it wary. Uncertain. She seemed to have retreated into herself.

Meanwhile, amazing aromas were seeping through the front door and out onto the street. My stomach growled, audibly. Myla burst out laughing.

"See? Tom will spontaneously combust if we don't feed him. C'mon." She linked elbows with Samira and literally pulled her into the restaurant. Given a choice between struggling with Myla on the sidewalk or going inside quietly, Samira picked quietly.

It smelled like an Indian restaurant times ten. Same spices, but way more intense. The air seemed thick with the smell of frying. One wall was papered with laminated eight-by-ten photos of the food, each numbered so you could order a particular plate. Goat curry heaped on colorful rice. Chunks of chicken served with a bread called *chapati.* Fried triangles stuffed with something.

"Those look like empanadas, with a different shape," I commented to Myla.

"They look like samosas, with a different shape," she replied.

"They are *sambusas*," Samira said. She had her back to the other customers and spoke to us in a low voice. "They are dough. Which you fill with meat, and spice, and then you fry. They are very traditional. You should get them."

"Yes," Myla and I both said, then looked at each other. She laughed, even though it wasn't particularly funny, and, you know, she just looked so *happy*. Like there wasn't anyplace else she'd rather be at the moment. Suddenly the roller coaster was creaking back up again, so my arm slipped over her shoulders and rested there. She let it stay the whole time we were deciding what to order.

A very, very skinny guy waited for us at the register. As we approached him, I glanced over at the men sitting at the tables. One or two nodded at me when our eyes met. The rest minded their own plates. Perfectly friendly, but it felt like every customer in the place was watching us without staring directly at us.

"Could we have a three, a five, and an eight? And a side of *sambusas*, please?" Myla said to the skinny guy. He nodded, punched numbers into his register. He pointed to a case where we could get bottled drinks. Then he turned to Samira, who stood slightly behind us. He smiled at her and said something in Somali. She nodded. She looked relieved. As I pulled out my wallet to pay the man, he gestured to a small table behind his counter. Tucked away, out of sight of the other diners.

"I think you like this better?" he said to me and Myla. There was one free table in the open part of the room, but Samira was already making a beeline for the back. Myla and I followed.

I sat across from the girls. As we popped open our drinks, I watched as this little cloud descended on Myla. Her happy expression had been replaced by something else.

"Are we getting stuck back here because we're women?" she finally asked.

Samira's eyes grew wide.

"No! He asked me if I would like to sit here."

"And why would he do that?" Myla asked.

"He is very nice," Samira insisted. "He knows . . . I feel more comfortable here."

"Did he *ask* you to sit back here, or *tell* you?" Myla persisted.

"Ask! He asked," Samira said.

I reached across the table. I covered Myla's hands with mine.

"Hey, College," I said. "It's all good. Let's just eat."

She looked puzzled but let it drop. She also let my hands stay put, at least until the *sambusas* arrived. Which turned out to be the most delicious things I'd ever eaten. By the time the goat curry came, Samira had totally loosened up, declaring the dish only passable and claiming that her mother's was far superior.

"You must both come to our home and I will make it for you," she said, smiling. "Then you will see I am right." Samira likes to be right.

When dinner was over, we loaded up Samira with three Styrofoam containers of leftovers to bring to her brothers and walked her back to her apartment. After she disappeared up the winding stairs, Myla and I wandered back in the direction of The Center, where she'd parked her minivan. As we walked, I draped one arm over her shoulders again. She didn't object. Didn't seem to notice, either.

The minivan was her parents' and it had about 180,000 miles

on it. They'd told her that if she could get it from Minnesota to Maine, she could keep it at college, and somehow she'd managed to coax it all the way to Enniston without breaking down. She mostly used it to tote kids from The Center around town. Sometimes even their parents. Doc appointments. Meetings at the school. Away games. That minivan was like the Little Engine That Could, chugging all the way to 200,000.

"So what do you think was up with that back-table treatment?" she asked me as we walked.

I shrugged.

"No clue. Maybe he wanted to keep us white people out of sight? Could've been bad for business, putting us near the front window."

Myla laughed shortly.

"That's a thought. Or maybe he just wanted to keep us *females* out of sight."

"Yeah. Can't say I blame him," I replied. I glanced down.

My attempt at humor was totally lost on her. She looked annoyed.

"I'm kidding, College. You know? Joke?"

She sighed.

"I know. Sorry. I don't mean to be a grouch. It's just . . . sometimes I don't *get* her! Samira. Like, it's so obvious she's been shoved in the back, in this dingy corner behind the cash register, for God's sake, and she acts like the guy's being nice to her! It kills me, you know?"

The roller coaster wasn't just creaking down at this point. It was in full-scale free fall. Like, the part of the ride when everyone screams.

I stopped walking. Removed the arm. We'd reached her van. Time to figure out where the evening was headed.

"Can we not talk about Samira right now? I'm sort of feeling like the mayor. A little maxed out on Somalis."

To say she didn't get my second attempt at humor would be an understatement.

"That is so not funny, Tom, that I don't even know where to begin. Except maybe to just say good night and thanks for dinner." She fumbled in her shoulder bag, pulled out her keys, and pressed the automatic unlock button. She strode around to the driver's side and got in. Before she could pull out or relock, I jumped into the passenger seat.

"Get out. Call a cab, Bouchard," she said. She sounded almost tearful, she was that angry.

"You need to calm down, and we need to talk," I said softly.

"You need to stop being an asshole!" she said furiously. "Every time I start to think that maybe, possibly, you're cool, you go and ruin it. Some things are *not* funny, Tom! Some things are very, very serious. And what's going on in this city right now, and that stupid letter the mayor wrote? Not funny."

I was getting tired of this person calling me an asshole.

"You know what, College?" I fired back. "I don't need some pointy-headed intellectual from away telling me about my city. You think I don't get how serious this is? Trust me: I get it. Every time I walk into my school and see black kids wandering lost through the halls because the whole idea of changing classes—hell, the whole idea of *classes*—is foreign to them, I see a serious problem. I see Saeed doesn't have a doctor to sign his sports permission forms, and his mother can't speak English and she doesn't have a job.

Kids spray-paint 'Go back to Africa!' in the bathroom. And every day, every single day, more Somalis show up. And if people around here get a little tired of it once in a while, I think it's fuckin' okay to say we're a little tired! And it's okay to make a joke! Jesus. You and my aunt Maddie. *No* sense of humor."

We both sat there silently, breathing hard. I had surprised myself. I hadn't expected that sort of shit to come out of me. I hadn't realized it was all in there.

Myla broke the stalemate.

"You hate me, don't you?" she said. "Pointy-headed intellectual? Great."

"Actually, I have a mad crush on you. But don't let *that* go to your pointy little head."

"*Ahh!*" She slammed her fists on the steering wheel, then buried her face in her hands. "You are so aggravating!"

"Yeah. Back at you, College."

"Stop calling me College! Stop commenting about my height! Do you think I like looking like a twelve-year-old?"

"A very hot twelve-year-old. Maybe I should call you Lolita. Whaddaya think of that, College?"

That's when she punched me in the arm. Hard.

"Ouch! Knock it off, Myla!"

"Yes, thank you! That's my name. Myla."

Silence returned to the minivan. The thought crossed my mind that this "date" was almost as fun as watching *Survivor* with Cherisse and Aunt Maddie.

"I don't hate you," I said finally.

"You have contempt for me," she said sullenly. "You think I'm naive."

"I think you're smart and cute and you have a good heart," I told her. "I think you do the right thing and I admire it. I also think this situation in Enniston is very complicated and you need to give the people around here the benefit of the doubt. Even the mayor. I'll admit, she's not the sharpest tool in the shed. But she cares about her city."

I had been addressing most of this to the windshield in front of me. But then I heard this little choky sound and I turned to her. Two straight lines of tears streamed down her cheeks. This was so unexpected I didn't know what to do. It crossed my mind that maybe Myla was also tired. That maybe she was maxed out, too, but didn't think she was allowed to admit it.

"Oh God, don't cry. Please. That shit breaks me."

That's when the floodgates opened for real, and I was holding this sobbing girl in the front seat of a minivan. She buried her face in my chest and just let it all out while I stroked her hair. Shampoo. Fresh laundry detergent. All the little Myla scents floated up to me. So when she finally lifted her face to mine, there was really no question what would happen next: my lips found hers.

She kissed back.

We pretty much lost track of time after that, but after a while we broke for conversation.

"Can I ask you something?" she said.

"Sure."

"Are you still dating that girl . . . what's her name?"

"Cherisse. And no. *Not* in a relationship. Unless nasty texting counts as a relationship. I still get a lot of that from her."

Myla rolled her eyes.

"And . . . are you still grounded?" she asked.

"I have no clue. No one's ever said my groundation would ever end. Although they knew I was seeing you after homework help tonight. Why?"

Myla smiled, a little hesitantly.

"You feel like hanging out? Back at my room?"

I struggled to keep a neutral, nonchalant expression on my face. As if hot college girls invited me to hang out in their dorm rooms on a regular basis.

"I don't know. What did you have in mind?" I asked.

"I could show you my flamingos," she said.

Flamingos. In Maine. Intriguing.

"How can I refuse an invitation like that? Drive on, Lolita."

Chapter Eighteen

Not long after that, the skinheads got involved.

Okay, maybe it's not fair to call them skinheads. They were a . . . religious organization. The United Church of the World. They believed in white people. That was pretty much it. Which you had to admire for its simplicity.

Unfortunately for them, most of their members were in jail. And their founder had offed himself a while back. And their members who weren't locked up had shaved their heads, covered themselves with tattoos, and made some harsh videos about blacks and Jews and all the "mud" races, which pissed a lot of people off, so their recruitment numbers were down.

Which may explain why they jumped on our little family fight in Enniston. They needed some free publicity.

The mayor's letter had led to a follow-up letter by a group of Somali elders, which led to another group forming (Aunt Maddie and Co.) and leading these little marches and stuff, which made the news, and next thing we knew the United Church of the World decided the whites in Enniston needed their help. They

planned to rally here, which everyone assumed was code for starting a race war, and people began really freaking out (think: Aunt
Maddie) because, thanks to our beloved mayor and her stupid letter, the skinheads were coming to town.

This was what Myla had meant by "very, very serious."

Of course, Tom Bouchard had other things on his mind. In
particular, soccer and Ramadan.

Here's the thing I learned about Ramadan: it moves. Not like
Christmas.

Christmas comes at the same time every year. I'm sure no one
has any idea what day Jesus Christ was actually born (something
he shares with my refugee friends), but the day we celebrate his
birthday? December 25? Set in stone. Retailers the world over
count down to that day, and even if some archaeologist unearthed
a papyrus birth certificate in the sands of Bethlehem proving
that Our Lord was actually born on the Fourth of July, I doubt
anybody'd shift the date.

Ramadan, however, is a whole different deal. It's based on
the Islamic calendar, which is about eleven days shorter than the
Gregorian calendar, which, BTW, is *our* calendar, which means
that every year Ramadan begins eleven days earlier than the year
before.

I got that off Wikipedia. After Mike told me our next game
against Maquoit was during the fast of Ramadan. I looked it up.
Just to make sure.

So . . . yeah. My senior year. The year Saeed and Ismail and
Ibrahim and Double M were transforming our front line and
Chamberlain started stacking up X's in the win column, Ramadan
began on October 1.

We were scheduled to play Maquoit on October 8.

I got how an invasion of white supremacist skinheads was probably a bigger deal and should have taken up more space in my mental hard drive. But for me, Ramadan and calendars and the chances that I could convince the guys to break the fast, at least for the day we played Maquoit, had become my new obsession.

Mike said no way.

"Tom, these are *serious* Muslims." We were in the car, driving. We had had the early practice that day, and afterward Mike asked if I could take him to Harmon, the neighboring town. He wanted to catch the end of Ellen's cross-country race, which was being held there.

We'd been hanging out more, me and Mike. Partly because we had soccer, partly because I had AP calculus with Ellen Fitzgerald and Mike was in love. Neither of them had ever dated anyone before (which, when you're a senior, makes it even *more* awkward, because everyone expects you to have had *some* knowledge of the opposite sex), and somehow I had ended up as their personal romantic go-between. Not literally passing messages back and forth. But Mike would grill me for info about her, and wait for me after calc in order to pretend to walk with me to our next class (he'd actually be looking for an opening to speak with *her*). Ellen had suddenly become fascinated with every detail surrounding Chamberlain soccer and would slyly ask me questions about Mike's stats and whether he had scored.

I was tempted to tell her he'd probably score if she came to more of our games, but that was the type of double-entendre asshole comment Myla would have hated, so I kept it to myself. Anyway, between Mike and Myla and four AP classes and a hundred hours of community service, I hadn't seen much of Donnie. I mean, this usually happened during soccer season, but this year it really felt like he'd dropped off my radar. Sometimes there would be days I wouldn't even bump into him at lunch, and I wondered if he was skipping school.

Here's the thing about cross-country: there's really nothing to see until the end. Everyone runs off into the woods, you wait for them at the finish line, and about twenty minutes later they all start running out. Mike kept glancing at his watch as I broke the speed limit through school zones.

"Don't worry, I'll get you there," I told him. "And when are Muslims *un*serious, by the way?"

He laughed.

"When they're cafeteria Catholics," he said. "Picking and choosing what you want to do instead of letting the pope decide it all for you."

"Watch it; I resemble that remark."

"Then you know what I mean. You miss mass once in a while, or eat that chocolate you were going to give up for Lent, and it's like, hey, whatever. Not like I'm going to hell for a Hershey's bar. But Double M and the guys? They are serious. I was sitting next to them on the bench yesterday, and they were arguing over whether they can brush their teeth during Ramadan. And I'm like, 'What, is toothpaste food?' and they said, 'No, it's because you can't drink during the day, and what if you swallow some water?' And I was, like, 'Dude. Allah will understand if a drop slips down your throat.' And they all gave me this look, like, Allah will most certainly *not* understand. I mean, a *drop*, Tom. That's what they're worried about."

193

"You know your problem, Mike? You're a freakin' infidel. How would you know what Allah thinks?"

"Exactly. What do I know? So don't you get into micromanaging Ramadan for them, Tom. They won't appreciate it."

He had a point. I sure don't want anyone who's not Catholic telling me how to practice my religion. But just like the dates for Ramadan move, the ways you do Ramadan aren't set in stone. At least, according to Myla.

We had been talking about it the night before, on the phone. She thought Mike was full of shit.

"Give me a break," she said when I told her about the toothpaste. "I know plenty of Muslim kids who brush their teeth during Ramadan without worrying about swallowing a little water."

She also has this friend, Jackie, who lives in her dorm. She's a black woman from Pittsburgh, born and raised in this country, and she's Muslim. She wears makeup and jewelry and you can see her hair. She doesn't cover up with long skirts and a *hijab*; she dates and goes to parties and plays sports. But alcohol doesn't touch her lips. She doesn't get on the floor and face Mecca, but she does make a point to pray quietly five times a day. And during Ramadan, she doesn't eat or drink during daylight hours.

Unless she has a soccer game. See, she plays midfield for Mumford.

"Jackie says a lot of this stuff that some Muslims say is part of the religion is actually just cultural and not in the Koran," Myla said. "Like, when she's introduced to a man, she'll shake his hand. Not like a lot of our Somali girls, who won't touch a man who is not an immediate relative, and if they *have* to shake a man's hand—like, say, the principal handing them their diploma at graduation—they'll cover their hand with the *hijab* so they don't touch skin."

"Seriously? Samira wouldn't shake my hand?"

"We should ask her. I'm curious. Samira's . . . unpredictable." Myla's voice trailed off. "I think there's a lot she's still trying to sort out."

"So where are you now?" I asked.

"Lying on my bed," she replied. "Supposedly reading for my anthro class tomorrow. But then this *guy* called . . ."

"Hey, we're talking about Muslim cultural and religious practices. Sounds like anthropology to me."

She laughed.

"Do you have your flamingos on?"

"Of course," she said. "I wish you were here to appreciate them with me."

"Somehow I don't think *any* anthro would be happening if we were appreciating the flamingos together right now," I said.

"That's very true, Cap."

The flamingos are these small pink party lights, shaped like the long-legged birds, that Myla has strung along the walls of her dorm room. The overhead light in her room is this bright fluorescent thing, which she hates, so she bought herself a floor lamp that uses an energy-saving bulb, and these strings of flamingos.

The flamingos create some pretty intense atmosphere. I gave them two enthusiastic thumbs up the other night.

"But listen," she said, pulling me away from some pleasant, flamingo-lit memories. "What you've got to realize is that while American Muslims like Jackie might feel comfortable breaking the fast for a college soccer game, guys like Saeed might not. Somali people are pretty conservative, and refugees a lot of times get even stricter about religion when they leave home. They've already lost so much, you know? Religion is one of the few things they've got left."

I sighed.

"So basically you're telling me there's no chance I'm gonna convince these guys that the team needs them to be in top form when we play Maquoit and please won't they eat and drink *something* before the game?"

"I'm saying you can *try*, but don't get your hopes up."

As Mike and I pulled into the parking lot of the middle school, we heard a gun going off in the direction of the fields, followed by cheers. He glanced at his watch.

"I can't remember if the girls run first or second. If we hurry, maybe I can catch her on the second turn."

A cross-country race is like organized chaos. First you've got these runners all packed together along the start line. A gun fires, they take off, and it's like a cartoon mob of flying feet and pumping arms and you're just sure someone is going to trip and get trampled. But no one does, and within ten seconds or so they fall into an order of sorts, with a third going out strong, a third pacing themselves in the middle, and a third settling into a jog because they're clearly not concerned about their times and just hope to finish the race.

They run along a route that only makes sense to them (all the teams walk the course beforehand to make sure no one accidentally cuts corners or gets lost in the woods), and as they circle and loop round, disappear behind the trees and then reemerge, the line thins as gaps form between the fast runners and the kids falling behind. At various points along the course, clusters of fans gather, screaming encouragement, urging them forward, faster. Everyone is spread out for miles—you can work up a sweat just jogging between various points along the course to cheer—and it's only at the end that it gets truly crazy and intense, as the runners, who pretty much all look like they want to die, put on a last, final burst for the finish line. Everyone screams for everyone, and the biggest applause comes for the kid who crosses *last*. This is usually the most out-of-shape kid on the team, possibly in the whole school, but you've gotta hand it to him: he just ran a 5K and lived to tell about it.

When Mike and I reached the field, a pack of guys ran past. Two wore Chamberlain jerseys.

"Yes!" he said. "The girls must be running second. C'mon, let's go watch!" We took off at a slow run to a hill where we could pretty much see the whole race play out around us.

The runners were like different-colored jewels scattered on a green, green cloth. Mike and I positioned ourselves at the crest of a long, open part of the trail that the runners ascended slowly. It was probably the two-mile mark, the telling point, where you knew whether you still had something left or whether you'd gone out a little too fast and burned yourself up. A lot of people gathered here, cheering for their schools.

In the distance, I saw a black boy in Harmon's colors slowly approach. His breathing was labored; his legs moved almost in slow motion. Over and over, runners approached him from behind and passed him. He didn't acknowledge them, his gaze was fixed ahead, but as each runner passed, I noticed, they spoke to him.

When he got near me and Mike, fans began speaking to him

as well. Every fan, from every school. They clapped and shouted encouragement as he made his way up the hill.

"Good job, Ali! Attaboy! Don't give up!" His opponents, the kids from the other schools, cheered him as well. Some patted him on the back as they ran by.

"Nice job; good going. Keep it up, Ali!"

When he got close to us, I saw that he was bathed in sweat. He looked agonized; he didn't appear to notice the shouts of the people around him.

"Go, Ali! You can do it!" Mike yelled.

I stared at him.

"You know that guy?"

Mike looked surprised.

"You don't? That's Ali Suleman. He's Harmon's number one runner. Probably number one in the state. He's awesome." He'd passed us now, and I watched as he disappeared around a clump of trees.

"Number one has about twenty-five guys ahead of him," I commented. "He didn't look too happy." Mike shrugged.

"No, but he was looking good for someone who hasn't eaten or had anything to drink since dawn," he said. "C'mon, let's head to the finish."

We got there as the first runners crossed the line. At that point, it didn't matter which school anyone was pulling for: every runner was cheered. Some of them put on this superhuman burst of energy as soon as they drew close to the crowds at the end, which got a lot of applause for effort. When Ali approached, the crowd noise intensified several decibels.

His teeth were pulled back in a grimace and perspiration flew off him. The Harmon team, in a pack, chanted his name as he approached the finish line, and when he crossed they mobbed him. He staggered; they practically knocked him over. Mike and I were only a few feet away, so I heard what he said. It was almost a gasp, but I could hear him.

"Ramadan is pushing me, but I push back! I push back!"

The other finishers, once they walked it off and their heart rates settled, poured themselves paper cones of icy water from the big plastic coolers the organizers had set out. Ali took nothing. Hands on hips he walked slowly, shaking his legs out, stretching, loosening the lactic acid out of his muscles. The expression on his face was tired and relieved and . . . triumphant. Like he'd just won something big.

That's when I knew I wasn't going to ask Saeed and the other guys to break their fast the next week.

Chapter Nineteen

The boosters decided to spring for a fan bus to the Maquoit-Chamberlain game.

Granted, it was a school bus. But this was still the regular season, the first half of October, and the boosters usually only hired fan buses for the postseason. That is, if we were lucky enough to make it to the postseason and could convince enough people to travel all the way to Bangor to watch us get our butts kicked.

But this was the brave new world of Chamberlain soccer, and we were the team to watch (at least according to John LaVallee, sports columnist for the *City Cryer*). And a game between the Team to Watch and the Team to Beat, aka Maquoit, warranted a fan bus. Signups to reserve a seat started at 7:30 a.m.; by first period, at 8:00 a.m., the bus was filled and there was a waiting list two pages long.

Saeed came bounding into school the morning of the game. He had already been up for hours, doing his pre-dawn prayers and stuffing himself with as much food and water as he could before sunrise. On game day he'd planned to go to the mosque instead of just praying at home. So as I stood in the school hall, wishing I'd had time for a second cup of coffee that morning, for him it was like noon already.

"Tom! Big day!" he enthused, clapping me on the back. I was drifting with the herd toward homeroom when he came up behind me. We were both wearing button-down shirts and ties, standard issue for varsity game days.

"Big day, man," I agreed.

"Yeah! Everybody coming!" He gestured to the table in the lobby where kids had signed up for the bus.

"Even my parents are getting off work early to see the game," I told him.

"Me too. My family, too! Myla is driving." I nodded. That I knew. Myla's minivan service.

"Hey, Tom Bouchard." Silky voice to my right. Lila Boutin. Cherisse's BFF.

Saeed punched me lightly on the arm and disappeared in the crowded hallway. I fell into step with Lila, who's in my homeroom, a room full of B's: Bouchard, Boutin . . . "So what were you up to this weekend? We missed you at Carrie's. Epic *ray-jah*. At least one girl I can think of was pretty disappointed you didn't show."

"Didn't you get the memo, Lila?" I smiled at her. "We broke up."

Lila opened her eyes wide. The lashes were crusted so thickly with black mascara they looked like tarantula legs.

She leaned against me as we walked and spoke into my ear.

"I was talking about *me*."

There was absolutely no good answer to this. Whatever I said would be relayed to Cherisse ASAP. Minus Lila's come-ons, of course.

"I didn't do much this weekend," I told her. "Unless you count community service hours and homework."

"All work and no play," she said, singsongy.

"Makes Tom a dull, dull boy," I said sadly.

Lila smirked at me wickedly.

"You're lying, Tommy. I can tell. You're no good at it. Cherisse told me you're seeing someone else."

I shrugged.

That's what I'd come up with the night Cherisse got voted off the island. It wasn't particularly kind, but given what I could have said, it was humane: "I realize this probably isn't the best timing in the world, but you should know I'm seeing someone else."

The timing in question was the end of that evening's episode of *Survivor*, after which Cherisse flicked off the lights in the den and attempted a little lip-lock action before my mom started prowling around. Maddie had never come back.

It's probably not great to break up with a girl midkiss.

"Who??" Cherisse demanded. "Who is she?"

I thought it was interesting that her first instinct was to discover who the competition was, rather than to mourn the end of our relationship.

"It doesn't matter. You don't know her," I said.

"I know *everyone*, Tommy," she said between her teeth in a fairly scary and not particularly attractive way.

"Not this girl. And besides, I'm not going to tell you, so give it a rest."

There was some pretty colorful language after that. Mom

heard, and came busting in just as Cherisse was busting out. She slammed the door as she left the house.

"What was *that*?" Mom exclaimed.

"Hurricane Cherisse," I said. "Be happy. I'm gonna go upstairs and study physics now."

I hadn't said a word to anyone at school, but I hadn't needed to. Don't telegraph: tell-a-Cherisse.

"So go on. Who is she?" Lila persisted. We'd reached the classroom. I shrugged at her again, smiling, and took my seat. Lila looked pretty annoyed. I didn't know what she was hoping to gain from our little conversation . . . information? A date? . . . but she came up empty-handed.

Given that I supposedly can't lie, it was pretty funny that Cherisse believed the one I told her about seeing someone. Which, ironically, morphed into the truth. I pretty much at that point considered myself to be seeing Myla.

Anyway, the afternoon of game day was perfect. I don't usually stop and smell the roses, so to speak, but you couldn't have asked for more perfect weather to play soccer: the trees still held all their leaves, and against the blue, blue sky every one was some shade of orange, yellow, or red. The air was cool and smelled like cut grass. The gorgeously manicured Maquoit fields were deep, rich green.

Deep. Rich. Like the Maquoit soccer team. Whose second-string benchwarmers could probably have defeated most of the boys' varsity teams in Maine.

An insane number of spectators showed up, for both sides. Usually I spot my parents on the sidelines or locate Cherisse and her posse (not anymore), but it was like a sea of people on that side of the field and you couldn't tell who anyone was. The Maquoit fans formed the biggest bloc, in their black and red, but a legit number of Chamberlain fans had staked out blue territory.

The ride over was quiet. I don't know, maybe I should have been whipping the guys into battle readiness, a little foot stomping to piss off the driver and some Maquoit hate chants to get the adrenaline going. But I've never been that guy, and never been that captain. I'm more the get-in-the-zone sort of athlete. So I listened to my iPod. Got into game mode with Dr. Dre and Eminem . . .

Lose yourself in the moment . . .

You only get one shot.

As we stepped off the bus in the Maquoit parking lot, Saeed filed out right in front of me. He was a hell of a lot quieter than he'd been that morning. We walked together toward the field.

"How you doin'?" I asked him.

"Good," he said firmly, eyes fixed on the ground before him.

He's exhausted already, I thought. *Shit.*

Is this what you want, God? Allah? Whoever? Yet another victory for ever-victorious Maquoit by hitting us over the head with Ramadan in October? Thanks.

As we walked, neither of us spoke. I tried not to imagine how thirsty he might be. On the bus, nobody ate or drank, not even the white guys. All of us had made a point of not eating or drinking in front of the Somalis that month, so we made sure to chug some water and eat snacks away from the locker room. During the game would be an exception: you couldn't ask the non-Muslim guys to not drink at halftime, or on the bench.

Here was the bottom line: the brave new world of Chamberlain soccer needed Saeed. Full-throttle Saeed, in all his fast, crazy glory. And the other Somali guys, too, if we were gonna stand a chance. As we walked to the soccer field, I wanted to say something, anything, to communicate that to him.

I wanted him to know that I had faith that he'd deliver. Even if it was only a shaky half faith.

"Ramadan pushing you?" I said quietly.

Saeed raised his head and looked at me.

"Yes," he said. "Yes, Tom."

So I shoved him. Just a little.

"You push back," I said, and grinned.

He looked startled for a second. But when my words sank in, he smiled broadly.

"I push back!" he exclaimed, delivering a return shove that made me stagger.

Okay, then.

Me, Mike, and Jonnie jog-trotted to the center of the field. Alex and his goons were already there, with the refs. This was the coin toss to determine which team would start with possession, and the usual warnings to play safe, show good sportsmanship, et cetera. Plus we'd shake hands.

My stomach was doing unnatural things. Everything around me seemed intensified: the crowd noise was palpable; the colors were in high definition. I willed myself to breathe in deeply, to fill my lungs to capacity, then fought back the urge to exhale in a swift whoosh. Let it out slowly.

Coach had taken me aside.

"You look nervous, Tommy," he said quietly. I stared down at the ground. My cleats. The grass. I was trying not to look across the field at the packed bleachers.

"Yeah," I breathed. "I am nervous."

"Well, a little nervous is understandable. Even desirable. Don't want to be complacent."

I laughed.

"Against Maquoit? Never, Coach."

He looked at me curiously.

"So what's going on today?" he said.

"I'm just worried that Saeed and Ibrahim and the other guys aren't going to be at the top of their game. We need them today. We can't beat Maquoit if they're draggin'."

He shook his head.

"I don't think we have anything to worry about on that score," he said. "You'd be surprised at how their bodies adjust. I've noticed it just this week. They'll do fine. You concentrate on *your* game, and project confidence for your teammates. Tom, if they sense panic from you, it won't matter how well fed and well hydrated anyone is. Understand?"

I nodded firmly. Confidently. Or so I hoped.

The Maquoit guys were expressionless as we approached. None of their typical snide bluster, the mind-game crap they're known for in our league. Once, before a game, they were being such jerks a referee asked one of the captains if he'd like a yellow card right then and there for being rude.

"I could do it, young man," he'd said severely.

It didn't help that Maquoit had gone on to beat us six-zip that day. Even though most of the calls had gone our way.

I tuned out as the ref spoke; it was the usual riff, and I knew what was expected and how to behave. Instead, I tried to make eye contact with Alex . . . but he was staring intently at the ref, focused on his every word. Right. Like Stripes was saying something new and different? *C'mon, Alex, you see me. You know you want to flash me some attitude. Go on, do it, bro . . .*

And then he did it. The blink. Those rapid blinks like he had something caught in his eyes.

Wow.

Alex Rhodes was nervous. No, correction: I was nervous. He was *freakin'* nervous.

He thought we could win.

It was like someone whispered in my ear: *hope.*

They won the coin toss, but it's not like I cared. As we jogged back to the huddle, my mind raced as I tried to figure out some way to channel my amazing optimism. I only had seconds and I only had words, which are pretty useless most of the time. How would I tell them what I'd just seen so that they could feel what I felt? This overwhelming sense that our destiny was in our control and we were not going to get rolled that afternoon?

I realized I was just thinking too much.

"Get in close. Closer!" I demanded when I reached the guys on our side of the field. We laced arms around each other's shoulders. Our heads bumped.

"I got a secret for you boys," I began. "We *rock*."

"Yeah!" everybody started yelling. I waited until they settled down.

"I've got another secret," I continued. "Up until a minute ago, I didn't believe. Yeah, I wanted this. I worked for it, and all of you did, too. But deep down I never thought we could do it. Then one minute ago, I saw something that made me *believe*."

No yells then. I had their attention.

"They. Are. Scared," I said loudly. "I know these guys. You know I know them. And I have never seen such fear on their faces before. Never. Ever. Maquoit is never afraid, but let me tell you, they are petrified right now. Because they've seen us play, and they know: we can *beat them!*"

The guys ignited. Yelling, fist pumps, our usual chant. Yeah.

We headed out onto the field.

Within thirty seconds Alex made a mistake. He's a great ball handler, it's almost impossible to strip him when he's got possession, but for some reason he wanted to get out early and score right away. Even though no one challenged him, he tried to pass off to a man behind me. Who wasn't expecting Alex to pass just then . . . so I intercepted it. Stopped, settled the ball, and just beyond Alex and the encroaching Maquoit front line I saw our guys: Saeed, Double M, Mike Turcotte. I booted it, high.

The ball lofted over Alex, and Double M had it. He took off, while Mike and Saeed flew ahead of him. The Maquoit defense collapsed on Double M, and he looked for an open man. Someone who hadn't outrun the defense, because that would be offside. Saeed was screaming. He was way off to one side, his hand up, but he was so far out of scoring position that it seemed pointless to direct the ball that way. His closest defender didn't even think it was worth sticking too tightly to him there, and had given him plenty of space.

Double M knew better. As well as I knew Saeed's game at that point, and as much as I'd come to expect from him, I didn't see what he saw. I sure as hell wouldn't have done what Double M did: he waited, slowed the action so that the defenders, smelling blood, rushed him. Then he did this thing—I can only compare it to a chip shot in golf—where you strike the ball at such an angle it floats up, then out. Right to the unguarded Saeed, who turned it around instantly and sent one of his on-the-wings-of-angels shots toward the goal.

And of course it went in. High, in the corner, a perfect shot the goalie couldn't possibly reach.

We think we're all playing the same game, but we're not. Saeed and the guys? They try things we don't try. They have shots and they do stuff they learned playing dirt-yard pickup soccer in Kenya. Nothing they're teaching us here in Enniston, or from a private coach with a British accent in the heated dome in Portland. Maquoit couldn't defend against that. Couldn't anticipate it coming.

It was *so* sweet.

And that's how it went, for 110 minutes of play. Chamberlain pulling up with this unexpected, wild-ass soccer we'd never played before, and Maquoit battling back, because they were, after all, Maquoit. One hundred and ten minutes of running our guts out for two halves and two overtimes. One hundred and ten minutes of yellow cards, good calls, crap calls, and fans screaming themselves hoarse. And after those 110 minutes the score was tied, 1–1. Which meant it came down to PKs.

Penalty kicks. The most godawful, heartbreaking way to end a game. All that effort, and it's decided with the five best kickers from each team doing battle, one-on-one, against their opponent's goalie. They each line up, take aim, and fire the ball. It almost always goes in: it's nearly impossible for a goalie to block a penalty kick.

So you wait, pray, hope, for a mistake. Some kicker to blow the shot by going wide and ricocheting the ball off the side of the goal, or blasting it high over the top. Or aiming it directly at the goalie, who can't help but stop it. Sometimes the goalie makes an incredible save off an awesome shot, and that's cool. But pretty much a game that ends with penalty kicks is about someone screwing up.

Which sucks, no matter which side you're on.

Coach chose the five: me, Saeed, Ibrahim, Ismail, Mike Turcotte. Pete LeBourdais was in goal. We headed out.

Maquoit kicked first, with Alex Rhodes starting. Pete faced him, hands out to his sides, feet planted wide, knees bent. He was totally ready to dive, leap, whatever it took, when . . . *pow!* Alex fired; Pete hurled himself to the right. But Alex faked him out but good, because he'd just lasered the ball into the left corner of the goal. Maquoit: 1. Spectators screamed ferociously.

I was up next. Their goalie was a senior named Luke Hanson. Enormous guy with great reflexes. He played center for the Maquoit basketball team in the winter and could get some serious air when he tried. He was not as good down low, however. I took aim and shot in the opposite corner from where Alex had just shot. Luke didn't get anywhere near it: 1–1. Equally ferocious screaming.

If the score is still even after everyone has kicked, you send out another five guys and do it again. If the score is *still* tied, you get another five kicks. At some point it becomes sudden death . . . which means the first team to score after someone misses has won.

It's like sitting around a busy intersection waiting for a car crash.

Maquoit's second man scored; our second, Ibrahim, scored.

Maquoit's third man scored; our third man, Mike, kicked

it . . . wide. It missed the goalpost by a fraction of an inch. Mike dropped to his knees in despair as the black and red side of the crowd erupted with bloodthirsty yells. My throat clutched and I realized there was a very good possibility I would cry, in public, if this thing didn't go our way.

Maquoit's fourth man lined up. It was Sasquatch. I looked at Pete in goal: he's a pretty tall guy himself, but he looked like a helpless child compared to Sasquatch. I stifled the urge to pray, because we all know God doesn't take sides, at least not in the Penacook Valley Athletic Conference, and . . . *yes!* Sasquatch booted the ball over the goal. It disappeared into a clump of trees ten yards away. Now the blue side of the field lost it.

Our fourth man, Double M, scored. We were back to tied.

Maquoit's fifth man stepped up. He booted it . . . straight down the middle. Like he was aiming for Pete's gut. Pete couldn't have missed if he'd tried. He doubled over and wrapped his arms around the ball.

Chamberlain fans went so completely berserk that a couple of cops in charge of crowd control started pushing them back, trying to contain them. They wanted to rush the field already. They felt it, they felt victory, so, so close.

But it's not over till it's over.

Saeed stepped up.

My man was drenched in sweat. His jersey hung limply off his bony shoulders. Slowly, carefully, he placed the soccer ball on the ground. He seemed oblivious to the pandemonium around him. He was in some quiet place of his own, lost in the moment. I saw his eyes close, briefly. Like maybe he was praying.

What? What would Saeed say, ask, right then? *Please let us* win. *Please help me defeat my opponent. Please help me to do my best. Help me to not let my team down.*

Someone told me—Aunt Maddie? Myla? Mike Turcotte?—that the word *Islam* means "to submit." Not a concept we're used to in America, for sure. But it made me think maybe I do know what Saeed might say in his prayers. Especially since it's also a line in the Lord's Prayer.

Your will be done.

The four of us left on the field had our arms around each other's shoulders. I held my breath. Saeed liked to go high. That airborne, lofty shot that came out of nowhere and self-directed into the goal. Exactly what Luke Hanson was genetically suited to block. I realized, too late, that I should have thought of that, should have warned Saeed that Luke can't go low . . . but it was too late. It was out of my hands.

You only get one shot.

Saeed stepped back. He took one, two, three steps and . . . game over. Because it was in. Like a guided missile traveling mere inches above the grass, the ball flew low into the corner of the goal. Saeed stood still, staring at his own shot like he couldn't believe it. Screaming, we swarmed him. We lifted him. Meanwhile, the rest of the team had hoisted Pete, and we looked like an insane tribe carrying off a couple of victims. Except this was a celebration.

The cops couldn't hold the crowd back, and the sea of shrieking, blue-clad fans streamed across the field toward us. It was mad, intoxicating . . . a little scary, even. And somewhere in the melee I felt someone grab my arm.

There she was. I don't know how she found me in that crowd, but I'm learning to not underestimate short people.

"You did it, Cap!" she screamed.

I picked her up and swung her around. She laughed, her legs swinging out and bashing into people around us, but no one cared. When I returned her to earth, she turned her face to mine and I was kissing, kissing her, like I'd never kissed anyone else before. Except I had. A few nights ago, kissing someone just this way, surrounded by softly lit pink flamingos.

And it felt, like it hadn't felt in a long time, as if I was starting to get things right.

Chapter Twenty

John LaVallee is one of those guys everyone thought was going somewhere. The trophy case in our school's lobby is packed with hardware from the days when John played soccer, hockey, and baseball for Chamberlain, and guidance counselors still talk about the year he won the Maine state essay contest and got to have lunch with the governor at the Blaine House. Everybody figured John was going to end up as a network sports announcer or a reporter for the *Boston Globe*.

Instead, he sat in a stuffy little conference room across a table from me, Saeed, and Coach Gerardi. The *City Cryer* is the weekly newspaper you'd most likely use to light your woodstove in the morning, so I hadn't been expecting much. Even so, their setup seemed shabby. We'd walked up two flights of stairs to reach the *Cryer's* offices, which were located over a pawn shop on Main Street. Next door was a deli, and the staircase smelled like sauerkraut.

John and Coach go way back, which was why Coach agreed to bring us in that morning for an interview. John started all four seasons he played soccer at Chamberlain, and the year he graduated, 1989, they'd made it to the semis before losing to Bangor. He and Coach spent some time reminiscing about the old days while Saeed and I waited for the questions to begin. It was Saturday morning, and I was only half-awake. It'd been a late night. Or, as Uncle Paul would say, an early morning.

It had started on the ride. Jake had an iHome in the bus, so he cranked his pump-up mix all the way back to the high school. We were practically screaming lyrics and the bus driver didn't care. He didn't say a damn thing the whole way; I actually saw him smile.

Which made me realize: the whole freakin' town had wanted us to beat Maquoit.

The fan bus had left ahead of us, and when we pulled up to the school an impromptu party had taken shape in the gym. Somebody on the boosters must be pretty well connected, because three different pizza places, including Michelangelo's, delivered boxes. One of the Somali moms showed up with a tray of *sambusas*, which pretty much got eaten right away. Other parents brought big bottles of soda, the custodial staff set up tables, and you'd think we'd just won states, that's how pumped everybody was.

After the food was gone and the thriving in the gym had spun itself out, Mike Turcotte invited the team back to his house. I had just gotten the car keys from my dad and was asking around to see who needed a ride when I felt a tug on my sleeve.

"Victory is sweet, Tom-boy."

I hadn't seen Donnie up until that point. Not at the game, not even during the postgame party in the gym. Then he just materialized, with that stupid, lopsided grin on his face.

"Man hug," he said, then threw his arms around my shoulders.

"Where've you been?" I demanded. "Did you even go to the game?"

He laughed.

"Late, but then you guys helped me out by taking it to PKs, so I saw what counts. Even better: after the game I watched Alex Rhodes take major shit from somebody I think was his dad. You shoulda seen him. He was furious."

"Couldn't happen to a nicer guy," I said.

"Yeah, sucks for him," Donnie sighed. He glanced around at the thinning crowd. "Whaddaya say? A little celebration of the liquid kind?"

I shook my head.

"Team's heading over to Turcotte's," I said.

"No friends of the team allowed?" he said. I tried not to notice the edge of disappointment in his voice.

"Nah, his parents want to keep it to just the team. Sorry." I managed to *not* add that even if friends of the team were invited, Donnie Plourde wasn't likely to be in Mike Turcotte's guest book. Mike was still mad about the rock.

Don shrugged.

"That's okay," he said. "Probably not my kind of refreshments anyway. Call me later if you want to hang out." He put his hands in his pockets and started walking backward away from me. "And Tom . . . great job today. Seriously. You're the man."

In the *Cryer* offices, John and Coach finally finished their hey-have-you-heard-from-so-and-so's and turned their attention to me and Saeed. John looked like a softer, slightly rounder version of his jacked high school self. Less hair, bit of a spare tire hanging over his belt. There was a picture of him in the trophy case, accepting a plaque from someone I didn't know. Maybe a principal from three principals ago?

"So, great playing yesterday, boys," he began jovially.

"Thanks," I said.

"Thank you," Saeed said.

"Nothing quite like beating Maquoit," he continued. "Back in my day, that was as good as winning states." We nodded as if we knew anything about "his day." John directed his gaze at me.

"And I'll bet that win was particularly gratifying for you, Tom. Don't you have a personal grudge against Maquoit?"

I frowned. I wasn't sure what he meant.

"Grudge? No, not particularly . . ."

"Didn't you get into some trouble recently for defacing their school spirit rock?" John interrupted.

I looked at Coach. Color rose on his cheeks.

"That was a silly prank Tom got involved in, John," Coach said evenly. "It had nothing to do with the team or the traditional athletic rivalry between the two schools."

John nodded and smiled. Smirked, more like.

It occurred to me that I didn't like John LaVallee.

"A bit one-sided to call it a rivalry, though, don't you think?" he said. "C'mon. Don't you just *hate* those guys?" He looked at me like he was speaking in a code we both understood.

Hate. It's a strong word. A word I save for things like lima beans and getting stitches. And yeah, in the past, Maquoit. But our victory had somehow taken the edge off that and the question felt strange.

"I hate losing," I told John, "so yesterday was great." I glanced at Coach, who nodded ever so slightly at me.

John tried again.

"So, what was the difference yesterday?" he asked. "What's been the difference this season, for that matter? Because you boys are having a great season."

I pointed to Saeed.

"You're lookin' at the difference," I said. "This guy's amazing."

Saeed startled. He looked genuinely shocked. He shook his head emphatically.

"No! Tom is . . . the man. He the man! Yes, I am . . . very fast. We all Somali peoples play very fast. But Tom, he the middle and he is . . ." Saeed struggled for the word. He placed his hand on his chest.

"Heart. Tom is heart of team."

Never in my life had I felt more unworthy of praise. Especially coming from a guy like Saeed, with all he'd been through.

That's when Coach stepped in.

"The combination of both these young men is the difference," he said. "Listen, John, you know our program. We play fair, but we play physical. Thug soccer. That's what people have always said about us. Now these Somali kids come in, and they play a different sort of game. We've become a lot better technically because of them. So opponents like Maquoit, who have had us for lunch as long as I can remember, not only have to deal with players willing to be physically aggressive, but players who can handle the ball skillfully and quickly."

John scribbled all this down.

"So overall, you'd say the new Somali players have been good for the athletic program?"

Coach shrugged.

"I can only speak for soccer, but yes. Absolutely."

John looked up from his notepad.

"One bright spot in a sea of controversy and complaint," he said, unsmiling. "A lot of people in town don't share that opinion."

Coach stared steadily back at him.

"You know me, John. I don't worry much about winning popularity contests. Just games."

John laughed pleasantly.

"That's for sure. But, Coach, you can't ignore what's going on right now. I mean, it's national news, what with this rally planned. It's gotta have some effect on your job, the team, the—"

"No. No effect. The kids know better than to pay attention to a bunch of lunatics. The media would do well to follow their example."

The expression on John's face made me think he knew damn well Coach was including the *City Cryer* in "the media." Even if they did have crap offices.

"So, you were born in Somalia?" John suddenly, unexpectedly, aimed his next question at Saeed. Who looked as if he'd been drifting off.

Great, I thought. *Here comes the not-so-straight narrative. With major gaps.* I looked at Coach, hoping he might jump in again.

The expression on his face surprised me. Frozen. Moose in the headlights. He saw something coming, and he didn't much like it.

"Yes," Saeed said. "But then we goes to Kenya. To Dadaab?"

John nodded like he actually knew what Dadaab was.

"And you played a lot of soccer there?" he continued.

Saeed nodded enthusiastically.

"Yes, in Kenya, we play every day. It always warm and we go outside. Even when it rains, the rain warm. So I play soccer all the times."

John wrote this down. Then he looked up.

"And how old are you, Saeed?"

It came out of nowhere, that question. Well, nowhere to me. Coach sure as hell knew what was up, because he stood. Took his windbreaker off the back of his chair and slipped his arms through the sleeves, preparing to leave. I followed suit, and Saeed, hesitantly, because he wasn't sure whether to walk out with us or answer the question, stood.

"I am eighteen," he said quietly. John, who remained in his chair, didn't remark on the fact that his "guests" were leaving. He didn't seem at all surprised.

"How do you know you're eighteen?" he asked.

"Boys, please wait for me outside," Coach said sharply.

I took Saeed by the arm and half pulled, half led him out. I closed the door to the conference room behind us, but not before John fired a final question our way.

"Saeed, are you sure that's right? Are you sure you're not twenty years old?" he called out. The door closed.

We should've probably headed down the sauerkraut-stinkin' stairs and waited outside, but instead we listened at the door. We heard raised voices. Well, one raised voice. Coach. We barely heard John.

"Why the *hell* are you sandbagging my player?" Coach demanded angrily.

Blah blah blah, calmly, from John.

"They have no grounds, no grounds whatsoever, and this is

only going to undermine his confidence. Undermine the whole team. How can you not see that? Why are you participating in this?"

Blah blah. Blah blah. Blah.

I turned to Saeed. He looked very worried.

"Do you know what's going on?" I asked him.

"I think," he replied, "some peoples is asks my age. They think I too old. But I got green card, Tom, that says my age! So I don't know . . ."

"Who?" I interrupted him. "Who is asking your age?"

He shrugged. "Coach says I should don't worry. But I worry, Tom! What if they says I too old?"

The door swung open, abruptly. Coach was red in the face and looked surprised to find us standing there.

"What are you two doing lurking out here?" he growled. "I thought I told you to go outside." He didn't wait for an answer, but stomped down the stairs. We followed.

Out on the sidewalk, Coach exhaled deeply. He looked up and down the street, as if he were trying to remember where he parked his car or what he was supposed to do next.

"I'm sorry about that, boys," he finally said. "I should have known better. John LaVallee is a small-minded guy. Always has been. I guess I didn't realize how small."

"What's going on?" I asked. Coach shook his head.

"Nothing you need to worry about. I handled him. So listen: can I give either of you a ride home?" Saeed pointed down the street.

"I walk. My house right here."

"Okay, see you Monday, son," Coach said.

Saeed turned and trotted in the direction of his apartment. I held my ground.

"What?" I repeated. He wasn't going to get rid of me that easily. I could see him trying to decide whether to get into it or not.

"Some people are questioning the eligibility of all our immigrant players," he finally said. "They're clever. They know better than to just target Saeed, because that would reveal their true purpose, which is to get him off the field. Instead, they're going after everyone, on principle, to make it look like they're worried about rule infractions. So they've got the ball rolling to formally challenge the boys' eligibility. If it turns out they're not eligible, our entire season will be thrown out and we won't be allowed to compete at states. Even if they are eligible—which they are; their green cards are absolute proof of date of birth—the challenge alone could get them removed from a couple of postseason games as the matter is being resolved."

I couldn't believe what I was hearing. Why would anyone care so much about high school soccer that they would go through all this trouble?

"Who?" I asked.

But of course, I didn't need to.

"Maquoit," Coach said bitterly. "Alex Rhodes's father is leading the charge. He's a lawyer. He's got the whole athletic department over there whipped up."

It made sense. You don't drive thousands of miles and spend thousands of dollars over eighteen years to sit back and do nothing while a handful of barefoot-soccer-playing immigrants pluck the state championship trophy from your son's hands his senior year.

You sure as hell don't just let the kids *play*. That would leave too much to chance.

I got Mr. Rhodes. I got people like him, and Alex, and all the rest of them who needed to keep us in our place. Greasing the skids for their kids' sports, their kids' college, eventually their kids' jobs. My guidance counselor and my parents—shit, even Don—kept wondering why it was taking me so long to step up and apply to college. Take my place in the world with the Little Lord Fauntleroys and the rest of the rich pricks. Yeah, right.

Here's who I didn't get: John LaVallee. The hometown guy. Who should've understood, more than anyone, what a state championship meant for us.

Why wasn't he on our side? What, in his mind, could possibly outweigh beating Maquoit?

Chapter Twenty-One

I sent Alex Rhodes a message on Facebook. We weren't "friends," so I attached my message to a friendship request. He took several days to respond, but when he did, he agreed to meet me at a Starbucks halfway between Enniston and Maquoit.

Donnie thought I was crazy.

"Certifiable, Tom. And I know nuts, let me tell you. I straddle that line."

We were walking to The Center together. Donnie had done nothing toward racking up community service hours, and I'd convinced Myla that while Mr. Plourde would probably be an impediment to after-school homework, he'd be a lot of fun for the younger kids who just wanted to play. Don was more than happy to go along. He didn't seem grateful or resentful that I was practically holding his hand and telling him what to do about his service.

He just seemed happy to be hanging out. Almost relieved.

"Listen, Alex and I are gonna talk. The two of us, neutral territory. Maybe if we can just *talk*, without any adults around, we can get to the bottom of this."

"Why would he want to get to the bottom of this?" Donnie exclaimed. "He'd love it if our Somali guys got thrown off the team! Then his team might actually win!"

Donnie didn't know Alex. Hell, I didn't either. Not really. But I'd at least spent some time with the guy, played on the same side of the field with him, and . . . I needed to try. Needed to follow up on my gut feeling that he wasn't his dad.

Myla wasn't there when I dropped Donnie off, but Samira waited.

"Hello, Tom," she said to me as her eyes strafed Donnie. Her nose wrinkled, sniffed the air. "Myla said I should show your friend around and introduce him to the kids. She's not coming until later."

"Oh. Okay. But you do know I'm not staying, right?" I told her. I looked around the room. Plenty of kids, but no other adults. "It'll just be you and Don until Myla gets here." I wasn't sure if that was something she'd be allowed to do: working alongside an unrelated guy without another woman or adult.

"And I'm a handful," Donnie said to her. With his lopsided grin. Which, at that moment, went perfectly with the lopsided, overlong hair.

Samira stared right back at him.

"You are Tom's friend, Don Plourde, yes? I am Samira Bashir. Myla told me you want to get community service hours here?" She waited for a response.

"Yes," he said, sincerely. A bit too sincerely. "Otherwise they won't let me graduate. And let me tell you, I *don't* want to spend another year in high school."

Samira shrugged.

"There are worse places than Chamberlain High School," she said quietly.

The expression on Donnie's face went from flippant to chastened in less than a second. Seriously, I'd never seen him knock off the attitude so fast in my life.

"We thought you could play games with some of the older kids," Samira continued. "We have a volleyball set up outside. You want to come?" She turned on her heel and walked out, expecting Don to follow. He glanced over at me, shrugged, and followed her.

"Later, Tom-boy," he said.

Alex sat in one of the deep brown-leather armchairs that makes Starbucks such a comfortable place to settle in and drink expensive caffeinated beverages. Everything in the place was a shade of coffee. I dropped into the armchair facing him.

"You wanna get something to drink?" he said. Funny how both of us dispensed with "hellos."

"I've already had enough," I told him. We both smiled at each other. He held up a big to-go cup.

"French roast. Grande," he said. "I've got practice in the dome tonight and AP calc to study after that. Me and caffeine are big friends." He took a swig of his poison, and we both settled into looking across the little round table at each other. I called the meeting, so I broke the silence.

"You guys practice at night? In the dome?"

He shook his head.

"Premier team does. School team practices in the afternoon." Right. Premier. United Maine, with all their matching gear, guys driving hours for practices that would get them home at 11:00 p.m.

"Yeah. Anyway. I guess I don't have to tell you what I want to talk about," I said.

Alex smiled easily at me.

"Yes. And just so we don't waste any time, let me assure you: it's *not* happening."

"Really? You've dropped the challenge?"

Alex looked puzzled.

"Um . . . there never actually was a challenge, Tom. Just because you decided to make some demand in front of everyone, to get your guys pumped, doesn't mean we have to keep playing your stupid games. Drop it. Move on. Get over it."

I was completely confused.

"Demand? What demand?" I said.

"To paint 'You rock, Chamberlain' on our spirit rock. What the hell do you think I'm talking about?" Alex sounded annoyed.

"Oh . . . that." The whole thing with their rock seemed like ancient history. Was it really only a few weeks ago that shit was important to me? "Right. We made a deal."

"No deal, Bouchard. And for the record? I already went to our principal, and he said to tell you: blow."

I tried to imagine that low, stubby guy saying "blow" to anyone, and couldn't.

"I thought you had more integrity than that, Alex," I said. Something flickered across his face, some expression I couldn't read. He shrugged, but my comment had bothered him.

"Whatever. So, are we done here?" He acted like he was going to get up.

"Actually, that's not why I wanted to meet. We need to talk about the challenge to some of our guys' eligibility."

Bland smile from Alex.

"I'm afraid I can't help you, Tom. I don't know anything about it. What else is new?"

"Your dad is heading it up."

"Who told you that?"

"One of the guys who's fending him off."

"Well, then maybe you should be speaking to my father. Although good luck with that. He's a big talker but not much of a listener." Alex looked steadily at me when he said that. Took another swig.

I tried again.

"Alex. These Somali guys. They're eligible."

"So you say."

"They have green cards that show the date of birth. It's all legal and they're eligible."

"If they're so eligible, why are you so worried that you'd ask to meet me here to talk about it?"

"Because *your father* is making a stink right before we head into the postseason, and our guys might have to sit out a few games while it all gets resolved! It's bullshit, and you know it, Alex."

I wanted to smack him. I wanted to hit him on the side of his big blond head and knock some sense into him. *Don't you see what you're doing, you self-centered, entitled prick?* I wanted to yell.

Which might have been fun, but would only have succeeded in getting me thrown out of Starbucks. I took a deep breath.

"Alex. I'm gonna be straight with you, okay? Saeed. That's the guy we're talking about here. He has no birth certificate. He's a refugee and before coming to this country he pretty much lived in something like a yurt. So no records, no paper. Which means when he was answering questions about his birth date? He estimated. He gave them his best guess. He thinks he's eighteen. His green card says he's eighteen. But he might be younger. And he might be older."

"Thank you, Tom. That's the point. He might be older."

I shrugged.

"And you're gonna prove that how? No one can. So the green card rules. Which means this is all a waste of everybody's time."

Alex didn't reply. He glanced out the window at the parking lot. The strip mall stores. The UPS Store. The Athlete's Foot. A sub shop.

"Can I ask you something, Tom?"

"Okay."

"What happened to you? How come you never played with us?"

It took me a second to figure out what the hell he was talking about. Then I realized: the club team. Back when we were in eighth grade.

"What, United Maine? Simple. I couldn't afford it."

Alex gave a short, dismissive laugh.

"C'mon. The club offers scholarships. You could've gotten one. We *wanted* you. Tons of guys try out, only a few make it, but you? We *invited* you. And you walked away."

I knew I was supposed to be impressed and grateful for that revelation, but instead I felt a little disgusted. These guys were so friggin' pompous. They thought everyone was just dyin' to be one of them.

"A five-hundred-dollar scholarship barely makes a dent in the twenty-five-hundred-dollar fee, Alex. And it doesn't cover all the hotel and food and gas expenses my parents would have had to take on to get me to games. It wasn't personal, man. It was financial."

Here's what I didn't tell him: *I wanted to. I wanted to play with you guys so bad. I wanted to play great soccer, with the best. And sometimes I wonder if the reason I want to beat all you people from Maquoit so much is because I need to prove that I'm as good as you.*

"Why do you give a rat's ass whether I played for United Maine or not?" I said instead. "Seems to me you've done fine without me."

Alex didn't answer right away.

"I don't know. I guess I just never understood," he finally said. "Maybe if you had, we wouldn't be sitting here like this right now."

I stifled the urge to laugh. It struck me that Alex Rhodes was missing something big: whether I played for United Maine with him or not, we'd have *always* ended up here. Maquoit versus Chamberlain.

"So can I ask *you* something?"

He nodded.

"Is winning states so important to you that you'd be willing to play dirty for it? Because that's what this is. It's a bullshit technicality that might knock us out of contention. Seriously, man, is that how you want to win? Because even though I love beating your ass, I've always respected you and thought you were better than that."

His face fell.

Bingo.

This was where he lived. He might be a privileged, full-of-himself jerk, but he was no dope. He knew that beating us without Saeed on the field was no victory at all. Everyone would always wonder whether Chamberlain would have won if they'd had their best player. It would be a hollow victory at best. And Alex was, first and foremost, a competitor.

"I *am* better than that," he said quietly. "And for the record, I know we can beat you, and I welcome the opportunity to do it with your whole team on the field. If it makes you feel any better, I said that to my father." His tone changed. "Not that what I say matters. He's running this show. Pretty much runs the athletic director and the principal, too. So you see, Tom, you're talking to the wrong Rhodes. I may play the game, but my father calls the shots."

I didn't know what to say. I've got a father who always comes to my games, but other than that he's pretty indifferent to sports. I think he would have preferred if I sang in the chorus, to be honest. For the first time in my life I actually felt sorry for Alex Rhodes.

I hoped that feeling would pass.

I stood.

"Then I guess we don't have anything else to talk about," I said.

"Guess not," he said. He didn't get up. As I walked toward the exit, however, I thought of something. I turned to him.

"About that Osama crack. Back at the rock? That sucked, man."

Alex looked surprised. I wasn't sure he even remembered he'd said that.

"That's, like, hate speech, Alex. You can't go around doing that. Even if you were just trying to bug me."

An incredulous smile spread over his face.

"C'mon, Tom, let's not exaggerate. I just said it to piss you off. But you're right: it wasn't nice. And I'm better than that, too."

I stared at him for a moment. The feeling had passed. Probably faster than it should have.

"So you say," I told him. Then I left.

Chapter Twenty-Two

We were on the letter M when all hell broke loose. Varsity had the late practice, so I went to The Center right after school to put in an hour of service. And . . . for other reasons.

Unlike C, M was turning out to be easy. We did *money* and *malab*, which means "honey." As Abdi drew the pictures, I attempted some humor.

"My grandmother has a saying: 'No money, no honey,'" I said. "I guess we could change that to 'No money, no *malab*.'"

Blank stare from Samira.

"It's a comment about relationships," I explained. "Honey, in this case, could mean love. Romance. A few other things, which we won't mention in front of Abdi here." Our guy was actually paying no attention to me at all. He loves to draw. The only time that foot stops swinging is when Abdi's got some crayons or colored pencils in his hands.

"So the phrase is a funny, rhyming way of saying that without cold, hard cash in hand, you can pretty much forget about *holding* hands. Isn't that right, College?" I said that last bit loudly, in the direction of the glassed-in cubicle where Myla was doing some paperwork. Her head shot up, and she smiled at me through the glass.

"What's that?"

"No money, no honey," I called to her. "You've heard that before, right?"

Myla got up from her chair. She joined us in the big room.

"Hmm. Can't say that I have," she said. "But it sounds about right." She was trying not to laugh.

Samira frowned at her.

"But what does it mean?" she asked.

"It means," Myla said, "that it's easier to love a rich man than a poor man."

"It does not!" I exclaimed. "Samira, don't listen to her."

Myla stepped behind me and put her hand over my mouth.

"It means," she continued, "that if a guy wants any affection or attention from a girl, he'd better show up with a very full wallet." She burst out laughing at her own joke. Samira, meanwhile, looked very serious. Pondering.

I pulled Myla's hand off my face.

"It means," I said, looking pointedly at Myla, "that getting along with girls is hard as it is, and being broke only makes it harder." I still had hold of her hand, and I pulled her toward me. She gave me a look and tilted her head toward Abdi. I released her. We'd agreed to cool it with the boyfriend-girlfriend thing around The Center because we didn't want to make anyone uncomfortable. Samira knew what was up, but she was the only one.

Finally she spoke.

"It means," she said slowly, "that life is hard, and if you don't have money you work all the time. To pay your bills and feed your children. But if you have enough money, you can stop work and do the fun things. And that is the sweetness. The honey."

Myla looked at me.

"And just think: English *isn't* her first language."

"Done!" Abdi cried. He slapped his pencil down and held up his sheet. Around the words and definitions he'd drawn a big jar of *malab* and a green one-dollar bill. "I go now, right?" Before any of us answered, he was out of his chair and flying toward the exit. He almost crashed into Saeed, who'd just arrived.

He looked terrible.

If despair were an expression, he'd have been wearing it. His eyes lit on me and he walked right over to our table.

"Tom. I can talk to you?"

Myla and I exchanged a glance and she wordlessly pointed to the office.

I closed the door behind us. There were a couple of chairs, but when I went to sit, Saeed remained standing, so I stood, too.

"I off the team."

Damn. Damn, damn . . . damn. This was bad. I'd known they'd try, but deep down I hadn't been able to believe those Maquoit ass-holes would actually get him thrown off. How the hell had Coach let it happen? Principal Cockrell? Were those guys completely asleep at the wheel?

"Who told you?"

"Coach. Before school end, he call me down. He say we gots to fight, and he say we will win it, but today I off the team. No practice. Nothing."

"Did he say how long you'll have to sit out?"

"He don't know, Tom! I don't know. I ask, 'You need to see the green card?' but he says no. So I don't know!"

I put one hand on his shoulder.

"Saeed, Coach will fix this. You'll just have to miss a couple days of practice probably, then it'll all be worked out."

He nodded, but he didn't look too convinced.

"How are the other guys doing? Ismail, Double M? Are they okay?" Saeed shrugged.

"Yeah, they still plays. They is okay." I wasn't sure I'd heard him right.

"The other guys are still on the team?" He nodded.

"Only your eligibility has been challenged?" I heard my own voice rising.

"Coach say somebody say my age? On my green card? Is maked up. The peoples in Maquoit tell Coach somebody tell them I makes up the age! I don't!"

Oh God. Oh no. Fuck. Fuck you, Alex Rhodes. You two-faced son of a bitch.

I'd handed it to them. Told him Saeed had no papers back in Africa and he estimated his age and might actually be older. I said that. I didn't say it about the other guys, just Saeed. And that's what they were using.

They must've had nothing. Absolutely nothing. Until I opened my big, stupid mouth.

Certifiable, Tom. Even Don had known I was nuts to talk to Alex.

I had to find Coach. I had to tell him what happened.

I beat it out of there, scarcely saying goodbye to Myla and Samira. I got to the fields at least a half hour before JV practice ended, but Coach was nowhere to be found. The JV coach said Coach Gerardi had a meeting and wasn't coming to practice and so he was going to work with us. Told me I could try calling him at home that night or track him down at school the next day.

So I went through the motions at practice, expressing disgust and anger with all the other guys over Saeed's eligibility case. I said nothing about speaking to Alex, nothing about how my fingerprints were all over it. I buried my guilt and my rage and took it out on the ball. Ran a couple extra laps when practice was over, and prayed I could get some sleep and the night would pass quickly.

Then the storm hit.

Chapter Twenty-Three

A nor'easter is a winter storm, but we can get them in Maine as early as October.

It forms when warm air spiraling up the East Coast mixes with cold Canadian air, creating a meteorologist's nightmare. Heavy snow and rain pelt the ground. Winds whip, taking out power lines heavy with wet snow. It usually gets really cold right after a nor'easter, freezing the rain and turning the snow into a sharp crust that makes things especially fun for all the emergency crews trying to restore power and all the people creeping out of their homes to survey the damage and chainsaw the fallen trees blocking roads and driveways.

When you live in Maine, you pretty much get used to weather. My dad likes to say there's no such thing as bad weather, just improper dressing. But a nor'easter is serious. It was a nor'easter that finished off George Clooney in that movie *The Perfect Storm*. When there's one in the forecast, you count on a snow day from school.

You bring in extra wood, stock up on batteries and candles

and lamp oil. Make sure you have plenty of PB and J in the house, because you might not be cooking for a while.

Here's what you don't do: you *don't* go out driving. Especially not with George Morin.

Practice was canceled because of the forecast, and when the final bell rang and kids streamed out of the building toward the waiting buses, it was getting dark. The sun had already been setting earlier and earlier every day; by late November, it would be pitch black by four-thirty. But that afternoon, with the storm coming? Dusk fell early. The clouds were low and thick overhead, and everything was awash in a gray half-light. *Le crépuscule,* in French. I've always loved the feel of that word, like something soft is closing—and end of day is like shutting the lid on a velvet box.

Of course, that's how *le crépuscule* feels at the end of a good day. On a bad day, like that one? It felt like closing a coffin.

I had just come from seeing Coach.

His office is a glorified closet not much bigger than a confessional. It felt like a confessional, with him sitting in there alone, waiting. We didn't have an appointment, but there he was. Seriously, I almost started out with, "Forgive me, Father, for I have sinned," which is the traditional opener. It precedes the long list of all the things you've screwed up and have to tell the priest, who then absolves you, tells you to knock it off ("go out and sin no more"), and assigns you a few prayers to mutter in the pews before you peace out.

My non-Catholic friends think this is the biggest pile of horseshit they have ever heard of. They're like, "Dude, so you can pretty much go out and do whatever because the priest is gonna wipe the slate clean for you on Saturday afternoon?" Which of course is not the point. The point is you're supposed to *stop* doing whatever it is.

But in the whole big Catholic cafeteria line, confession is the part I actually get. That and angels, which, after watching Saeed play, I'm a little more open to. I'm not so sure about the rest of it—the body and blood, the pope, saints—but when I walk into that little dark box and tell Father Whoever behind the grille what I feel guilty about, I'm pounds lighter. Like someone just took a sack of stones from my arms. It doesn't mean I won't mess up again, but for a while at least I believe I won't.

And that feels good.

Coach let me spill. He didn't interrupt once, just let me get it all out. And when I was through, he didn't yell. Didn't tell me what a complete dope I'd been. We just talked, man to man. And yeah, the stones I'd been carrying all day dropped from my arms one by one. Which didn't fix anything, but at least I didn't feel like shit anymore.

"First off," he said, "I want you to let yourself off the hook. You tried to do something to help a friend. That's nothing to be ashamed of. I do wish you'd come to me first, but . . . well, that's water under the bridge.

"Second, I don't think you and I can appreciate how much pressure that young man is under. It explains why he used you."

"You mean Alex?"

He nodded.

"His father was at the meeting I attended yesterday and . . . well, let's just say it can't be easy having him for a parent."

I thought of that summer day at soccer camp, and Mr. Rhodes

speaking to his son. The blinking. Alex was like a dog that's so well trained it doesn't need a leash: it obeys on voice command.

"Why was he there?" I asked.

Coach swore.

"That's what I wanted to know! Why is the president of some private soccer club involved with a public school sports program? But no one seemed interested in answering that question, and it turned out to be a foregone conclusion that they were going to challenge Saeed's eligibility. I don't know why they bothered to waste my time with a meeting."

I felt gut-punched. This was mind-blowingly unfair.

"So Saeed's off?" I said.

Coach shrugged.

"My guess is we'll work this out in a couple of days, but in the meantime, he's benched. I did get *that* concession from them. He can suit up and sit with you guys, but I can't put him in."

A couple of days. We were scheduled to play our first post-season game in a couple of days. And if we lost . . . we were out. Our season would be over.

"Also, Tom, given what you've just told me . . . there's a chance you might get asked some questions."

"What sort of questions?" I asked.

"About Saeed. Whatever you told Alex. They may try to use that against us." Coach said this calmly. Matter-of-factly. As opposed to the adrenaline flips my stomach was doing.

"What do I say if they ask me?" I said.

Coach smiled.

"Do what you always do, son. Tell them the truth. Tell them

to the best of your knowledge, Saeed is eighteen. Exactly what it says on his green card."

To the best of my knowledge. Key words there. Pretty much everything I knew about Saeed was "to the best of my knowledge." Which was none too clear. Bits and pieces I could barely string together. Stories from Myla, a few things from Samira. Plus the dude himself. Laughing, eager, friendly. Fast. What could I say? I liked him.

But I hardly knew him.

"There is some good news," Coach continued.

"Yeah? Surprise me," I said.

"The weather. If the storm we're getting tonight is as bad as they're predicting, we might have a foot of snow dumped on our field. That might push the schedule back just in time to return Saeed to the team."

When I came out of Coach's office, Mike was waiting for me. He sat slumped on the floor, back against the wall. His backpack, stuffed full, lay beside him.

"Hey," I said, surprised. He got to his feet.

"So what's the word?" he asked.

"Say what?"

"Saeed," Mike replied.

I shrugged. I headed down the hall toward the exit. Mike followed.

"He's off. For a while, anyway. Probably long enough to miss the next game or two."

Mike stopped.

"So we're pretty much fucked, right?" he said.

"Pretty much," I agreed. ·

Mike shook his head in disgust and we continued walking.

"How'd you know I was talking to Coach?" I asked him.

"I didn't," he said. "Jake said you'd gone in this direction, and I was gonna ask, since practice was canceled, if we could go over the physics. Torque wrecked me on the last quiz. I really can't figure out the moment arm." He sighed. "I've got the car today. How 'bout you teach me the physics and I'll give you a lift home?"

As we drove to my house under darkening skies, he basically interrogated me the whole way about what Coach said. I didn't have much to tell him, especially because I left out the parts about my meeting with Alex. I just didn't have it in me to explain what had happened there. Mike respected me and I didn't want to lose that.

Even if I didn't deserve it.

At my house, there was a note from Mom taped to the fridge: *Hands off the lasagna. I'm bringing it to Tetu's tonight.*

"Hmm. I don't think she's going to any potlucks tonight, but whatev," I said to Mike. Our first order of business was surveying the microwaveable options in the Bouchard kitchen. Hot food, we agreed, was the goal, because once the storm took out the power it'd be cold sandwiches for the foreseeable future. We started out nuking a bunch of frozen burritos; then I was unsheathing a couple of steaming pasta alfredos from their plastic containers when my cell phone vibrated. My hands were covered in sauce.

"My phone is ringing," I told him. "Right back pocket."

He gingerly reached into the pocket and slipped the phone out. He frowned, glancing at the display.

"It's Plourde," he said. He snapped it open.

"Hey," he said.

"Tom-boy!" I could hear. Donnie was practically shouting.

"Don-boy!" Mike called back. "How the hell are ya?" Pause.

"Who is this?" I heard Donnie say.

"Mike Turcotte."

"Turcotte, you loser. Where's my man Tom?"

"Yeah, nice talking to you, too," Mike said. "Tom's a little tied up. How can I help you?"

"You can put Tom on is how you can help me. Bye-bye, Mikey."

As I rinsed my hands, Mike held the phone out toward me.

"Your buddy's high as a kite," he said grimly.

"Great," I said, taking the phone. I put it to my ear. "Don?"

"Tom-boy!" I heard once again. "Where you and little Mikey at?"

"My house. Fixing something hot to eat before the power goes out. What's up?"

"Man, the power isn't gonna go out. What a bunch of sissies. It's still October! Whoop-dee-doo, it's gonna rain!" Laughter.

Yup. Stoned.

"Tell you what. Call me when you return to earth."

"No, no, don't go! Seriously, bro, I need you." He fought back laughter. I opened the fridge but kept the phone to my ear. There was also some leftover Chinese we could reheat. I gestured to Mike, whose eyes lit up when he saw the white carryout boxes lined up next to the milk.

"What do you need, Don?"

"Hey. So, are you gonna see that little Myla tonight?"

I sighed. He was stalling. Just trying to keep me on the phone.

"Probably not. I don't know if anyone told you, but this is a *real* storm heading our way. Might be a good night to stay home."

"Dude . . . no. That's why I'm calling. We're going out to the speedway. Morin says someone took the gate down."

The Millsap Plains Speedway is about a forty-five-minute drive from Enniston. It's a short track, a third of a mile of semi-banked asphalt where kids from age eight to age fifty go to race. People head out there on Friday nights, with coolers loaded with whatever, and watch cars buzz around. It's not my thing. I like to watch sports where people compete against each other, instead of engines and tires competing against each other. But hey, to each his own.

You're not supposed to drive on the track when the speedway is closed. And it's suicide to drive fast on a banked road that's glazed with ice.

I looked at Mike, who was shoveling heaps of General Tso's chicken into one of my mother's microwaveable bowls.

"He says they're going to the speedway," I told him.

He shook his head, then leaned toward the phone in my hand.

"Do you have a death wish, Plourde?" he said loudly into the receiver. "Pass."

"You're a *woman*, Turcotte!" Don yelled in return.

Mike went back to spooning out the leftovers.

"Don?" I said into the phone. "No way, man."

"Oh, c'mon," he wheedled. He was so out of it. He usually didn't call me when he got like this. "We never do anything together! We used to do everything together, but now it's like, you're always playing soccer, or hangin' out with that *woman*, Turcotte, or with some girl. I mean, I get that. The girls. And Myla? She's nice, Tom-boy. Definitely your type. An in-tel-lec-tu-al." He emphasized each syllable, then started giggling like he'd made a great joke. I couldn't decide whether he was pissing me off or worrying me.

Then I realized: pissing me off. More than usual.

"Let me ask you something, Don. Have you ever noticed that shit happens? All the time. To people who are just walking around, minding their own business. They get cancer. Or lose their jobs. Or they're just out there in the fields, taking care of a cow or something, when out of the bush comes a dude with a gun who burns their house and chases them to a refugee camp. Shit finds us. But you, buddy? You actually go out looking for it. And it blows my mind, because it's not like you don't already have a boatload of shit to deal with!"

I could hear sounds coming from his end, so I knew he was still on the line. I think I surprised him. He didn't realize what a day I'd just had.

"Now, I should probably just tell you to fuck off, good luck, whatever, but I'm stupid enough to put up with your sorry ass. So screw Morin and come over here. We can hang and watch ESPN until the television goes out. You know my mom loves to feed you. You can sleep over."

There was another long silence as he considered my offer.

"Nah. Thanks, but I shouldn't come over right now, if you know what I mean. Besides, I don't have a car. Do you have a car?"

"My parents aren't home from work yet, but Mike's got his car. We've got some homework to do first, but if you can sit still long enough, we'll swing by and get you later." Mike flashed me a look that pretty much summed up what he thought of being transformed into Donnie Plourde's cab service. Whatever.

"I'll be long gone later, Tom."

I glanced out the window. In the fading light the first flakes fell. They turned in the air, spiraling down, hinting of the wind to come. This was so useless.

"Well, then I can't help you," I said shortly. I heard him breathing on the other end.

"Yeah. Well, it was worth a try, right? You have a good night, bro," he said.

I snapped the phone shut without saying goodbye. The microwave beeped, and when I opened the door the smells of ginger and soy sauce wafted out. As Mike and I divvied up the Chinese food, he glanced at me curiously.

"He need a lift?"

I shook my head. I didn't want to talk about it.

We carried our plates and textbooks into the den. As we walked by the big picture window in the living room, I glanced outside again. Already a light dusting of snow had covered the handrails on our front porch and turned the driveway white. It was blowing hard enough to obscure my view of the mailbox. Passing cars had their wipers going and had slowed their usual speed.

In less than five minutes, it had become winter.

Chapter Twenty-Four

The first call that night was from Myla.

My cell vibrated on the nightstand, waking me. I could tell right away that the power had gone off: my face felt cold. The house was silent, empty of the usual background hum from the furnace and the fridge. At the window I heard the soft, bristly sound of sleet brushing the glass. I snapped the phone open.

"Hello?"

"Tom, it's Myla. You awake?"

"Sort of. What time is it?"

"Twelve-thirty. I'm sorry. I keep forgetting you live in real-people time, not college time."

Real-people time versus college time was one of the odd little hurdles we'd had to negotiate in our new in-a-relationship status. Myla, and everyone else at Mumford, it seemed, lived like a skunk. Nocturnal. It wasn't unusual to find her and the rest of her dorm studying at one in the morning. Updating her Facebook at two. Popping Orville Redenbacher at three. In real-people time, aka living in the Bouchard home with parents who went to work and a kid in high school, the lights were usually out by eleven.

"What's happening, College?" I asked.

"Have you heard from Saeed?" she said.

The question was so totally out of the blue that I was a little disoriented at first. *Saeed. Right. Soccer.* I was conscious, I could respond . . .

"Heard from him . . . when? Tonight?"

"Yes." Myla sounded rushed.

"No. Now that I think of it, I didn't see him at school today. I mean yesterday. Yeah, that was yesterday . . . this is tomorrow." Wow. I was *so* not awake. I heard her breathe impatiently.

"I'm sorry. Is something wrong?" I asked. I sat up. The air in my bedroom felt really cold.

"He's missing. Samira just called me and they are really worried about him."

Missing. What the hell did that mean? Just not home and didn't call in? Or wandering outside in a storm?

"Did anyone try calling him?" I asked.

"Yeah, but he's got one of those crappy Tracfones they all use. It's the end of the month, so he's out of minutes. Do you have any idea where he might be? His mother is pretty upset."

"Jeez, Myla, I don't know who he hangs with outside the soccer team. Have they called Ismail, Double . . . er, Muhammad Muhammad, or Ibrahim?"

"I don't know. Do you have their numbers? Not that they have any minutes left, either."

"Yeah, sure, hold on. It's in my phone." I scrolled through my contacts, found the guys' numbers, and read them to her.

"Thanks, Tom," she said when I was done. "You can go back to sleep."

"Whoa," I said. "Don't wake me up, drop the I'm-freaking-out bomb, then sign off. What's going on?"

"I'm not freaking out. I'm just in a hurry to get them these numbers."

"You sound sort of . . . freaking."

She sighed.

"They depend on me for a lot, you know? They don't really know what to do and I think this storm is adding to their panic."

I sighed. Definitely freaking.

"I hate to break it to you, College, but these are competent people who have survived civil war and a transatlantic migration. And that was before they met you, so take a deep breath. Now, don't you think he's just at a friend's house and can't call them 'cause his phone's out of minutes?"

"Probably. I don't know. They're worried he's been in an accident."

"Has anyone called the police to see if there's been an accident?" I asked.

She didn't answer right away.

"Somali people don't call the cops," she finally said in her I-can't-believe-what-an-idiot-you-are voice.

"Uh . . . why the hell not?" I asked her. She wasn't making sense.

"Okay, you know what? I don't have time to explain the whole post-9/11 universe to you, but when the lights go back on, we'll talk. Good night, Cap."

"Myla," I said, but she'd hung up. Great. I obviously said

something that bugged her. Whatever. I was just trying to be helpful. I pulled the comforter over my head and drifted off.

The second time I woke up because someone was banging around downstairs. Chopping wood, sounded like. At—I flipped my phone open to check the time—2:00 a.m.? Seriously? I tossed the covers off and swung my feet over the side of the bed. Cold air enveloped me. Like it was January in my bedroom. I pulled on a sweatshirt and some socks, then made my way to the stairs, hands brushing the walls, searching for the railing in the dark.

A halogen glimmer came from the living room, where I found my dad wearing an L.L. Bean headlamp and wielding a hatchet. He balanced a fat log, end up, on the hearth, and attempted to drive the blade into the cracks. He was making a terrific noise, and there were wood chips scattered on the carpet.

"Whatever you're trying to do, Mr. Bouchard, is not working," I said.

He startled. He hadn't heard me walk in.

"Tom! I'm sorry. Did I wake you?"

I didn't bother to respond. Instead, I threw myself into an armchair and surveyed the mess.

"It's freezing," I said.

He nodded.

"I'm trying to get the stove going but we didn't have any kindling. Stupid. I brought wood in for just this reason, but forgot kindling."

"I'm beginning to understand why you never made Eagle Scout," I told him. He shook his head ruefully. My father is not a hands-on guy. Before he could aim another whack at the log, I got up and took the hatchet from his hands.

"I'll cut kindling if you find matches and newspaper," I told him.

Before long a small fire popped in the open grate of the woodstove. Dad fed the flames with the thin, dry sticks I had shaved from the log, and I handed him the slightly larger pieces of wood. Once we got it roaring, we closed the iron door and let the heat pulse through the room and up the stairs.

I love fires. I love the smell of woodsmoke that permeates our house each winter, love the way my face feels hot from sitting near the stove. I could stare for hours watching the orange-yellow-blue flames lick the edges of the logs and softly dissolve them. I can so get why we've been gathering around fires together since caveman days. Why we form a circle and tell stories or toast marshmallows or chuck pieces of dry pine branches in the middle to make sparks.

So it made sense that sitting here with my dad, feeding the stove and warming the house, I would finally tell him everything that'd been going on with Saeed and the soccer. With Alex and my incredibly stupid attempt to fix things.

His face was still in the firelight as I spoke, and he never interrupted. When he did finally break his silence, his words surprised me.

"I still remember how disappointed you were when your mother and I didn't let you play on that club soccer team," he said.

"Uh, that was a while ago, Dad. I'm pretty much over it."

He looked up.

"Are you, Tom? Or was it the first step along a path that's made you bitter? I worry about that. I worried about that when you went after their rock. Donnie, God bless him, is a goofball. But you? You know better. What motivated you?"

Good question. And hard to answer. Because in hindsight,

it looked so incredibly boneheaded, while back then it seemed so incredibly funny. Badass. *Eff you, Maquoit*—that sort of thing. Which was . . . yeah. Bitter.

"Maybe I am," I told him. "But not about soccer. About everything. These people suck, and they always win. Why does a jerk like Alex go to Amherst while a guy like Saeed gets kicked off his high school team? Why does it feel like half the kids at my school have parents out of work, while everyone in Maquoit drives a Lexus?"

"Everyone in Maquoit doesn't drive a Lexus, Tom."

"Okay. A Hummer, then," I said. He laughed. But I was only half kidding.

"Do you know," he said, "that right before you were born, when your mom and I were looking to buy our first house, we almost bought in Maquoit?"

"Seriously?" I said. He nodded.

"And do you have any idea why we chose Enniston?" he continued.

"Because you didn't want me to grow up to be an asshole?"

He laughed again.

"Because Enniston is where we wanted you to grow up," he said. "Let me ask you something: Why did Alex Rhodes tell his father what you said about Saeed? He told you himself that he wanted to play you guys straight up. So why was he willing to go along with this plan to have Saeed kicked off?"

Pressure. Desire to win. Can't think for himself. Basically a jerk.

Those were the obvious answers, and probably all true, to a certain extent. But I knew the real reason.

"He doesn't know Saeed," I told him. "He doesn't know any

of our guys, and what playing on this team means to them. So it was easy."

Dad nodded.

"Things get a little more complicated when you know somebody's story," he said. "Yeah, it's messy. People get mad when Somalis parked outside the mosque block their driveways. Folks get nervous when a bunch of black men gather to play soccer every evening on fields near their houses. White supremacists show up trying to start a fight . . . it's a mess. But then some Somali lady teaches Maddie how to make *sambusas*. You teach Abdi his ABC's. Saeed teaches you how to kick a goal from midfield."

"I wish," I muttered.

"But you understand," he said. "It's hard to fear someone, or be cruel to them, when you know their story. And aren't you lucky? Knowing all these stories that Alex never hears? Tom, the fact is, life *isn't* fair and bad things happen to good people. But there *are* angels in this world, and sometimes the good guys win."

"You were with me until the angels part, Dad," I said.

He shrugged.

"Don't you think that Myla friend of yours is Samira's angel?" he said.

I gave a short laugh.

"I don't think Myla'd appreciate hearing that," I told him. "She's not much into the religion thing."

"Won't she be surprised," he said, more to himself than to me. He got up to put another log in the stove.

A blast of hot air washed over us when he opened the metal door. I was actually starting to feel a little sleepy again, and thought maybe I'd just crash on the couch. One question still nagged at me, however.

"Did you ever regret it?" I asked him when he sat.

"Regret what?"

"Buying the house in Enniston." He smiled.

"Never. Although sometimes I do worry."

"About?"

"You. And how I don't want you to wind up like your uncle."

"What? Not rich? Working with his hands instead of going to college? That sounds awfully snobby, Dad."

He shook his head.

"Bitter," he said.

That's when my cell went off for the second time that night. It vibrated in my sweatshirt pocket . . . yeah, I'm that guy, the one who's always within reach of his phone . . . and when I pulled it out I saw it was Donnie.

"Dude," I said when I flipped it open.

"Hello?" Woman's voice. Hesitant.

"Who's this?" I asked.

"I'm looking for Tom Bouchard," she said.

"Speaking."

"Oh, good. Tommy." The voice broke. Whoever it was, she was crying. "This is Ruth Plourde."

Donnie's mom.

"Hey, Mrs. Plourde. Is everything all right?" I looked across at Dad. When he realized who I was speaking to, he sat up straight.

"We're at St. Anthony's Hospital," she said. "There's been an accident."

No. No. C'mon, please, no.

"How bad?" I didn't need to ask any other questions. I knew what he'd planned.

She didn't answer right away. I heard her breathing hard, as if she were trying to calm herself.

"Can you get over here? I think he'd want you to be here," she finally said.

"Is Donnie dead?" I asked. Dull sound to my voice. Surreal. I couldn't believe I was saying the words. Asking the question.

"He's in surgery right now," she said. "The phones are out everywhere. I tried calling your house, but the phones are out. I finally asked them if they found Don's phone, because I knew he'd have his numbers in it. . . ." That was it. Mrs. Plourde dissolved.

"We're on our way," I said, not sure she even heard me at that point. Not sure how we'd get across town to St. Tony's in the middle of an ice storm, but I saw that my father was already standing. I snapped my phone shut.

"Oh Jesus, Dad," I said, my own voice catching. "He's finally done it."

Chapter Twenty-Five

Mrs. Plourde sat in a corner of the waiting room, hunched over, as if she wanted to disappear. Dad strode right to her, put his hands on her shoulders. She looked up, her red face puffy and damp. Dad sat, held her as she wept. I stood three feet away, frozen, feeling my hands form these tight, balled fists.

How could something so predictable feel like such a shock?

He'd shattered bones; that much we knew. Especially in the places where the bone actually poked out through the skin. Like a snapped chopstick jutting from his arm.

"Only it was sharp at the top," George Morin explained.

George Morin, the driver. The survivor, who somehow managed to stay in the spinning car after it crashed into a retaining wall, and escape with nothing but spectacular bruising from the airbags. While Don, whose door flew open, inexplicably, even though his airbag inflated? He didn't stay in the car.

"Don't. Don't even speak. You stoner asshole," I said to him, but too late. He'd seen us arrive. He'd come right up to me and started talking. Polluting my imagination with visions of a broken Donnie.

Thrown from a fast-moving car. How do you have any skin left after something like that?

"Why hasn't someone arrested you? Who let you past security?" I demanded, loudly, to his startled face. Heads turned. The entrance to the Emergency Center is flanked by an intake window on one side and a glassed-in cubicle with a security officer on the other. The Sisters of Charity founded the place. God help me, but I didn't feel very charitable at that moment. My father looked up, Mrs. Plourde's face buried in his chest. He frowned and shook his head: *Stop*.

I walked away from George Morin, my father, and Mrs. Plourde and found a seat at the opposite end of the waiting room. I willed my imagination away from those closed double doors that led to the operating rooms. I tried to focus on the past, good times when we were growing up, but even in my memories, Donnie had no luck.

"I've got a lot of uncles, Tom-boy," he used to say about the parade of boyfriends trooping through his mother's house after his dad moved out. "Mom lost her watch again," he'd comment when she was late or a no-show for school concerts and baseball games. "Cleaning lady's on vacation," he'd say with a grin when you'd walk into his kitchen to find an empty vodka bottle in the sink and stale pizza crusts on the counter.

When we were little, my parents usually insisted Donnie come to our house, rather than the other way around. I can count on one hand the number of playdates I had at the Plourdes'. When I did go, Mrs. Plourde would feed us a lot of stuff I wasn't allowed at home, like Twinkies and Milk Duds. She smoked cigarettes, and there were butt-filled ashtrays throughout their house, but she always took her smokes outside when I came over. And no matter where we were—in Donnie's room, or in the yard, or curled on the couch watching television—she'd come over unexpectedly and snatch him up in her arms, swing him around, and squeeze him. "Boys are the best," she'd say, laughing.

If my mother'd done that, I'd have blushed beet red. I'd have wriggled away, told her to stop, I'm playing. But not Donnie. He'd squeeze her right back.

She'd let go before he did.

A nurse at the hospital had called her. After they'd cut away Donnie's clothes, someone found his wallet and ID'd him. Enniston's a small city—hell, the whole state of Maine is a small town—so it was no surprise that a nurse knew his mother and how to reach her.

She'd sat alone while they worked on him. She'd called his dad, but no answer there so she left a message. She'd called her sister in Thomaston, but the sister couldn't head over until the storm stopped. At some point, as she'd told me, she thought to call us, but the phones were out. She'd asked if anyone had recovered Donnie's cell phone, because she knew she could track me down through his contacts.

She'd been holding it together pretty well, but now, as she sat collapsed against my father, sobbing, she was losing it. For a moment I wondered if they could sedate her or something, but then realized that wouldn't work because she was the only relative on hand if . . . decisions needed to be made.

What can you say about waiting?

I guess if it's a new baby on the way and you're hanging out with a bunch of relatives holding balloons and chocolates and little stuffed bears, pacing and impatient to get their hands on the new member of the family, it's pretty cool. That's probably the best sort of waiting there is.

But emergency room waiting? The worst. Time is a lunging dog on a leash when you're in an emergency room. It yanks you forward in ways you can't control, and even though you want to haul it back an hour, two, and change the direction of . . . everything . . . you can't. You can't control it. You can't control anything.

In the limbo, while you wait, you pray anyway. What the hell, right?

Please. Please please please please.

Hours passed. I remember my father pacing. I think Morin left—a rare sign of intelligence. He knew it wasn't a good idea to be in the same room as me. I don't remember talking. At least not out loud. But a steady, one-sided conversation kept going in my head.

Please. God, if you're there, please.

The barest suggestion of morning light penetrated the windows when the doctor walked in. It had stopped snowing and raining. It looked still and cold outside. Frozen. Typical nor'easter. Rips through your town and leaves an icy calling card. The doctor wore scrubs and his eyes darted to the corner of the room where Donnie's mom dozed. He walked over to us.

Please please please please.

"Mrs. Plourde?" he said. Her eyes opened immediately. She nodded. He sat in an adjacent chair.

Oh Christ. He's sitting. That's not good. He's breaking the news to her. Please! Please!

"Your son is in recovery right now. We've stabilized him. . . ."

I missed much of what followed. Partly because Mrs. Plourde broke into hysterical weeping and the doctor, this young-looking guy who was clearly better at setting bones than comforting emotional mothers, eventually had to stop speaking because she couldn't hear him anyway.

Alive. That's all my brain could process. It didn't matter how alive, or what he was left with. He was still with us.

Thank you.

When she calmed down, my dad repeated for Mrs. Plourde everything she'd missed, translating some of the medical jargon for her. He soothed her when fresh sobs broke out, the tears of relief giving way to horror when she realized just how bad off he was.

Donnie had broken bones in seven places. Three breaks were compound, with the bone coming through the skin. The worst was his right leg, and that was the one that had kept him in surgery so long. He would probably be able to keep the leg, the doc said, but even then it would be a while before he'd walk on it again. He'd broken a couple ribs, but as far as they could tell at that point, there was no other internal damage.

The biggest question, he said, was Donnie's brain. He hadn't cracked his skull, but until he regained consciousness they wouldn't know for sure what damage he'd done to his brain.

That was when I had to turn my own brain off and stop imagining. Because while it was hard to imagine him limping or scarred for the rest of his life, it was impossible to think of him as . . . not Donnie. I couldn't go there.

"Can I see him?" Mrs. Plourde asked at last. The doctor

nodded, and she rose unsteadily to her feet. My dad had one arm wrapped around her shoulders.

"Tom, wait out here," he said. "After Ruth has seen Don I'll come back out for you." He didn't wait for a reply; it wasn't a question. They walked slowly from the waiting room and turned right toward the elevators.

Thank you. Thank you. Thank you. Thank you.

My throat was dry. I had the sort of headache you get from clenching your jaw for hours. A Poland Spring cooler at the other end of the room, near the windows, caught my eye, and I got up and filled a paper cone with icy water. I stared out the window as I drank. The sun was rising and the lights of the parking lot had just begun to dim. The clock on the waiting room wall said 5:45. A very early morning for Tom Bouchard. Or was it a very late night?

I crushed the empty cone, tossed it in the trash, and looked up as Jake Farwell walked hesitantly into the waiting room.

"Jake!" I called out.

He looked relieved when he saw me. He took long, fast steps in my direction.

"Kind of early for you, man, don't you think?" I said. Okay, so it probably wasn't fair to joke around with Jake right then, who looked sick with worry. I put one hand on his arm.

"He just got out of surgery and his mom is with him. He's pretty banged up, but the doc says he'll live." The tension in Jake's face melted into relief. He looked like he might cry, actually. Hell, I knew the feeling. I threw my arms around his shoulders, and we did the man hug thing. We held on for a lot longer than the usual man hug thing.

When Jake broke away, he was wiping his eyes.

"Morin texted. It woke me up; I had left the phone on. What *happened?*"

"Seriously? Did he manage to tell you he almost killed Don?" I said angrily.

Just then Lila walked in. She ran over when she spotted us.

"Oh my God, do you guys know how Donnie is?" she exclaimed tearfully. She looked like she just rolled out of bed. Probably had. High school peeps don't do 5:45 a.m. unless they've got ice hockey practice.

"Morin texted you, too?" I said.

"He's texted everyone," she said.

"Are you *shittin'* me?" I exclaimed.

"Tom. Chill," Jake said. "The guy feels terrible. He's telling everybody so that *you're* not here alone. And besides, no one holds a gun to Don's head and forces him to do stupid shit. This stuff is usually his idea, and it's just random George didn't get hurt much."

I wasn't quite ready to let George Morin off the hook, but before I could say anything else, I saw her. Down the hall, talking to someone at the emergency registration desk. She was all bundled up in a coat I didn't recognize, but I did recognize the little spiky-heeled boots. "Be back in a minute," I said to Jake and Lila, and walked toward her.

"Myla," I said, and she turned. Her eyes widened.

"What are you doing here?" she said at the same moment that I said, "How did you find out?"

"Excuse me," she said to the woman at the desk. "I'll be right back." She pulled me down the hall and turned left into a little waiting alcove. There were chairs, some magazines.

"You first," I told her.

"Find out what?" she asked instead.

"About Donnie," I replied.

She looked confused.

"What? I don't know anything about Donnie."

"There's been an awful accident," I began. Then, dammit, I couldn't believe it. After holding it together for, what? Hours? Tears. I was blubbering like a baby, in front of this girl who I'd been trying to convince that I was mature. Great. *Epic fail once again, Bouchard.*

But then her shoulders dropped, and she looked so sorry. I felt her arms around my back, and I buried my face in her neck, and . . . it was okay. It was okay to feel really, really sad. And somehow we ended up sitting, away from the main entrance and people walking in and out, and Myla listened.

When I was done, she was just quiet, because what could she say, really? Then something occurred to me.

"Wait. If you didn't know about Don, what are *you* doing here?"

"I'm with Samira," she said simply. "They still haven't heard from Saeed."

This confused me.

"You're looking for him at the hospital?" I said.

She shrugged.

"Actually, it's the first place I thought of," she said. "To check here and see if someone matching his description was in an accident."

I shook my head.

"Myla, you are probably the nicest, most generous person in

the world. But *why* are you doing this? For God's sake, the cops know all the accidents. Make the call!"

She frowned and said in a low voice, "Tom, there's definitely some stuff going on that I don't really get. But I do know this: the police are a last resort to these people. They don't want any trouble, and their experience is that guys who carry guns are not necessarily out to help you."

"So you're turning yourself into their personal *CSI: Enniston?*" I said. "C'mon, College. Not practical. Or even very helpful."

"I know," she sighed. "But it's not like this was far, you know? You can practically see my dorm from this place. I've told them if Saeed doesn't turn up by lunchtime, somebody needs to call the police."

"Okay," I said. She glanced back at the registration desk.

"I never got a chance to talk to that woman," she said. "Wait here?"

I nodded, and Myla returned to the counter where I found her. I leaned back in my chair, rotated my head on my neck, and felt stiff ligaments crack. Man, I was tired. My eyes settled on a figure standing alone, leaning against the wall no more than a dozen feet away from me. I don't know how I missed her, standing there in her blue *hijab* with the bomber jacket over it, but Samira had been in the alcove, too. Waiting for Myla. I walked over to her.

"Hey," I said.

"Hi, Tommy," she said quietly. We stood there awkwardly.

"I heard you and Myla," she finally said. "I'm sorry about your friend. Is he going to be fine?"

I shrugged.

"Depends on how you define *fine*, I suppose. But he's alive, and that's what counts, right?"

"Where there is life, there is hope," she said seriously. Which was a cliché, but I knew she meant it. It's the funniest thing: all the Somali kids I friend on Facebook are always posting that sort of little wise saying. Like the plaques on the walls of that Somali restaurant. I mean, it's all good, wholesome stuff. It's just this . . . way . . . they have.

I finally thought of something to say.

"You know, your brother? He's a smart guy. I'm sure he's going to be okay."

Samira glanced away. A thin line formed between her eyes. She stared with great concentration down the hall where Myla had gone.

"I mean, he didn't survive civil war in Africa and cross an ocean only to get screwed up in Enniston, Maine, you know?" I said, attempting to lighten her mood. But then I saw her lower lip quiver. Tears spilled from her eyes, tracing down her cheeks in two lines she didn't bother to wipe.

"He has been so upset, Tom," she said. "About the soccer."

"We're all upset," I told her. "But it'll work out. Coach is on it."

"It is so unfair," she continued as if I hadn't spoken. "It makes him angry. And I worry . . . that he is angry."

That surprised me. The Saeed I knew was always smiling.

"I've never seen your brother mad," I said.

"Saeed can be angry," she replied. Her voice cracked.

Maybe it was all the hugging and the crying and the emotion I'd been swimming in for the past few hours that explains what happened next. Maybe it was sleep deprivation. Temporary insanity. Or maybe I just wanted to be nice. Whatever. I didn't think. I just *did*. So I put my arms around her and gave her a big hug.

Samira smelled like perfume. Not like my mom's. More like the stuff at the natural foods store. So maybe that's not perfume at all, maybe it's more like . . . incense? At any rate, it wasn't a girl smell I was used to. Cherisse always smelled like chewing gum. Myla smells like Altoids and her shampoo. Mrs. Plourde smells like cigarettes. Anyway, just something I noticed, no big deal . . .

She stiffened. Her arms remained firmly at her sides, I heard a soft intake of surprised breath, and I realized: I'd crossed the line.

Somali girls is different, I heard in my head. I hadn't known what Saeed meant when he said that, but just then, at that moment, I stepped closer to understanding. I released her, and we both moved away from each other. I looked at her, apology at the ready, but something stopped me. She stared over my shoulder with this frozen, frightened gaze. I turned.

Cherisse and Lila stood not three feet away from us. They looked pretty funny, actually, each of them with their mouths open in these little round O's. Like a cartoon, or something out of a really bad sitcom.

But I knew that what they'd seen and what they thought were anything but funny.

Chapter Twenty-Six

Aunt Maddie tells this story about a friend of hers who works as a physician assistant at a clinic in Portland.

She treats a lot of refugee and immigrant people, and one day she was assigned this really difficult patient no one else could deal with. He was a Muslim guy, African, and barely spoke English. He was experiencing some serious symptoms, but because of the language barrier, plus he seemed emotionally unbalanced, no one could work with him. He would get belligerent when people didn't understand him. He would storm out of appointments, then return unexpectedly and demand to be seen. If he was given orders or a prescription, he'd rarely follow the advice or take the medicine. Some at the clinic thought he was bipolar. Maddie's friend thought his behavior was understandable for a traumatized, displaced person.

For some reason, the two of them hit it off. It took a while, but he trusted her, and slowly she began to get correct information out of him, and she could prescribe the right treatments for him. He began to open up to her, tell her things about his past and his family. He came to the clinic a lot, sometimes just to ask her questions that had nothing to do with his health.

One day, after a good visit, she made a mistake. As they said goodbye, she impulsively threw her arms around him and gave him a brief, friendly hug. Like you'd hug a brother. Or a friend. She saw his eyes cloud over. Saw the pleasant, easy expression on his face change. He left, abruptly, and never came back. To this day she has no idea how he's getting his meds, or whether a doctor sees him. Others report seeing him around Portland, but no one really knows how he's doing.

For the friend, it was like he disappeared.

"The rules are complicated," Maddie said. "They always come back to the same thing: it depends. Is it against Islam to touch a woman who is not a family member, or is it just a cultural taboo? Depends on who you ask or what country you're from. Should a Muslim girl cover up or not? Depends on how strict her family is. Do you have to pray at certain times each day, or can you save it up until after school? Depends."

Myla and I would try to get straight answers out of Samira. One day, while Abdi colored, we asked what she would do when she graduated in a couple years. Myla had wanted an answer to the handshake question.

"It is not all right for skin to touch skin," Samira explained.

"Okay," Myla said thoughtfully. "I'm gonna play devil's advocate here. In America, shaking hands is a sign of respect. It's a *good* thing. So aren't you disrespecting the principal and the whole school, basically, by refusing to shake?"

"So a compromise is made," Samira said simply. "You shake the hand with the *hijab* covering it. You shake, but skin does not touch skin."

"Is that what you'll do?" Myla asked.

"I don't know," Samira sighed. "Probably."

Here's the thing: she was trying to figure out the new rules as well. Trying to figure out what was religion and what was culture. *Haram* versus *halal.* In a strange new world where she was trying to fit in as a new American, but also as a good Muslim. Meanwhile, all the Somali boys around her were sure as hell touching skin. Dressing like rappers, playing sports, hanging out. Like Ibrahim, on my team? Last summer he went to Upward Bound at some college in Massachusetts, and all over his Facebook page he posted pictures of himself with other kids, white girls in skimpy T-shirts included, smiling at the camera with their arms around each other.

The "rules" are freakin' confusing. So did I screw up, like Aunt Maddie's friend? Maybe. Maybe not. It's not like I was making a move on Samira. So I had to trust that we'd get past it.

The big question was: would we get past Cherisse?

In the hospital, there was this slow-motion stupid second where the four of us just stood there looking at each other. Then Samira came to life. She fled down the hall toward Myla.

"Yeah, you run, bitch," Cherisse seethed.

I took one step toward her.

"That was *not* what it looked like," I said.

She laughed.

"Things are always what they look like," she retorted. "You surprise me, Tom. I didn't know you liked chocolate." The anger I felt toward her right then was so intense I could practically hear it. Like waves crashing, and someone turning up the volume.

"No wonder you wouldn't tell anybody who your new girlfriend was," she continued.

I got up in her face.

"You are a stupid bitch. And no one—*no one*—wants you here."

Genuine surprise flickered across her eyes. Then they narrowed. But before Cherisse spoke again and made me do something I'd regret, I quick-stepped away from her. I headed toward the waiting room, the registration desk. At the end of the hall, I spotted more kids from school. Word had spread about Don, and the tribe was gathering.

I could also see Myla and Samira, with Samira speaking urgently to her and pulling her by the arm toward the exit. Myla caught sight of me and stopped. Yanked her arm away, actually. Samira ran from the building.

"Tom, I'm sorry, but I've gotta go," Myla said as I approached. "She's, like, hysterical to get out of here for some reason."

Get her out, fast, I managed to not say.

"Saeed?"

She shook her head.

"Not here. We're going to drive to the housing project where a few of his friends live. See if they know anything. I'm sorry. I'm really sorry I'm not staying with you." She slipped her arms around my waist and squeezed. The top of her head brushed my chin.

"It's okay. Really, I'm fine," I said. We were standing just outside the waiting room, and I caught the eyes of a couple of my classmates who had just arrived. I read it in their expressions as they watched this little interchange: *What?* I stepped back. "Call me as soon as you hear something, okay?"

She stood on tiptoe and kissed me.

"You too," she said. Then she headed out to the parking lot and Samira.

Someone came up behind me. Jake.

"You're the only guy I know, Tom, who can meet girls at a hospital," he said.

Hours passed. Dad and I waited for Mrs. Plourde's sister to arrive from Thomaston because Dad didn't want to leave her alone. People came and went, most notably Cherisse, who, shortly after Myla beat it out of there, stormed through the exit door, texting all the way. Lila scurried after her like an indignant lady-in-waiting. In the back of my mind warning sirens sounded, but I was too dog-tired to respond and too relieved to see her go.

At some point my father took me in to see Don.

It was bad.

First thought that popped into my head when I walked into his room: *It's not him.* He was that unrecognizable. That wrapped. Not just the one busted operated-on leg, but his chest, wound tight (the broken ribs), and his head and face mostly covered. The bits of him that were exposed were swollen and purple from bruising, and tubes snaked out of more places on him than I cared to count.

He was unconscious, but I spoke to him anyway. Quietly, in his ear.

"I love you, bro. I'm here. We're all here." I waited for a sign. An eyebrow twitch. Slight movement of the head. Some indication that he heard me.

"Even Sister Marie is here," I said. A total lie, but if anything could make Donnie get up from that bed and walk, maybe even run, it was Sister Marie. I moved back slightly, half expecting his eyes to flutter open.

But he was really out of it. I tried not to let myself imagine the possibility that he'd *stay* out of it.

Back in the waiting room, I was glued to my phone. Myla texted: *Still no Saeed*. Mom called: she'd brought Grandma to our house to sit by the warm stove. She said Paul had come by to see if we were all right. He was out with his chainsaw cutting limbs and trees that blocked driveways and making some cash. Devon, who doesn't even like Don, texted: *Howz the boi?* Aunt Maddie called: she was fine, just checking in. Mike Turcotte texted: *WTF Tom is C kidding?* Mom called: our power was back on.

Mrs. Plourde's sister and the second call from Mom arrived at the same time. I was actually waiting for a response from Mike, because I'd texted *???* in response to his *WTF*. Dad patted me on the knee.

"Time to go," he said. "A hot shower and warm bed await." I closed the phone and shoved it in my pocket.

As we drove, we got a good look at the storm's damage. A lot of lines were down, some sparking dully on the ground. Twigs and branches were pretty much everywhere, but in some places whole trees and big limbs had crashed on roofs and landed on parked cars. Ice and snow were melting wherever the sun struck, but in the shady places clusters of trees remained glazed. They sparkled. Beautiful and treacherous at the same time.

And like a good neighbor, State Farm is theeeeeeere, played inside my head as I looked out the car windows and checked out the damage. Man, you know you're beyond exhausted when the insurance jingle takes up space between your ears. Sleep. I needed sleep.

My phone vibrated in my pocket. Another text. I flipped it open. Mike finally got back to me.

C posting shit about u and a Somali girl. What up??

I stared at the words on the screen. It was the last thing I needed.

Posting what? where? I texted back. Waited.

Facebook. Texts too. ?????

I pressed furiously with my thumbs.

What shit? Waited again. A while. Damn.

Then, finally: *"Bouchard's new girlfriend is a Somali slut." C + L saw you making out w/her at the hospital. ?!?!?*

"Ha!" I burst out. Dad glanced at me.

"Something funny?" he said, smiling faintly.

"Not in a good way," I replied as I keyed a response to Mike. It was all so ridiculous. The girl was so stupid. No one would believe such crap. It occurred to me that it might have been a very good thing that Jake had seen me and Myla together at the hospital.

Total lies. I'm dating a girl from Mumford.

I don't know why I left out a few key details. Maybe because I knew how innocent the hug was but how pointless explanations would be. Subtleties are wasted on the Chamberlain High School mind. Better to keep it simple: nothing happened.

Of course, something had. But not what Cherisse thought.

The phone vibrated.

C just posted a picture.

"Of what?" I exclaimed involuntarily. Before I got out of the car I texted him a line of question marks. My father stared at me curiously as we headed into the house. I practically tripped on the stoop because I was watching the screen and walking at the same time. Finally he texted back.

New girlfriend wears head scarf?

I raced up the stairs to my bedroom without speaking to my mother or saying hello to Grandma, who was sitting in the living room. I fired up my laptop, logged on to my Facebook account and . . . there it was. A brand-new post on my wall from Cherisse Ouellette, who was oh so kind enough to "share" it with her 1,584 "friends." A photo taken with her Verizon Wireless phone.

You couldn't see Samira's face or her jacket; they were blocked by my shoulder. But you could clearly see her bright blue *hijab* and see that she's black. And you could tell it was me. I was wearing my team T-shirt, with my name and number blasted right on the back. We'd bought them with money we raised selling candy bars and cookies and bottles of Poland Spring water at the refreshment shed.

Here's the thing about luck: it's a bitch. Curls up next to you one minute, then bites you the next. You meet a Myla and think, *Damn! I'm a lucky guy!* Then you turn around and there's Cherisse, phone at the ready. She's like one of those Hollywood stars you see in *People* magazine who have a Starbucks in one hand and a very visible cell in the other.

I mean, what were the chances? But that's luck for you.

I thought, *Is this what you want, God? Did Tom Bouchard not have enough on his mind? Was life getting too easy and predictable for Samira's family? Fine. Hurl us headlong into the shitstorm of gossip Cherisse has created. So long, life.*

I waited. Seriously, I waited for my answer. Because you know what? It had been a *bad* night, and some *bad* stuff had gone down, and I was thinking it was about time somebody upstairs started coughing up answers.

That's when I heard him.

Not God. I never hear God. I heard Dad, calling from the stairs.

"Tom! Come quickly. It's Ruth on the phone. Donnie is awake!"

My aunt Maddie has this really annoying habit, whenever life spins out of control, of saying, "God speaks in mysterious ways."

Uncle Paul says that's just another way of saying, "Shit happens."

Chapter Twenty-Seven

I spoke, while across town Mrs. Plourde held the phone to his ear. She told us he could blink—twice for yes and once for no—if you asked him a question. He couldn't talk. Too many stitches around his mouth.

"So I sit in the emergency room for, what? Almost nine hours. And you decide to wake up *after* I leave? You know, Plourde, it's a relief to know you're still an asshole."

My parents both startled when I said that. We stood in the kitchen, within earshot of Grandma in the living room. I looked at them and shrugged.

Grandma had grown up in a mill town. She'd heard worse.

"Tom?" I heard from the phone. Mrs. Plourde. "I don't know what you just said to him, but it looked like he . . . laughed. Keep talking."

I turned to the window so I had my back to my folks. Outside, everything was melting. Cars swished past on the wet road.

"By the way, don't expect flowers from me. I am seriously pissed at you, man. To begin with, thanks to you, now I have to go out and murder George Morin. And you know I'm going to get caught, and murder charges are really going to screw with my future. So, thanks. I'm going to wind up in prison instead of college, and it's all your fault.

"Second, don't even *think* about dying. You hear me? I need you to walk out of that hospital and come home so I can beat the *shit* out of you. That's how mad I am, you stupid jerk."

My father came up behind me. He reached for the phone. Angrily I twisted my arm around, away from him. I glared and he stepped back.

"Don't you know? Don't you realize that people *love* you? I don't know why, 'cause you're such an asshole. But your mother? You're all she's got. And you don't know it, but half the freakin' high school came by the hospital to see how you were. Stupid, right? Everybody all upset about a guy who doesn't give a rat's ass about himself?

"Which probably makes me the dumbest of them all. Because I love you. You're my family." My voice broke. I was losin' it.

"So here's what's gonna happen. You're gonna get better, which, by the way, will hurt like hell, because you screwed up your leg and will probably needs tons of physical therapy. Then, after you get better, and if I don't beat the crap out of you, you're gonna graduate from our shithole of a high school. You and me. We are crossing that stage together. Even if I have to push you in some damn wheelchair, you're doin' it. You hear me? Blink twice." I stopped talking. With my free hand, I rubbed my face. My hand came away wet.

I waited. No one spoke.

"Blink harder. I can't hear you." There was a noise from the other end. Like a grunt or a groan. Then, Mrs. Plourde.

"Tommy? We should probably stop. He's trying to talk, and that's not a good idea right now. But I think he heard you, dear. He's blinking his eyes a lot. So that's good. It's good he understands, you know?" She sounded like she was crying, too.

"You'll come by later?" she asked. "With your folks?"

"Yeah, for sure," I said. She hung up.

When I turned to face my parents, Mom was boo-hooing as well. I placed the receiver on the counter and wrapped my arms around her shoulders. Dad put a hand on my back.

"Well," he said, "you might want to reconsider your plans and pursue a career as a motivational speaker."

Later that afternoon, when I was on the phone with Myla, she put it another way.

"You're just a real warm and fuzzy guy, aren't you, Cap?"

I was stretched out on my bed, the curtains drawn. It was late afternoon, and I'd just woken from a nap. That was all I'd managed since speaking with Don: a shower, bed. I'd even turned the phone off. When I did wake up, there were three messages from Myla.

"I know, right? Regular teddy bear. That's me."

She laughed softly. Which was a relief. Myla gets me. And right then I really needed that.

Because I had some serious explaining to do about the Cherisse and Samira thing.

We talked about Don for a while. Then switched the topic to Saeed. They still hadn't heard from him.

I sat up.

"Myla—" I began.

But she cut me off.

"I know. I know. And yes, I did it. They were not happy with me, but I didn't back down. I actually took Mrs. Bashir and Samira down to the police station to report that he was missing and to give them a photo."

"And?" I said.

She sighed.

"We wait," she said simply.

"No, I mean, how did it go? With the police?"

"You know . . ." Her voice trailed off. "To be honest: weird. I mean, they took it seriously, which is good. They didn't just blow Mrs. Bashir off, like she was some worried foreigner making a big deal out of nothing. In fact, it was just the opposite. They kept us there for a while and asked a lot of questions I didn't quite get. Like, about their mosque, and whether Saeed spent a lot of time there. Really bizarre. Or that's how it seemed. I don't know, I was so tired. *Am* so tired."

"Tell me about it," I said.

"Hey, at least you got to take a nap today," she said. "I drove around town for hours in crap weather."

"Story of your life, College."

"Hey, how about some sympathy? I mean, I like Samira, but sometimes? I feel like calling me is part of her daily routine, like brushing her teeth. But she always seems to have something urgent to deal with."

"Yeah," I said hesitantly. "Speaking of that . . ."

"Bad intro, Cap. Especially when I'm this tired."

I climbed out of bed and went to my desk. The computer was still on and open to Facebook. I checked my wall.

There were fifty-seven comments on the photo Cherisse posted. The first two were immediately visible.

Bouchard, you wild man! Who is she?

WTF, Tom.

"Uh, are you near your computer?" I said to Myla.

"I'm always near my computer. Why?"

"Open Facebook. Go to my wall. Then I'll explain."

I heard the rapid staccato of Myla keyboarding as I scrolled through the comments. As I went down the list of all fifty-seven comments, the "discussion" deteriorated. What began as jokes and questions morphed into meanness as Cherisse's girlfriends chimed in. Morphed into obscenity as some of the guys tried to get funny. Racism. Sexism. Then fighting and personal attacks as people called each other out for all the isms. It was a street brawl, right there on my wall. Then, near the end, comment number fifty-three, if I counted right: the red flag.

Who is the girl, Tom?

Ismail. We were Facebook friends. Hell, I'm friends with all the guys on the team.

"Oh. Wow." Myla had opened the page.

"I can explain," I said to her.

"That'll be interesting," she said. "Oh. My. God." She was reading through the comments.

"You know when you went to the desk, to ask about Saeed?" I said quickly. "She was crying. I mean, she never cries! She's always so . . . tough. Distant, especially with me. And I just felt *bad* for her, Myla . . ."

"That was why she practically ran out of the place!" she exclaimed. "I was wondering what was up."

"Cherisse saw us and took a picture. I know, crazy, right? What were the odds of that? But it happened, and . . . Myla, you *know* this is all bullshit. I have nothing going on with Samira."

"Tom. Please. Don't even go there. The problem is way, way bigger than that."

I already thought the problem was pretty big, so Myla's comment didn't make me feel too good.

"Wow," she repeated. "This is baaaaad." She was reading through more comments. "How glad am I that I'm not in high school anymore? Yours in particular."

"These people suck," I muttered.

"Not all of them," she commented. "In response to 'So Bouchard's screwin' a fucking raghead? Who gives a fuck?' one very enlightened person replied, 'It's not a rag it's a burka you fucking moron and Tom can screw whoever the fuck he wants!' Now *there's* a great person to have on our side. Although I am tempted to type in a little response myself and clear up this burka thing. Don't they realize it's a *hijab*?"

"Myla. Seriously."

"Tommy, if I don't joke around right now, I'm gonna cry. This is so, so bad."

"Really? I mean, why so so bad? Why not just . . . bad?"

"Uh-oh," I heard her say.

"Now what?" I asked.

"Who's Ismail?" she said.

I sighed. She'd made it to comment number fifty-three.

"Guy on my soccer team," I said.

"Friend of Saeed's?" she asked.

"Yeah, sure," I said. There was a long pause, and I heard more keyboarding.

"Bad. Bad bad bad bad bad . . ."

"Okay, stop it, you're freakin' me out. What?"

"Are you friends with Samira? Facebook friends?"

"No."

"I am. There's one comment on her wall from a Somali girl named Fatuma. I don't know her. She's written, 'You shame your family.'"

There was a long pause as I processed this information.

"I'm sorry. What?" I finally said.

"Shaming the family is huge. I can't tell you how huge. And a big part, probably the biggest part, of a family's reputation, is the purity of its women. How your girls behave, how they dress, what people think of them, is a direct reflection on the family. This comment by this Fatuma means the Somali kids on Facebook have seen the picture and someone recognized Samira. The wolves are circling."

"But, Myla, Samira did nothing. *Nothing!*"

"What she did is irrelevant if people say otherwise," Myla replied. "Welcome to the hell of Somali gossip. In a close-knit community like this, it spreads like wildfire. And on Facebook? We're talkin' viral. At least, within your high school."

My head spun. This was so stupid.

"So what do we do?" I said.

"I hate to say this, because I've got serious amounts of reading to do before my class on Monday, but I think we're heading over to the Bashirs'. Like, now."

Chapter Twenty-Eight

Until you've been on the other side of it, you don't know how scary The Law can be.

I thought I knew. Thought me and Don's brush with The Law over the rock was some life-altering moment in the up-to-that-point fairly charmed life of Tom Bouchard. But I didn't know shit. I didn't know real fear at the point of a gun. I didn't know what it meant to be powerless, to stand by helplessly as your life blew up before your eyes.

If I'd had any clue about any of that, I never would have pushed Myla to report Saeed missing. And maybe if she hadn't been so tired and so worn down by it all, she might have given me a bit more pushback. Because her instinct was to wait, to not rush to the cops.

Turns out she understood these people way better than I did.

We arrived at the apartment building to babies crying, doors open, nervous families peeking down the hall, and two plain-clothes detectives sitting in the Bashirs' living room. Aweys answered when we knocked, just cracking their door and peering through the space. When he recognized Myla, he threw it open wide.

"They is police here," he whispered to her as we kicked off our shoes. His eyes were enormous, round.

"Police?" Myla whispered back.

He nodded solemnly.

"They is want Saeed," he said.

"What the fuck . . . ," I heard her mutter under her breath as she strode in the direction of the living room. Aweys and I followed her.

Everyone was sitting. Two men wearing dark suits, in chairs I recognized had been dragged in from the kitchen. The rest of the family—Mrs. Bashir, Samira, two little boys who seemed younger than Aweys—in a stiff, silent line on the couch. The low coffee table, which was usually strewn with toys, had been cleared for a ceramic teapot and mugs. Somali hospitality. Mrs. Bashir would have been sure to offer her interrogators a hot drink.

"Hi," Myla began. "Is . . . uh, this a bad time?"

One of the men stood.

"This is Myla! The one I tell you about!" Samira said.

Her voice was altered. Not only was her grammar off, but the sound was higher-pitched, the words rapid. She wore clothes I didn't recognize: a dark *hijab* and a skirt to the floor. In the dim room, she and her mother seemed shadowed and small.

The man held out his hand.

"I'm Detective Lloyd Parker, this is Detective John Baylor." He tilted his head toward the other guy. "We're following up on a missing-person report. Are you the young woman who brought the Bashirs to the station earlier today?"

"Yes," she answered. Simple. Short. Telling the truth without volunteering information.

"And this is . . . ?" His eyes met mine.

"Tom Bouchard," I said. I held his gaze.

"He is friend to Saeed!" Samira said.

Parker looked at me with a bit more interest.

"You know Saeed Bashir?" he asked.

"Yes," I said. His glance flickered briefly to his partner, who nodded at him. Made you wonder if police school had taught them how to communicate telepathically.

"Why don't we step into the other room, Tom. I'd like to ask you a few questions. If you don't mind."

Wrong. Wrong wrong wrong. Everything about the whole scene felt wrong. The family was scared. Petrified, actually. Mrs. Bashir looked practically catatonic. Samira was a wreck. Even Aweys seemed to sense that this was not good.

Trouble was, I didn't have a good reason for *not* speaking with him. I followed him into the kitchen.

It seemed like there were pots and dishes everywhere; a lot of cooking had been going on. Smelled like frying. Lloyd sat in one of the remaining kitchen chairs and gestured to another. I sat.

"So, how do you know Saeed?"

"We play soccer together at Chamberlain High School."

"Teammates?"

"Yes."

"Have you known him long?"

I shook my head.

"I just met him this fall."

"So this fall was the first time he'd gone out for soccer?"

"He just moved here."

"From . . . where? Where was he before he moved to Enniston?"

"You'd have to ask his family. Or check with our school. I can't comment on what Saeed did or where he was before I knew him."

I think it was the "I can't comment" comment that signaled to Detective Lloyd Parker that I wasn't fooled by his friendliness. He leaned back in the chair and eyed me critically. Like he was sizing me up.

"How *well* do you know Saeed Bashir, Tom? And please . . . think carefully before you answer."

I shrugged.

"I don't know him well. He doesn't speak very good English and he's only been at our school since September. The people I know well I've known all my life. But here's what I do know: He's a good teammate. He gets along with everyone. He plays soccer really, really well. He's friendly. I mean . . . that's it."

"Religious?" he asked.

I frowned.

"He's Muslim, if that's what you're asking."

Parker laughed softly.

"No, I knew that, Tom. But I'm wondering if Saeed struck you as *particularly* religious. Did he go to the mosque more often than usual? Belong to any religious clubs? Seem to be . . . rigid? Or orthodox in any way?"

I shook my head.

"I don't know. I mean, he's a practicing Muslim. Like, they've been fasting for Ramadan, all that. He doesn't drink. I know he went to the mosque to pray before our last game. He did tell me that."

Parker smiled.

"And did Allah hear his prayers?" he asked.

I stared at him.

"As a matter of fact, he did," I said. *Do you want to know the score?* I managed to not say. I took a deep breath instead.

The detective changed directions.

"Do you know if Saeed was upset about anything? Anything bothering him recently?"

"Actually . . . yeah," I answered truthfully. "He's been benched. Another team, the one we beat last week? They've challenged his eligibility, claiming he's too old. So Coach can't play him until the whole thing's resolved."

Parker nodded.

"And how did Saeed react to that?"

"He was pretty disappointed. He loves soccer."

"Was he angry?" he asked.

I laughed.

"Are you kidding? We're all angry. You want to see *really* angry, you should go talk to our coach."

"No, I mean Saeed in particular," he said, cutting me off. "Did you see him get angry about this?"

I thought about that for a minute. Actually, I hadn't seen Saeed angry about it. I saw him upset. Worried. Sad. Really sad that he'd been taken off the team.

But Samira . . . she'd said he was angry. Could get angry.

If I hadn't seen it myself, was it fair to tell the cop?

"Why are you asking me these questions?" I said instead. "Shouldn't you be asking me, like, when was the last time I saw him? Answer: K Street Center, two days ago. Where does he like to hang out? Answer: the Somali store on Market Street. They watch international soccer pretty much 24/7 over there. How about, who are his other friends? Answer: I can tell you who I know, and give you their numbers.

"Meanwhile, shouldn't you be *looking* for him?"

Parker was silent. He seemed to be trying to make up his mind about what to say next. Maybe trying to decide whether I was keeping anything from him.

But I didn't have much to keep.

"Do you know what's been happening in the Somali community in Minnesota?" he asked.

I shrugged.

"No clue."

"Young Somali men, mostly teens, are disappearing. Into thin air, with no word to their families. Recently, federal authorities tracked down a few of them. They were in Somalia, where they'd joined up with an Islamic militia. Apparently they'd been recruited through their mosque in Minneapolis and were training to be terrorists."

Whoa. The guy was serious. This wasn't Alex tossing around rude Osama comments. This was . . . real.

"Are you a fed?" I asked without thinking. First thing that popped out of my mouth.

He shook his head.

"No, we're Enniston detectives. But there's a very clear protocol we have to follow in cases like this. So if we don't start getting some answers about your friend, Saeed, very soon, our next step is to contact federal agents."

"Hold it! Hold on. You think Saeed is a *terrorist?*" The word sounded strange in my ears.

"We don't assume anything. But he's beginning to fit the profile. Young, observant Somali male. Recently suffered a big disappointment. Disappears without a word to his family—"

I cut him off.

"You've got to be kidding me! Saeed is, like, the last guy who would ever do something like that! He likes this country and he loves being part of things here. Being part of a team."

"The last young man who blew himself up in a shopping area in Somalia was an honors student at his high school in Minnesota and ran varsity cross-country. He took out ten people with a homemade bomb strapped to his chest."

Parker said that without a trace of emotion. He wasn't trying to convince me I was wrong. He just knew I was, and didn't care what I thought as long as I told him everything.

I shook my head slowly, trying to shake my thoughts clear. Like one of those little plastic boxes with the tiny silver balls you roll into the indented spaces. You had to be deliberate, careful, if you wanted to set everything straight.

I looked up at Detective Parker then, completely ready. To tell all. Anything. Everything I could possibly dredge up, from the handful of very confusing conversations I'd had with Saeed over the past weeks. Maybe there was something he could use. Some random detail that didn't mean much to me but revealed everything to him.

That's when I saw him. Standing in the kitchen entrance.

He had his backpack slung over one shoulder, and his clothes looked crushed. Like he'd slept in them all night. He looked tired.

"Hello," said Saeed, his eyes resting on Lloyd Parker. "Who you are?"

Chapter Twenty-Nine

The Chamberlain High School soccer team wasn't the only one Saeed played for. In Portland, someone had organized a league of immigrant kids, and whenever he could manage to find a ride, he'd go there for games.

Something I didn't know, and his family and Ismail and the other guys didn't think to mention. Or that the detectives would think to ask. Maybe, if they were actually looking for a missing teenager, instead of building a "profile," they'd have pulled that sort of information out of someone. Realized he was in Portland, with a bunch of his *other* teammates, when the power went out and his Tracfone ran out of minutes. Too clueless about the weather and what a nor'easter was all about to realize he should have stayed put. Unable to find a ride back to Enniston until late the following day.

Here's the thing that really sucked: they'd almost got me believing their story. They'd almost convinced me, despite everything I knew and *felt* about Saeed, that maybe, deep down, he couldn't be trusted.

Myla and I beat it out of there pretty soon after he turned up. Even the cops didn't seem to want to hang around when Mrs. Bashir lit into her son. You didn't need to speak Somali to get her drift, jumping up from the couch and throwing her arms around him when he stepped reluctantly into the living room. Her cries of relief quickly switching to something more like hysterical anger. The universal language of worried, pissed-off moms. No translator required.

I waited until the next day, Sunday, to call him. Did he want to go out, get something to eat? I'd pick him up?

We went to McDonald's. He loves Big Macs.

It was the same McDonald's I'd gone to with Donnie the night of the rock. I thought about that as we carried our plastic trays and bags of food to a table. Donnie with his wrinkled flannel shirt that had bits of wood chips sticking to it. He'd partied most of the night, stacked wood all day, then sat here with me to plot more action. Made you wonder: was he incapable of sitting still, or was he afraid to sit still? Was all his restless bouncing from thing to thing beyond his control, or was it a way to keep from thinking too much? Feeling too much? It's hard to think when there's a lot of background noise; easy to think when you're alone and it's quiet.

He was going to have plenty of quiet time on his hands now. I'd stopped by the hospital on my way to pick up Saeed. They'd moved him out of the intensive care unit, but no one could tell him when he'd get sprung from the hospital.

Saeed seemed tired. He had sunken half-moons beneath his eyes. He told me he'd slept on somebody's couch the night before, and when the power went out it had gotten cold. He hadn't known, until he arrived home, that everyone had been worried about him. He was sorry about that. He was sorry that Myla had had to drive his sister around looking for him.

We'd taken about a dozen ketchup packets, and squirted most of them over our fries. Saeed also got a big Coke. I got a shake.

"Did Samira tell you what happened at the hospital?" I began.

He nodded. He looked out the window.

"How your friend? Don?" he asked.

"Bad," I said. "I mean, he'll live. But he's pretty hurt."

"He drinking," Saeed said. Not a question.

"Yeah. He won't be drinking now. Not for a looong time." I took a big swig of shake. It was so cold it made the back of my head hurt.

"In Islam, is *haram*. Forbidden. To drink," he said seriously.

"Not a bad rule," I said.

"Is good rule," he said.

I took another pull on the shake.

"Samira didn't break any rules," I told him, redirecting the conversational ball.

"Tom. In Islam, there is many, many rules—"

"Samira didn't break any rules," I repeated, a bit more slowly.

He sighed. He didn't seem very interested in his food.

"Samira is a nice girl. She's smart. She works hard. You know she's a good kid, Saeed. You know."

He looked me frankly in the eyes.

"Yes, I know this, Tom."

"I broke a rule, Saeed. Not her. Okay? She was worried about you, and she was crying, and I . . . felt bad for her. Like I felt bad for Donnie's mother. Same thing."

"Somali girls is different, Tom," he said quietly.

I threw myself back in the plastic chair. I was hitting a wall here. A glass wall, and I couldn't figure out how to bust through and make him *hear* me.

"I get that, okay? I know I screwed up. But there is nothing going on between me and your sister, and that picture is a lie. I mean . . . the picture isn't a lie. It happened. I hugged her. But the posts and the captions? Total lies. That's my old girlfriend, Cherisse, making that stuff up."

"I think she not nice girl," he said.

I laughed.

"That's one way to put it." I wasn't gonna get into all the other choice adjectives I could've used to describe Cherisse. "That's why I'm not seeing her anymore. I'm going out with Myla now."

He looked at me skeptically.

"Samira say that. I think, Tom, you with lot of girls."

"I only go out with one girl at a time. I'm a serial monogamist." He frowned. Of course he didn't know what that meant. And why was I making jokes at that point? I think I just wanted to erase the closed, shut-down expression on his face. It was so not the guy I knew.

Saeed pushed his food to one side and leaned forward. His hands on the table formed this little teepee as he spoke.

"Is good that Samira smart. Is good that she work hard. I know these things, Tom, of my sister. But for Somali peoples is one most important thing. And that is religion."

I nodded.

"Okay. I get that. So . . . ?"

"In Islam, it say woman must not show hair, or the skin, to man outside family. Woman must not touch man outside family."

"She didn't. I did. And for the record: she ran." He nodded gravely.

"Samira say that. I believe, Tom. My sister is . . . true. But in picture, Tom, she don't run. And picture is what peoples see."

And a picture's worth a thousand words, stupid. In spite of what I know about my sister, and what I know about you, my friend, the world and its pictures tell a different story.

"What are we gonna do?" I asked him. *About everything. About your sister. About soccer. About this. Misunderstanding, wide as the ocean.*

"I don't know," he said. "Is bad. I get message from Ibrahim. He say, 'What your sister do, Saeed?' I says to him: 'Nothing! You know Samira! You know Tom!' But is just me says that. We have no father. No family here. My mother? She cries and she says she wish we had uncle. Or somebody." He unwrapped one of the Big Macs. It smelled of onions and special sauce.

"Just keep telling the truth," I suggested.

Saeed looked me in the eye. He raised one brow skeptically.

"Hmph," he said, biting into his sandwich. One little *hmph*, which pretty much summed up how well he thought the truth stacked up against what people wanted to believe.

Chapter Thirty

Cherisse didn't look too happy to see me.

When you hear your name called over the loudspeaker, asking you to report to the main office, you never know what's up. Sometimes it's good news, like you left your lunch at home and your mother just dropped it off. But usually . . . not. A buddy of mine, last year? He got called down in the middle of class to find a cop waiting for him.

"Christopher LeVoie?" they'd asked when he walked in.

"Uh, no, I'm Christian LeVoie," he explained. They let him go back to class while the main office secretary hunted down Christopher, who, it turned out, had been reported speeding by one of the bus drivers.

So yeah, nobody likes to get called down to the office, so when the conference room door swung open and Cherisse walked in, she wore this expression like she was ready to face the lion in the den. But then she saw me, and her jaw dropped.

I think she would've been happier to find a couple of cops. Or a lion.

"Good morning, Miss Ouellette," Mr. Cockrell said. He was there, too. Along with Mrs. Swift, Mr. Haley (Cherisse's guidance counselor), Coach, and some black guy named Mr. Aden. I wasn't sure why he'd been invited. He was slim, dressed like a teacher. Light-skinned, with a long horse face and a thin nose.

"Please, have a seat." Mr. Cockrell said, gesturing to the empty chair across the table from me.

Cherisse slipped into it without a word.

The girl's a pro. She knew better than to speak before they asked her a direct question.

A red flush had started at her neck and slowly crept up her cheeks. I glared at her, watching it spread, but amazingly, she could look everywhere in the room except at me. Mr. Cockrell began.

"Cherisse, we have heard a very disturbing report this morning from Tom. He says you've been cyberbullying another girl at Chamberlain High School."

Cherisse's big, blue, darkly rimmed eyes widened.

"I don't even know what that is," she said.

I heard Coach snort.

"It means bullying on the Internet," Mr. Cockrell explained. "Or on the phone."

Cherisse shrugged.

"I haven't bullied anyone. I don't know what Tommy is talking about."

There was a cell phone on the table before Mr. Cockrell. Mine. He flipped it open and pointed the screen at Cherisse. Right there on the display was the photo she'd taken of me and Samira, with the caption she'd texted to all her contacts: *Somali slut*.

"This is Tom's phone. This is a message you sent to Tom

on . . ." He looked at the date and time. "Saturday at one-thirty in the afternoon."

She shrugged again.

"So? Is there a law against me sending a photo to my boyfriend? I didn't send it to *her*. I don't even know who that girl is! It's just a joke!"

"I'm *not* your boyfriend" flew out of my mouth. Which wasn't helpful. Cherisse finally looked at me.

Drop dead, the big blues said in no uncertain terms.

"Tommy and I are in a fight," she said evenly. "I sent him that picture to make him mad. That's all."

"Then why did practically every other kid in this school get it?" I demanded.

She shook her head.

"I don't know," she said. "Did you send it?"

I looked around the table, incredulous. The adults were listening carefully to her.

"Are you really that stupid?" I said.

"Tom," Mr. Cockrell said warningly. "Let's keep this civil."

"Every person who got that text can read where it came from, and it came from you," I continued. I looked around the table. "You guys know how that works, right?"

Before Cherisse came in, I had had to walk them through Facebook as well as basic texting. They'd had no idea you could simultaneously send a message to every contact on your phone. And include a photo. Only Mrs. Swift has her own Facebook page.

Only the Aden guy seemed to understand Facebook. He had no questions about texting.

"Great. Prove it," she said. "Bring in all their phones. And by the way, how is it bullying someone if you don't even know who they are? I mean, do you people know who the girl in the picture is? You can't even see her face!"

"We don't know who she is, nor will Tom tell us," Mrs. Swift explained. "We wanted her in here as well, but he's afraid that if you learn her identity, you'll go after her more viciously."

"I haven't gone after her at all! I don't know her!" Cherisse exclaimed.

Mr. Aden spoke.

"I am wondering, Miss Ouellette, if you do not know this girl, why you identify her as Somali?" His accent reminded me of Saeed's.

"Well, because she's wearing that head thing," Cherisse said. "They all wear it. The Somali girls."

Mr. Aden nodded thoughtfully.

"Most of them do. Some do not. Also, many Sudanese girls wear *hijab*. But you do not write *Sudanese slut*."

Cherisse rolled her eyes.

"Sudanese, Somali, what*ev*," she said. "I don't know her. All right?"

Mr. Aden leaned back in his chair and glanced at Mr. Cockrell, who reached behind him and picked up a slim laptop. He opened it, gave it a few swift keystrokes, then turned it to face Cherisse. Her Facebook profile was displayed. With the photo and all the comments, which now numbered 108. I had opened it for them before they called her down.

"You seem very interested in discovering the identity of this girl," Mr. Cockrell said. "And very interested in encouraging cruel, obscene statements about her."

She sighed.

"Like I said, Tom and I are in a fight. I was jealous, okay? Yeah, I'd like to know who she is. But I don't. Is it my fault that other people are mean?"

"We are not in a fight!" I fumed. "We are not in anything. There is no 'we.'"

"If this isn't a fight, then I sure don't want to be around when you two do get angry with each other," Mr. Haley commented dryly. The adults laughed, even Coach. Unbelievable.

"Well," Mr. Cockrell said, "the bottom line is that the remarks are incendiary. They enter the realm of hate speech, and I'm afraid they could lead to some real trouble. Now, Cherisse, even if that wasn't your intention, you see where it's led, don't you?"

Cherisse nodded.

"What do we think needs to happen here?" Mr. Cockrell asked.

"You want me to take down the post? Fine," Cherisse said. She grabbed hold of the laptop and began to pull it toward her. But this Mr. Aden guy, who sat alongside her, took hold of it himself.

"One moment," he said. He rummaged in a battered brown briefcase at his feet and pulled out a thumb drive.

"Before the young lady deletes her post, I would like to make a screen capture." He looked at Mr. Cockrell, who nodded.

As Mr. Aden saved Cherisse's wall post—it took a while because he scrolled through all the comments and saved them, too—Mrs. Swift spoke up.

"What about the phone messages?" she said. "Even if you erase the Facebook post, those messages are still out there, and every person who received them could resend that picture to someone else, who can then send it to someone else . . ."

"There's no way to delete texts that have already been sent," I explained to her. "Nice job." I directed my last comment at Cherisse.

"It was just a joke!" she repeated. "It's not my fault if other people are mean!"

"So what's *your* excuse?" Coach said angrily to her. "You know, every day I ask my boys to step up. To set an example. To be tolerant of others and work hard to be a community. I'm pretty damn proud of what they've accomplished; it hasn't been easy. So it pisses the hell out of me that that this sort of mean-girl crap, directed at someone you only identify as 'Somali,' could undo everything we've worked for. Pardon my language, folks. But this is bullying. Racial bullying, if you ask me."

Everybody started speaking at once. Mr. Haley couldn't seem to get his head around either the bullying concept—"How can you bully someone you don't know?"—or global texting. Mrs. Swift wanted to figure out how to kill the image on the phone. Mr. Cockrell was asking Coach if he thought Cherisse should be suspended, because if so, there were very clear procedures. Mr. Aden seemed very preoccupied with copying all the comments on the Facebook post.

Meanwhile, Cherisse sat silently. She looked at me across the table. Subtly, she raised her right hand, pointing her index finger straight up and her thumb at a perfect right angle. A big letter *L* aimed in my direction.

Loser.

She wore this tight white undershirt with lace at the top and thin straps. She had a hoodie over it, but she'd only zipped the bottom half, so there was plenty of boob on display. Raccoon-like circles rimmed her eyes, and her hair was highlighted to a crispy yellow.

Did she and Samira really attend the same school? Inhabit the same planet?

Mr. Aden looked up from the laptop.

"Okay, she can delete now, if that's what you want her to do," he said. Mr. Cockrell glanced around the table, and everyone nodded. They at least agreed on this much.

Cherisse swiveled the laptop to face her. She logged out of my Facebook account, logged on to hers, then quickly deleted the post with the photo of me and Samira. The 108 comments evaporated.

There was no trace of what she'd set in motion.

"Are we done here?" she said, looking at Mr. Cockrell.

"Whoa. Wait," I said. "That's it? She hits Delete and walks away?"

"No, of course that's not it," Coach growled. "There are consequences."

"Can we first please decide how we're going to handle the phone messages?" Mrs. Swift chimed in.

Cherisse let out an exasperated sigh.

"Okay, listen . . . I'm not saying I sent that picture. But if it will make you all feel better, I can text all my contacts and tell them to just forget the whole thing. Sort of a global JK, you know?"

"What?" Mr. Haley asked.

"Just kidding," Cherisse and I said at the same time.

"I believe something along those lines, perhaps with a bit more explanation than JK, is in order," said Mr. Cockrell.

"Like?" Cherisse asked.

"Perhaps you and Mr. Cockrell can work that out together," Mrs. Swift said. "I'm sorry, but I'm supposed to meet another student in my office right about now. . . ."

"Unbelievable," I said.

Mr. Cockrell frowned at me.

"Excuse me, Tom?" he said.

I shook my head.

"She's gonna walk away from this," I said. "Punch the Delete key, send a text, end of story. You know what? I'm outta here." I pushed back my chair. Coach rose, too.

"One moment, please." Mr. Aden.

"Tom," he said, "I understand that you want to see this girl"—he gestured to Cherisse—"punished. But how do you think that will help the girl in the picture?"

Everyone was quiet. Including me. It was a good question. Even if we took Cherisse out to the school parking lot for some tar and feathers, it wouldn't erase the image she'd spread. The caption under the picture.

"I don't know," I said.

"And I don't, either," he said, smiling slightly. "I think the best thing for your friend in the picture is to leave her alone. Less attention, not more attention."

He was right. The last thing Samira needed was for Cherisse to be turned into some sort of example. Turn her coven of nasty girlfriends into a bunch of avenging angels. The whole thing would just drag on and on. . . .

"I think we can all agree that handling this quietly would be best," Mr. Aden said. Everyone nodded.

"So with that in mind," Mr. Cockrell said, standing, "Tom,

thank you very much for bringing this to our attention. You can go to your first-period class now. Cherisse, you'll stay with me a little longer. Everyone else: thank you, I think we're set."

I felt Coach's hand on my elbow.

"Let's go," he said quietly, steering me toward the door.

Out in the empty hallway, we both exhaled at the same time.

"You okay?" he asked.

I looked at him.

"That *sucked*," I said. "She's getting off . . . with nothing! Absolutely nothing. And she has *ruined* Samira. Coach, this sort of shit is bad."

To his credit, he didn't correct me for swearing.

"Listen, Tom. I hear you. But Mr. Aden's right. We need to not make this worse for your friend."

I looked down the long, empty corridor. My throat was dry. I was even tempted to visit the water fountain, germs and discarded cigarette butts and all.

"I've got good news," he continued. "We're all set with Saeed. He can play."

"Since when?" I asked. After the past forty-eight hours, I was having a hard time believing good news.

"I got an email this morning," he said, grinning. "The committee reviewing the Maquoit complaint jumped right on it because I told them we're in postseason play. They decided in our favor within ten minutes. That's what a buddy of mine on the committee says, at any rate. So we've got our full team back, and a game tomorrow. Things are looking up."

As he said this, Mr. Aden emerged from the conference room. He walked quickly toward us.

"Tom," he said, "I wonder if I could speak with you?"

"Sure. What's up?"

He looked hesitantly at Coach.

"Nothing you can ask me that Coach can't hear," I told him.

"Yes," Mr. Aden said. "Well, I wonder, can you please tell me who is the girl in the picture?"

"Oh for crying out loud, Abdullahi. Why?" Coach burst out. I hadn't realized they were on a first-name basis.

Mr. Aden stiffened.

"I promise you, I will not tell the young lady in there," he said, tilting his head toward the conference room where Cockrell and Cherisse had yet to emerge. "My only concern is for this girl and her family."

Coach shook his head slowly from side to side.

"Right," he said quietly. "Always got to stick your finger in it, don't you?"

Mr. Aden smiled.

"But I am paid to stick my finger in it! This is my job," he said.

"I'm sorry, but are you a teacher?" I asked Mr. Aden.

He held out his hand.

"I am Abdullahi Aden, and I am the cultural liaison for schools. I work with the new immigrant students and their families."

"So you're a teacher?" I repeated.

"No, but I am an employee of the school system," he said. He spoke precisely. Chose his words carefully.

"Why do you want to know who she is?"

"This is very disturbing, what that girl in there did," he said. "This would be very upsetting to one of our Somali families. If I can be helpful to them in any way, I would like to do so."

Coach was looking at me while Mr. Aden spoke. I might have been wrong, but . . . I thought I saw him shake his head.

"Tell you what," I said to the guy. "Do you have a phone number? I'll give it to the girl and her family, and they can call you."

He didn't like that answer. But what could he say? Abdullahi Aden gave me his card—sure enough, it said right there that he worked for the school department—then headed for the exit, nodding curtly to Coach as he left.

Coach smiled grimly at me.

"Well done," he said, clapping me on the back but offering no other explanation. "See you at practice this afternoon."

Later that day, after practice, Abdi and I floundered. We were close, really close, to finishing his little alphabet book, but we needed someone who could help us bridge the gap between his challenges and my cluelessness about the Somali language. And Samira was a no-show.

Not that we had a set date and time for working with Abdi. It's just that she was pretty much always at The Center, so I'd counted on her. Myla hadn't come, either. The events of the weekend had set her back, and she had a paper due.

The little dude swung a foot and looked at me like he really couldn't believe how stupid I was. We were on the last three letters, X, Y, and Z, and while Abdi easily came up with a Somali word, *xaaqin*, which means "a little straw brush," I struggled to think of a good English one. My mind kept jumping to *Xerox* and *xenophobe*, which, for obvious reasons, wouldn't work and wouldn't reproduce in Crayola.

"Man, don't you know anything?" he said crossly. For some

reason he was in a rotten mood. So was I. Practice sucked, and not only because we were missing Saeed. Something was up with the other Somali guys.

No one seemed to know where Saeed was and whether he'd gotten the message that he was back on the team. He hadn't come to school that day, and Ismail, Double M, and Ibrahim, who all had classes with him, had no explanation.

I got the feeling that they knew more than they were letting on. They didn't seem surprised or upset. They responded clearly and politely to Coach's questions about Saeed, but it was as if some curtain had dropped and they had disappeared behind it.

When I tried to talk to Ismail myself, he wouldn't look me in the eye.

"Is everything okay?" I finally said to him. He nodded. I decided to just cut to the chase.

"I saw your comment on that stupid post Cherisse Ouellette had on Facebook. You do know that was total crap, right?"

He shrugged and looked across the field. "Yes," he said. But his face was unreadable.

The rule at Chamberlain is that if you miss a practice, you miss a game. Coach was pretty frustrated that Saeed hadn't gotten the message that he was back on, because we needed him for the next day's game against Whittier. When practice ended, he pulled me aside and asked if I'd heard anything at all from Saeed. I promised to stop by his apartment on my way home from The Center.

"I know a lot of things," I said to Abdi, "but not everything." He didn't seem satisfied with that answer. He needed me to know everything, in that way little boys needed big boys to be smart and powerful.

He was in for a disappointment.

Here's what I did know, and what I finally figured out: the whole dictionary idea was pretty much a fail from the start. That's because there is no direct correlation between the English and Somali alphabets. Sure, we could match the words *apple* with *aqal* and *boy* with *babaay*. But their letters don't go in the same order as ours, and when you get a little deeper into it, nothing lines up. I mean, the letters *P*, *V*, and *Z* don't even exist in Somali, and some of their sounds are written by doubling our letters. Even writing Somali using the Latin alphabet was only invented forty years ago. By some African guy. I looked it up on Wikipedia.

It's like we'd tried to fold the two alphabets together, like the opposite sides of a single card, but because each half was a different shape and size the thing would never stand straight and the edges wouldn't match up. We'd have a collection of same-sounding words and pictures in the end, but it wasn't close to a dictionary.

I'm not sure Abdi cared.

"So, what is an X-word I can draw?" he insisted.

I thought of something.

"Hey, in your music class do you guys have a xylophone?" He frowned. "It's an instrument that makes sort of a ringing noise, and you play it with a little mallet?" He still didn't get it, so I drew a line of rectangles that started out big, then diminished in size. His face lit up.

"Yes! Is xylo! I play it in school." Using a different color for each bar, Abdi excitedly drew his version of a xylophone. It reminded me of the Playskool version my grandmother gave me when I was little. I could tap out "Twinkle, Twinkle, Little Star" on it.

End in sight, Abdi rapidly drew a *yaanyo* (a big red tomato) and a squiggly circle with a tail (ball of yarn, sort of). There is no Z in Somali, and no Samira to help us come up with a good phonetic Z-word, so I suggested *zebra*, and before you knew it, we were done.

He slapped the black crayon down on the table after he colored in the final stripe on a four-legged creature that looked like a cat with a horse tail. The crayon cracked in half.

"Yes! I go now. See you later, Tom." Abdi grabbed his pack and dashed out The Center door without a backward look at the project we'd spent weeks finishing. The other completed pages were in a file cabinet drawer in the glassed-in cubicle, and I added these final three sheets to that pile, then slid the metal drawer closed. I figured Myla and Samira could take a look before Abdi brought it to school.

When I left, I walked around the block to the Bashirs' building. The sidewalk was practically deserted. The sun had set, it was getting cool, and the air was filled with the scent of dinners cooking. Cumin. Frying meat. Just before I mounted the stairs I saw a man, his back to me, walking in the opposite direction. Not in any hurry, but walking purposefully to the corner. He was slim and wore nice trousers. He carried a briefcase.

I climbed four flights to the Bashirs' and knocked. The building was alive with sounds, with children in hallways, with doors open so you could see into families' private lives around the television or dining table. As I stood outside the Bashirs' closed door, I swore I heard noise on the other side, but no one answered. I knocked again, but when the door refused to swing open, I told myself it was the neighbors I heard, and Saeed and Samira were not home.

Chapter Thirty-One

And like that, they were gone. They slipped back into the nowhere they came from. As if they'd never existed and the past few months had never happened.

The neighbors would tell us nothing, and Myla and I had some long debates over whether they truly didn't know or there was some conspiracy of silence. They just shrugged and wouldn't reply when you asked them where the family went. And we asked. We knocked on doors, Myla and me, and even though at most of the apartments the kids, especially the little girls, were excited to see her and threw their arms around her waist, the adults told us nothing.

Same story with the guys on the team: Ismail, Ibrahim, and Double M knew nothing. Guidance had heard nothing; the Bashirs were simply missing in action. And even Coach, who I figured would go postal when he heard his star player had apparated, kind of just . . . moved on. Standing outside the bus, clipboard in hand, as we loaded in for our first playoff game against Whittier, he was his usual unsmiling pregame self. All business and calm.

"Saeed?" I said to him before I climbed the stairs.

Coach shook his head.

"We'll be playing this one without him, Tom," he said simply.

Losing that one without him, more like. Whittier beat us, 3–2. And like that, our season was gone, too.

I felt like I was in some Jason Bourne movie, or a remake of *The Manchurian Candidate.* I wanted somebody to tell me how I'd gotten here and which one of the seven passports with my picture in it was authentic. Tell me what had really happened and who I really was, because my current life was feeling like a bad dream. With moments that morphed into nightmare.

For example: sitting in a vinyl armchair, watching Don feed himself beef stew. He kept spilling, because his right arm was in a cast and he was trying to manage a spoon lefty. Lines from a Talking Heads song my dad always plays kept running through my head: *You may ask yourself: how did I get here? You may say to yourself: this is not my beautiful life!*

I managed to not share that with Don.

"I think you're getting more on your chest than in your mouth," I commented instead. He grinned at me, which was fairly horrifying because his mouth was full and the side of his face where he got all the stitches was still swollen and bruised.

"That's why I've got this nice bib," he replied. Uncle Paul had tucked a wad of napkins around Don's neck, so it did look like he was wearing a papery bib.

Paul had been coming to the hospital as much as, if not more than, Mrs. Plourde. Don told me that when he drifted off at night, Paul was usually in the armchair, and when he woke up, the nurses would tell him Paul had only just left, or promised to be right back.

Paul had always liked Don. I watched as he leaned over him and gently wiped traces of brown sauce from his chin.

"Don't let pretty boy here get to you," he said. "You've gotta practice using your left hand. The right's gonna be out of commission for a while." As if to prove the point, Don raised another shaky spoonful to his mouth. That one delivered the full load, no spills.

"Hey, who you callin' pretty boy?" I said.

"You," they both replied.

"Sure as hell isn't me," Don added. This was too true to be funny, so no one laughed.

Paul returned to his chair on the opposite side of the bed from me. He crossed one foot over his knee.

"So tell us again what happened yesterday," he said.

"We lost," I repeated. *"C'est tout."* That was it. All of it. Over. My energy for reliving the Whittier defeat was pretty low.

"But you beat 'em good in the regular season."

"They showed up ready to play and we didn't," I replied. They beat us to the ball nine times out of ten, I didn't add. They played with desire. We played in a fog.

We were missing our star. And sure, we still had plenty of solid guys on the team who could score, but mentally we were hurting. Winning begins with attitude, and we were defeated before the bus even pulled out of the Chamberlain parking lot.

"Didya ever find out what happened to Saeed?" Don said.

Paul looked at me quizzically.

"Were you missing people?" he asked.

"Only our best player," I said. Not a topic I wanted to bring up with Paul. I looked at Don. "No word from him. It's like they vanished."

"That sucks," Don said, then took another bite.

"Somali guy?" Paul asked. I nodded.

"Yeah, well, what do you expect?" he said with a laugh. "Here today, gone tomorrow."

"Don't."

The word came out of my mouth like a gunshot. Quick. Percussive. Unexpected. I didn't know what would follow, but I did know I wasn't going to listen to this crap from my uncle anymore.

"I'm sorry . . . what?" Paul wore a stunned expression I didn't recognize.

"Don't start running the Somalis down. It's bullshit, Uncle Paul. And you're better than that."

His face reddened.

"I think, Tommy, that I know something about—"

I cut him off.

"You don't know anything about Saeed," I told him. "He's not just a great player. He's a team leader. And even though he's had to deal with more shit in his short life than you, me, and Don combined, he still manages to be a good guy. And he happens to be my friend. So drop it, Uncle Paul."

There was silence as my uncle stared unflinchingly back at me. I'd seen him spar with my aunt enough to realize that he was not silent because he was at a loss for words. He was trying to decide how to respond. Because what came next would be the maiden steps in some new territory we'd just entered.

Don put his plastic spoon down on the tray with a quiet click. He pushed the rolling hospital table away. Paul glanced at him, cleared his throat, and rose.

"I'll take that out of here," he said. "I'm also gonna get myself a cup of coffee. You guys want anything?"

"No, thanks," I told him.

"Hot stone massage?" Don suggested. "Preferably given by the red-haired nurse who came on duty at five?" Paul shook his head, half smiled at him, and walked out with the tray.

Don looked at me with wide eyes.

"Tell us what you really think, Tom-boy," he said.

I sighed.

"Was I out of line?" I asked.

Don leaned back into his pillows. Just the effort of eating had exhausted him.

"Nah," he said. "I mean, Paul's the man. But he's definitely got some blind spots when it comes to people."

Abdullahi Aden was not expecting me. Still, he was way friendlier and more polite than the woman who worked the reception desk at the superintendent's office. I didn't have an appointment, and she chewed a piece of gum as I introduced myself. It was green. I watched it dance between her teeth as I spoke to her. Her nails, which clicked as she depressed phone keys and called down to Mr. Aden, were long and shellacked dark purple.

"Can I ask what this is regarding?" she said.

"It's a social call," I told her. "Me and Mr. Aden go way back." She raised one eyebrow but held the receiver to her ear.

"There's a student out here who wants to see you," she said. "Tom Bouchard." Pause. "Should I send him back?" Pause. She hung up.

"He'll be right out." She didn't invite me to sit or tell me how long I'd have to wait. She turned to her computer, and the nails began clicking rapidly over the keys. I wandered over to the windows and stared out at the street and passing traffic.

It was Donnie who suggested that Mr. Aden might know where the Bashirs had gone. After Paul left the hospital the night of the beef stew, I hung out way past visiting hours. More than the pain, Don hated being alone: "I've got my little friend here for the pain," he said, pointing to the morphine drip with the magic button he never let out of his good hand. "I need you for the rest of it, Tom-boy."

He lay in his bed, the lights dim, his eyes closed, and listened to me mind-dump about Saeed and Samira and everything that had happened, trying to find clues that would fill the holes in the narrative. I kept thinking he'd fallen asleep, but if I got up to leave, he'd say something that drew me back into my chair. Finally, from the drug-induced fog where my words swirled, Donnie came up with the answer.

"That guy, from the big powwow with Cherisse? He knows." In my mind I scrolled through the attendees at that meeting.

"Who, Mr. Aden? He had no clue what was up."

"Yeah, but he stopped asking you, didn't he? Means he figured it out. Adults only bug you if they're trying to get information. Once they've got what they want, they leave you alone."

And like that, I was back on the chilly, dark street, watching a man with a lumpy briefcase walk away from Saeed's staircase.

What had he said to the family to make them close their door to me?

"Tom?" I heard. Mr. Aden entered the waiting room. He smiled pleasantly. He wore a crisp white shirt and a nondescript blue patterned tie. His black shoes were scuffed. I imagined he did a lot of walking around broken sidewalks and up dusty staircases in those shoes. He gestured for me to follow him, and we walked down a long, beige hallway that wound through a rabbit's warren of small offices.

He worked in a cubicle within a larger office. There was just enough room for both of us to sit, and he motioned me to one of two chairs.

"How can I help you?" he said.

I skipped the formalities. He knew I knew he knew. Meaning the identity of the girl in the blue *hijab*.

"I was wondering if you would tell me where the Bashirs went. See, they left pretty suddenly and some of us who are friends of theirs would have liked a chance to say goodbye."

He registered no surprise at the directness of my question. From the moment Ms. Clicky Nails told him I was in his waiting room, he'd known why I'd come.

"That I do not know. But I believe the Bashirs would let their friends know where they had gone, would they not?" He lingered, briefly, on the word *friends*. As if it were a club that didn't include me.

"Yeah. You know, I'm having a hard time believing you don't know where they went," I said.

His eyes widened.

"It is not good to suggest that someone is a liar, Tom."

I shrugged.

"It's not good to be sneaky," I told him. "I know you went to see the Bashirs. I saw you. Leaving their apartment."

Mr. Aden didn't flinch. He held my gaze steady.

"Yes, but that is not a secret. After you refused to tell me the identity of the girl in the picture, I found others who would. So I visited the family. Later, like you, I learned that they had left. They did not tell me where they were going."

"But you sure as hell know why they left, don't you?" I said.

He frowned.

"We will not continue this discussion if you are going to speak obscenely and insult me by calling me a liar."

I took a deep breath. If I blew this chance, I'd never find out what he knew.

"I'm sorry. I don't mean to be rude. I'm just upset, is all. Saeed and Samira are . . . were . . . my friends, and I want to know what happened. I want to know what you said to make them leave."

He laughed shortly, without smiling.

"I did not say anything to make them leave. I do not have that sort of power."

"It makes no sense!" I blurted out. "I mean, c'mon! Saeed wouldn't just walk out on us. He loves soccer. He loves the team."

Mr. Aden leaned back in his chair. He looked at me curiously.

"But if you are Saeed's friend, then you would understand that there are many things more important than soccer."

"Of course. But for Saeed, soccer is really, really important."

"Not as important as one's family. Or one's faith. Soccer is a sport; that is all." Something changed in Mr. Aden's voice when he said that. Like he was reciting words from memory. From lines he'd read a zillion times over and learned by heart. I tried again.

"You say you don't know where they went. But do you know *why* they went?"

318

He got up from his chair and walked over to a water cooler just outside the cubicle. He poured two paper cups' worth, returned to his seat, and handed one to me without asking if I was thirsty. I drank it down.

"Do you not understand the seriousness of the implications made about the sister?" he said.

"No, I don't," I told him. "Anyone who knows Samira . . . and knows Cherisse . . . knows it wasn't true."

He looked slightly amused.

"Truth is a difficult word. One person's truth is another person's falsehood."

"And people believe what they want to believe," I fired back.

"People believe what appears to be true and what they feel is true," Mr. Aden corrected. "Tell me, Tom. What do you believe is true about Samira?"

"She's smart. She works hard and gets good grades. She seemed pretty religious. She never really liked me. Which is pretty ironic, given how things turned out."

He nodded.

"Yes, that is what you would see, and that is your truth. But there is another way to see things. You say she works hard, but does she help her mother? After school, she was often at the K Street Center visiting with the American student, not cooking or watching her younger brothers and sisters. You say she is religious, but some days I would see her at school not wearing *hijab*, only a small scarf. Sometimes she had on big gold earrings. One day I saw her with a jacket I thought was a boy's."

I knew the jacket he was talking about. Myla told me it had come into The Center with a big load of donated clothes. It was leather and lined with woolly fleece. It was really warm, and Myla had put it aside for Samira the minute she saw it. She was always worried that the Bashirs didn't have decent winter clothes.

It was what Samira had worn the first day I saw her.

"Wait a minute," I interrupted. "You're saying that wearing that leather jacket made her somehow *not* a good Muslim?"

"No," he said firmly. "I am saying that wearing certain styles of dress that appear immodest might leave a girl open to questions about her morality. People might be more willing to believe bad things about her character. And Tom, she had few defenders besides her brother and her mother. She has no father. The rest of her family lives elsewhere."

My mind spun. Arguing with Abdullahi Aden was like boxing smoke: I couldn't land a punch and I couldn't see clearly.

"So you're saying she got what was coming and the family left in shame?"

He shook his head.

"There were many problems, Tom. It was not only about the sister. The brother was upset that he was taken off the soccer team. Mrs. Bashir could not find work. They had no family in Enniston. And of course, the neighbors were very upset that police came to their apartment. These are law-abiding people who do not want trouble."

This sick feeling rose in my throat. Images of faces, partially obscured by half-open doors, peering down the hallway to the Bashirs' apartment and the detectives. Who looked like cops despite the ordinary clothes they were wearing.

"I simply suggested to the mother that, given their difficulties, her children might be better off living near an uncle or other male relative," Mr. Aden concluded.

I stood up. I had my answer, and I needed to get out. The air in there suddenly felt stale. Suffocating.

"And you won't tell me where that might be?" I asked.

He stared into my face politely and steadily.

"Do you have a number? If I hear from the family, I will tell them you wish to contact them, and they can call you."

Chapter Thirty-Two

The library at Mumford turned out to be a prime college-app-writing location.

That's partly because when I tried to write essays at home, I was distracted by thoughts of what I'd rather be doing. Thoughts that usually involved Myla. But at the Mumford library, she was usually across the table from me, staring into some book with this frown that wrinkled along the bridge of her nose, and I figured if she could concentrate, then I sure as hell could, too.

Plus we sometimes broke for coffee over at the student center, and wow. Nothing like a little caffeine to keep you going. I'm so destined for addiction.

But the library worked for me in other ways. Jocks and hipsters and white girls with dreadlocks and black women in team jackets and tour groups filled with kids my age and professors trailing eager students moved in a constant stream through the library's main floor . . . and I could still concentrate. Go figure. The only times I got pulled away from my work was when I was literally pulled away from my work.

Like, by Myla's friends.

The first time, we were studying when a few of them came by our table to collect her for a meeting they were going to. And invited me to come with.

"What sort of meeting?" I asked them.

"Stand Up, Enniston," one of the women replied. "We're planning the counterdemonstration."

The United Church of the World had picked a date in January. They were coming to Enniston to rally in support of all of us poor oppressed white people . . . which everyone knew was just code for "We're coming to break heads and make trouble." So another group had formed, calling itself Stand Up, Enniston, to plan another demonstration. This included anybody from Mumford people to Somalis to church groups to Aunt Maddie–type town activists. Their plan was to stage a sort of peace rally for the same day, all very politically correct and touchy-feely.

Myla was really into it.

"It's *empowering*, Cap," she tried to explain to me. "It's something we can do, you know? Instead of just standing by and watching a bunch of hater freaks jump around in front of the news cameras and make the rest of the world think Enniston buys into their crap."

I got that, even though I'm definitely not the protesting, marching sort of guy. It's funny: until the skinheads decided to invade our town, I never realized I was much of an I-love-Enniston sort of guy, either. But they seriously pissed me off.

So I started doing Stand Up, Enniston with Myla and her friends. A few of them knew I went to Chamberlain, but the rest? We just let them think I was some townie Myla had met.

323

Which turned out to be fine with me. For some reason I didn't look at them and see a bunch of rich kids driving around in their parents' old SUVs. I didn't think of Alex and wonder whether any of them were sports recruits. I didn't hear my uncle's voice in my head, making snide remarks about how they might all have $200,000 degrees, but they'd still need to call him if their sinks got blocked up.

They just all seemed like . . . Myla.

Sometime during the first week in December I started feeling bummed that it was all going to end. Myla was scheduled to take her last exam on December 15, then fly home to Minnesota for break. She'd be back for the rally, plus there was a possibility I might go out there for New Year's if I could scratch up enough dough for a ticket ("Tell your folks you want to tour Carleton," she suggested slyly), but still. Hanging out with her had been, like, my recovery from all the crap that went down in the fall, no less than physical therapy had been for Donnie.

He was still not back at school at that point, but he was off pain meds ("Seriously? Tylenol instead of Percocet? I'm *dyin'* with the pain, doc!" he'd argued, but no one bought it) and able to get around pretty well with an electric wheelchair. Plus he slept a lot and was completely off the booze, so except for the jagged scars on his face and the casts, he looked healthier than he had in months.

Strangely, he seemed happier, too.

"I mean, what can go wrong?" he said to me when I visited him at home one afternoon. "I can't OD. I can't drink. I've already been in a near-fatal car crash, so what are the chances of *that* happening again? I guess if the house burst into flames I'd be pretty much fucked, but maybe I could roll out in time. Strange as it sounds, Tom-boy, this is the safest I've felt in years. I actually sleep nights."

Which was more than I could say for myself. It wasn't like I had bad dreams or anything. But my mind raced. Thoughts came crashing down on each other like a rickety house of knobby sticks. Angry thoughts. Things I should have left behind, but instead propped up against each other, arranged and rearranged.

Maquoit went on to win the state championship, and the Enniston paper carried the photo. Not the formal team picture, the players lined up nicely by height with the coaching staff, and the trophy displayed in the center. No, they used the victorious "bro pic," with all the guys in their black and red jerseys screaming in triumph, hoisting the trophy over their heads.

Correction: in the photo, Alex Rhodes hoisted the trophy over his head, while his teammates lifted *him*.

The day that picture came out, the sports section was the first I used to light the woodstove.

Cherisse Ouellette continued to come to school and hang out with her coven of mindless friends like nothing had happened. Maybe something had; I didn't know. Maybe her guidance counselor wrote in her file that she was an awful person who wrecked lives.

Then again, maybe Mr. Haley still hadn't figured out whether it counted as bullying if you didn't actually know who you were bullying.

The guys on the soccer team, even Mike Turcotte, went on as if nothing had happened. Sure, people were disappointed, and when Maquoit won there were plenty of rude comments to go around. But most of the guys just drifted into their winter sports, hockey or indoor track or basketball, and the subject of the Bashirs never came up.

That was about the time it occurred to me that if I didn't make some serious changes, I would lose my mind.

So I set to work planning my escape. And just in time, 'cause pretty much every college I was applying to had a January 1 deadline. Same day as Saeed's fake birthday. Hell, same day as every Somali kid's birthday. I told Abdi I'd get him a cake. We'd celebrate his green card birthday and my hitting Send all at the same time. He was cool with that.

Myla was pretty happy I'd finally gotten my act together with the apps. A little too happy, to be honest. She appointed herself my private college coach.

"Personal!" she kept saying. "This is supposed to be a *personal* essay. Reveal yourself. Tell them something they won't see on your transcript. I feel like you're holding back." She had this red pen I had grown to hate.

"I don't know if I can stand dating the freakin' grammar police anymore," I groused at one point when we nearly came to blows over whether to use *that* or *which* in a sentence. She didn't even raise her head, continuing to draw lines through whole sentences I had painstakingly composed.

"You love it," she murmured. And she was right.

One afternoon, when I'd arrived at the library before her and was already deeply involved in reworking a paragraph she'd trashed the day before, I felt her light tap on my shoulder. She slid into the seat beside me and placed a sheet of paper on the table.

"Minneapolis," she said simply. "They have an uncle there."

I looked at the paper. It was a printout of an email to Myla, from Samira.

"Read it out loud," she prompted.

"'Hello, Myla,'" I began.

So many times in my life I cannot say goodbye. When we left Dadaab, it was so quickly I could not say goodbye to all my friends. I said goodbye to my grandmother, but because I have no photographs I begin to forget what she looks like. When our father died, we did not expect it, and I did not say goodbye. When we left Atlanta, I did not say goodbye to my first teachers. All of these make me sad to remember.

But the worst was not saying goodbye to you and my teachers in Maine. You were my true lovely friend and there is a pain in my heart from missing you. I hope you are okay and not angry at me.

We live in Minneapolis now with my uncle's family. Their apartment is small and sometimes I think his wife is not happy we have come but my uncle tries to get us our own place, and that will be good. Minneapolis is a bigger city than Enniston and cold like Maine. There is a big mall here and the mosque and the school we can walk to. I am in school and so is Saeed and Aweys, but the schools are not as nice as Chamberlain and the teachers are not as nice. I miss Chamberlain very much but you know I work hard and get good grades.

I miss you but I praise Allah for my family and my kind uncle. My mother has work cleaning offices at night, and I come home after school to watch my little brothers and help my uncle's wife. My mother is often very tired but I try to help her.

Saeed was also very sad to go but already he makes new friends in Minneapolis. There are other girls my age in this apartment building but I don't like them very much.

My memories are my heart photographs. I have so many of you and they are all good. I remember your laugh and your patch of colored hair. I remember when I taught you to make sambusas and when you, me, and Tom ate at the restaurant. I remember riding in your van and you played your CDs and made me sing American songs with you. You kept telling me, "Sing louder, louder, Samira!"

Myla, there is a time to sing loud and a time to be quiet. Right now, I am quiet. I am quiet in my uncle's home and in this new school. But I promise you I will not be quiet forever. And when I sing, it will be so loud you will hear me all the way in Maine!

Even though many memories are sad, many are good. I remember anger but also laughter. I remember fear but also friendship. I remember feeling lost but also remember walking into The Center for the first time and finding you. I remember how I could not ride the moving stairs at the airport when we arrived in America, but I also remember the first time a teacher gave me an A. I remember my first snow and how it seemed like cold cotton falling from the sky. And I remember that even in Maine, where it gets so cold, warm rain, like tears, melts the snow and things grow again.

May Allah bless you my friend, until I see you again.

Samira

When I finished reading, I put down the paper with a shaky hand. Two lines of tears streamed down Myla's face. I wrapped my arms around her shoulders and instantly registered in some deep place in my chest how good it felt to hold her that way. My touch, more than my words, told her everything I wanted her to know. It was a language we both spoke and understood and trusted.

We stayed like that for a while, neither of us caring if anyone else in the library saw us. When we did move apart, she wiped her nose with the end of her sleeve like a little kid.

"Will you write back to her?" I asked.

"Of course," she said. "But not tonight. I need to give it some thought. Not during exam week, you know? I was wondering if I should try to see her when I go home. I don't live far from Minneapolis." I nodded.

"I mean, I don't know if her family will let her. Maybe they include me in the list of all the things they wanted to get away from. But I think I should try. Don't you?"

"Definitely," I said.

Myla peered at me curiously.

"So what do you think?" she finally asked.

I shook my head.

"Why isn't she . . . madder?" I said. "Why isn't she absolutely furious? I mean, she misses you, they live in a rotten situation with an aunt who doesn't want them, she's lonely. And she did nothing to deserve it!"

We were both quiet for a while, staring at the email printout that said so much and also left so much out. Finally Myla spoke.

"She's lucky, then."

"Huh?" I said.

"She's lucky to not be furious. Because she couldn't control it. None of it: not civil war, not losing her father, not Cherisse Ouellette, not Minneapolis, none of it. And yeah, it hurts and it's hard. But raging only makes things harder. So she's lucky to put that away and get on with her life as it is. She makes what choices she can, and she does it with grace. And hope. I mean, that singing part? She's not giving up."

I looked at her then. This funny little person who broke me and amazed me over and over. If the only good thing to emerge from the ashes of the season was meeting Myla, then I'd been luckier than I probably deserved. But of course, she wasn't the only thing. She was simply the best.

I looked over her shoulder to the scattered sheets of my essays streaked with red pen. Hopeless. Hopeless to continue with any of them now. I was ashamed of everything I'd written.

"You know," I said to her, "I'm really close to saying something right now that would be a real soul-baring game changer between us. But since it's study week and all, and you've got a lot on your mind, I'll just say you are probably the coolest woman I will ever know."

Her eyes widened.

"I know, right?" she said as she leaned forward and brushed her lips against mine.

We got back to work then, Myla and I. She folded the email in two and fired up her laptop. I pulled out a notebook and opened to a blank page. Trying to figure out what photographs I carried in my heart. What warm rain woke the frozen earth around me.

I began, again.

Epilogue

It is *so* cold.

Not quite spit-and-it-freezes-before-it-hits-the-ground cold, although that would be cool. I had to read Jack London's *To Build a Fire* back in eighth grade, which is the coldest damn story you'll ever read, and he describes what seventy below feels like and spit freezing. I mean, it's Alaska. Not Maine. We don't usually get *that* cold, at least not in Enniston. So while the weather on the day of the rally is in the single digits and windy, it's also sunny. Frostbite weather, for sure, but nothing Mainers can't deal with, especially if they're wearing the right socks.

And you gotta hope they are, because they stand outside the Mumford College auditorium for hours, waiting to file inside. Every type of Mainer you can imagine: little kids with their families, students, old couples, black people, brown people . . . everybody. All waiting to join the counterdemonstration, which we realized needed to be in a big space.

Because thousands turn up.

Thousands.

331

I was part of the crew that set up folding chairs the night be-fore, and Myla tells me more than four thousand had been ordered. I'd sent a Facebook message to the soccer team and every guy, every single guy, including the entire JV, turned up to help. Still, it took us hours, and we kept looking at each other and saying, "Seriously? This many chairs?" But we need every one of them.

Just inside the entrance I pass out programs and point people to empty seats. They file in with these big happy smiles, some carrying helium balloons, or tie-dyed flags with peace signs, or just holding their kids' hands. You'd think they were going to the circus or some massive party. As they wander in and see the size of the crowd, they grin, amazed, emotional. "Thank you," they say to me so sincerely. You'd think I was passing out twenty-dollar bills.

At one point, Myla finds me.

"Oh my God, you're not going to believe this," she says excit-edly. She holds out her phone, where there's a text message, but she's jumping around so much I can't see the screen.

"Just tell me," I say.

Turns out one of her roommates was across town at the Ar-mory, where the city had arranged for the skinheads (aka the United Church of the World) to have their rally. She was texting Myla as that meeting was going on. About thirty of them had shown up, minus their leader (seems he'd recently been arrested for plotting to murder somebody), and a couple hundred protest-ers had lined up, holding signs and chanting at them to go home. Cops were everywhere, but that was no surprise; we'd already heard that this was going to be the biggest law-enforcement callout in the state's history. So far, however, only one guy got arrested: some counterprotester who was heckling the skinheads.

"But now they've left!" Myla says. "She just texted me that

they made their little hate speeches to each other, then snuck out a back door into a bunch of vans and drove off!" Myla's so thrilled she practically bounces.

I hand her a stack of programs.

"That's awesome, College, but we've got some crowd-control issues here. Go stand on the other side of the door and pass these out."

She plants a kiss on my cheek and bounds over to the opposite side of the line.

At some point one of the security guys comes over to me and says all the seats are filled and I need to direct people to the standing-room areas.

"We're going to have to close the doors soon," he tells me. "Fire-code regulations."

"There are a lot of people still waiting to get in," I say.

He sighs.

"I know, but it can't be helped. We're piping the sound outside, so they can hear."

I don't bother to tell him that a lot of these people have driven from out of state and from northern Maine, for hours, and expect to be allowed inside. Myla's been handling phones, giving people directions and telling them where to park, all week.

But when the doors close and the security dude explains why they can't come in, they stay. They wrap around the outside of the auditorium in the bitter cold and seem grateful that the organizers thought to set up massive speakers outside so they can hear the speeches. Someone has donated tables lined with free hot chocolate, which helps. The kids, meanwhile, have a blast playing on these massive mounds of frozen snow.

For hours. Two and a half hours.

Inside, there's a long stage and a podium set up, and all these dignitaries—the governor of Maine, our two senators, Somali elders, church leaders—are lined up in their assigned seats. Sitting right up there with them are a few familiar faces: Ismail. Ibrahim. This Somali girl named Nasra who I used to see hanging around with Samira. Mike Turcotte. They're part of this leadership group Chamberlain has put together, kind of a diversity/anti-hate/anti-bullying thing. It's cool; they picked decent kids to be on it. Mike invited me to join. I turned him down.

"Nah, man, thanks, but I'm too busy," I told him. "Way behind on the college stuff right now."

He looked pretty skeptical.

"Yeah, you and the rest of the senior class," he said. "C'mon, Tom. It would mean a lot having you join. Team captain and all." But I held my ground.

I didn't have it in me to tell Mike that I didn't deserve to be in their group. That I got it wrong, so many times I lost count, with people who expected and needed a lot more out of me, and that I didn't feel like disappointing anyone . . . or myself . . . again. I decided to stay within my comfort zone of success: setting up chairs and passing out programs. Even Tom Bouchard couldn't screw that up. Beyond that: count me out.

Right before the doors close and the program begins, I see something that I really don't expect. In all his wheelchair glory, shaking hands and enduring sloppy kisses from all these mothers who recognize him, comes Donnie.

Uncle Paul pushes his chair.

"Wow. Look what the cat dragged in," I say, walking up behind them. I place one hand on Paul's shoulder and squeeze.

"Tom-boy!" Donnie exclaims, twisting in his seat to get a look at me. "Just the man we were looking for. Where are all the white supremacists, dude? This crowd is way too tame." He shivers as he speaks. His lips are blue. They've been waiting outside on that long line.

"That party's across town," I tell him. "But you've missed it. I hear they made their speeches and are booking it out of here."

Don laughs. He looks up at Paul.

"Guess we're stuck here with the 'Kumbaya' crowd, Paulie," he says.

Paul doesn't look at all surprised. His eyes dart around the auditorium, like he's trying to figure out where to go. He looks grim.

"Did you really wind up at the wrong rally?" I ask him quietly.

He flashes me this give-me-a-break look.

"No," he says firmly. "Don told me he needed a lift here today, and since I was already planning to come, it worked out. Just wish it weren't so damn cold out."

"Wow. Sorry, but . . . I'm in a state of shock, Uncle Paul. You were *planning* to come?"

He stares steadily into my eyes.

"You know, Tom, I don't agree with everything you people are doing in here. But I sure as *hell* don't agree with those bastards across town."

One of the security guards comes up and motions Paul to a roped-off section near the front marked HANDICAPPED ACCESS. He wheels Donnie away and they disappear in the crush of people.

The program is, I'll admit, a little boring. All the politicians need their turn at the mike, so there's a lot of blah blah blah. But hey, at least they came. The mayor, who got this whole thing started, is "out of the state," conveniently enough, and couldn't attend. When they make that announcement, people start to chant and holler, so that's pretty interesting. Then I notice Ibrahim has stepped up to the podium. He's the first high school student to speak. The first Somali kid, for that matter. The whole auditorium quiets down to listen.

He does a good job. He's reading from a prepared speech, and even though you can tell he's freakin' nervous—his voice shakes—he works to pronounce each word slowly and carefully. At first I don't quite catch it, because I'm standing near the back and there are some little kids messing around and making a ruckus, but then their dad silences them. That's when I catch what Ibrahim's on about.

He's telling them about our soccer team. He's talking about, of all things, pasta parties. Music jams on the bus. Beating Maquoit. Becoming like brothers, all part of one family. He gestures toward Ismail and Mike, and they join him at the podium. People clap. Then he waves his hand out into the audience and starts calling names, and one by one I see guys from the team get out of their folding chairs and head toward the stage. Double M. Jake Farwell. A bunch of the JV guys. The group around the podium with Ibrahim swells, and the clapping increases, as more and more of the guys step forward.

Then Mike Turcotte leans in toward the microphone.

"We'd especially like our captain to join us up here. Tom Bouchard."

Someone pushes me from behind. Myla. I didn't know she was there; she's been all over the place this afternoon.

"Go on, Cap. Your team needs you."

I feel like I have to walk a long way, between a lot of clapping people, my face turning redder with every step. Never have I felt less deserving of attention, of applause. It gets worse as the guys see me coming, and they start to applaud as well. For me.

This is it, God, I think. *The perfect time for the apocalypse. Or just a big, gaping black hole, right here, beneath your buddy Tom Bouchard. I'll step right into it now, and disappear. Okay?*

I reach the stage, mount the stairs, and stand at the podium with the guys. The view is awesome. It's a sea of smiling, clapping, cheering people. Some I even recognize. Coach. My parents, who scored good seats in the middle. My guidance counselor, Mrs. Swift. All these people I've never seen in my life, but who braved the cold in order to prove that we're better than hate, better than those guys across town.

That's when I hear him.

Not God. I never hear God. I hear *him.*

We the team.

I whirl around. Double M and Jake Farwell stand directly behind me, and I look past and beyond them, but . . . no one. I look down the length of guys, but everyone is cheering with the crowd and waving to their friends in the audience. My heart swells as I realize just how badly I would have liked to stand on this platform with Saeed. How right it would have been for him to be here with all of us.

And I realize that in some way, forever, I will always be looking and listening for him.

Acknowledgments

I could not have written this book without the selfless generosity of the men, women, and young people who shared their stories with me. I was inspired by you all and hope I have created something that does justice to your spirit and your work. I am especially grateful to: Winnie Kiunga, Caroline Sample, Sarah Aschauer, Mike McGraw, Rick Speers and Molly Ladd and the staff at the Lewiston Public Library; Julia Sleeper, Kim Sullivan, Fahmo Ahmed, Fatuma Abdirahman, Kelley McDaniel and the students of King Middle School; Karin Dilman and the entire Shardi family, who welcomed me into their home; Gail and Peter Lowe; Beth Caputi and the Williams College Alumni Association; and my dear friend Ruth Bouchard Klein.

Many thanks to my wonderful agent, Edite Kroll; my excellent editor, Nancy Hinkel, who helped me shift the tectonic plates of this book when they needed shifting; editorial assistant Jeremy Medina, who handles everything with skill, speed, and good humor; and copy editor Sue Warga.

Thanks to my ever-supportive husband, Conrad Schneider, and my daughter, Madsy Schneider, who spent countless hours/years listening to me talk about all my imaginary friends.

Finally, my very sincere thanks go to Shobow Saban and Jonnie McDonough. You inspire us and make us proud.

MARIA PADIAN is the author of the young adult novels *Jersey Tomatoes Are the Best* and *Brett McCarthy: Work in Progress*, which was chosen as an ALA-YALSA Best Book for Young Adults and received a Maine Lupine Honor Award and a Maine Literary Award. A graduate of Middlebury College and the University of Virginia, she lives in Maine with her family. To learn more about her, visit mariapadian.com.